ALSO BY VERONICA LI

Fiction
Nightfall in Mogadishu

Non-Fiction
Journey Across the Four Seas: A Chinese Woman's Search for Home

Praise for *Confucius Says*

"A story of a woman caring for her parents with as much filial piety as she can muster. Li begins her story with an elderly Chinese couple bemoaning their children's choice to place them in a nursing home, a conversation replete with quotations of Confucius and the virtue *xiao*, or filial piety. After Tak, the husband, swallows a bottle of vitamins in a suicidal gesture, they move to live in their daughter Cary's home .... Cary's journey through caretaking is paralleled by a deepening of her understanding of Confucianism, her parents' religion. A deep examination of what it means to see one's parents through the end of life, Li's book is also in many ways the story of a woman coming to grips with her heritage.
An affecting look at caring for aging parents and a story of the nuances of Chinese culture."
—*Kirkus Reviews*

"In this era of unprecedented longevity, this story of caregiving for elderly parents is most timely. While love for parents is a natural instinct, the Chinese codify it with a set of written guidelines. Through a humorous and entertaining story, the author uncovers the universal truths in Confucius' teachings and applies them to a modern-day family."
–**Yong Ho**, co-chair, Renwen Society of China Institute; author of *China: An Illustrated History* and a number of books on the Chinese language

"Veronica Li's *Confucius Says* is a wonderfully engaging book about a tough topic. With good humor and warmth, she takes us on an emotional epic journey of one family's experience with caregiving, providing insightful wisdom about how cultural values color our relationships. A must-read for anyone with elderly parents, but especially for all Asian Americans."

–**Gil Asakawa**, Asian American Journalists Association AARP Fellow; blogger and author of *Being Japanese American*; Manager of Student Media, College of Media, Communication & Information, University of Colorado

"I laughed my way in and cried my way out of this book. By turns hilarious and searing, mystery novel and textbook on aging, at its core this is a love story. As one of many who have taken on the task of caring for parents till the end, I'm deeply moved by this book."

–**Vilma Seeberg**, Director, China Studies and Education Project, and Associate Professor, Multicultural-International Education, Kent State University

"*Confucius Says* is a poignant portrayal of a Chinese family's adherence to filial piety and the impact of this tradition on everyone in the family (including the dog). The author captures eloquently the emotional roller coaster of parental caregiving—a ride that whizzes through the terrors of aging and dying interspersed with the exhilaration of love, life and liberation. Humor is sprinkled throughout the book, facilitating the reader's acceptance of the full range of emotions associated with this undertaking."

–**Ginny Gong**, host of the TV talk show *Ginny's…Where East Meets West;* former National President of OCA; and author of *From Ironing Board to Corporate Board: My Chinese Laundry Experience in America*

CONFUCIUS SAYS

A Novel

Veronica Li

Homa & Sekey Books
Paramus, New Jersey

FIRST AMERICAN EDITION

Copyright © 2015 by Veronica Li

All rights reserved. No part of this book may be reproduced, stored in a retrieval system, or transmitted in any form, or by any means, electronic, mechanical, photocopying, recording or otherwise, without prior permission from the publisher.

Library of Congress Cataloging-in-Publication Data

Li, Veronica, 1951-
  Confucius says : a novel / Veronica Li. – First American edition.
      pages ; cm
  ISBN 978-1-62246-017-5 (softcover)
  1. Chinese Americans–Fiction. 2. Middle-aged women–Fiction. 3. Aging parents–Care–Fiction. 4. Domestic fiction. I. Title.
  PS3612.I15C66 2015
  813'.6–dc23
                      2015005186

Homa & Sekey Books
3rd Floor, North Tower
Mack-Cali Center III
140 E. Ridgewood Ave.
Paramus, NJ 07652

Tel: 800-870-HOMA, 201-261-8810
Fax: 201-261-8890
Email: info@homabooks.com
Website: www.homabooks.com

Printed in U.S.A.
1 3 5 7 9 10 8 6 4 2

TO MY PARENTS, WHO TAUGHT ME
ABOUT LIFE AND DEATH

Author's Note and Acknowledgments

I would like to thank Joanna Taylor, my friend and editor, for helping me discover my funny bone and fine-tune my story to this shape and form. I never knew humor could be so serious. Special thanks also go to Paula Harrell, a historian and writer, who after reading an earlier draft, suggested that I turn a depressing memoir on caregiving into fiction. By transferring my experience to imaginary characters, I can see how ridiculously naive my expectations were when I started on the bumpy ride of reverse parenting. The fight over who's the parent and who's the child brings out our most irrational nature, and it's easier to laugh at both sides when the storyteller is removed from the drama.

I'm also grateful to Shawn Ye, editor of Homa and Sekey Books, for his advice and for introducing me to modern literature on Confucianism. Although Chinese is my native tongue, I, like most Chinese of my generation and after, have a hard time reading the classical language of the Four Books and Five Classics. Dedicated scholars have made these writings accessible, allowing me to understand and find relevance in a system of beliefs that infiltrates every Chinese soul. A Chinese is Chinese, regardless of where he's born, because of the messages encoded in his DNA, and the strands for filial piety are particularly strong.

Last but far from least, I want to thank Sverrir Sigurdsson, my husband, who gave me not only feedback on my drafts, but more importantly, the material for my story. Without his support, no way could I have cared for both parents at the most difficult stage of their lives.

Below is the reading list for my self-taught Confucius 101. These books are also the source of the Confucian quotations cited in my book.

de Bary, Wm. Theodore and Irene Bloom, *Sources of Chinese Tradition from Earliest Times to 1600*, New York: Columbia University Press, 1999.

Berthrong, John H. and Evelyn Nagai, *Confucianism: A Short Introduction*, Oxford: Oneworld Publications, 2000.

Fung, Yu-Lan, *A Short History of Chinese Philosophy*, New York: The Free Press, 1966

Gardner, Daniel K., *The Four Books: The Basic Teachings of the Later Confucian Tradition*, Indianapolis: Hackett Publishing Company, 2007.

Ho, Yong, *China: An Illustrated History*, New York: Hippocrene Books, 2000.

Legge, James, *Confucius: Confucian Analects, The Great Learning, and The Doctrine of the Mean*, Mineola: Dover Publications, 1971.

Ivanhoe, Philip J., *Confucian Moral Self Cultivation*, Indianapolis: Hackett Publishing Company, 2000.

Makra, Mary Lelia, *The Hsiao Ching*, New York: St. John's University Press, 1961.

Prologue

"I can't believe they want to move us into a nursing home!"

"Haiii, I've tried my best to be a good mother, but all my efforts have gone to waste. Since the moment they crawled out of me, I've been telling them filial piety is the number one virtue. Confucius says, 'If filial piety is not pursued from beginning to end, disasters are sure to follow.' Look at the storms and floods everywhere. It's because people don't love and respect their parents."

"The storms and floods are because of climate change. Confucius has nothing to do with it."

"Stop making fun of me. This is a very serious matter."

"You and your Confucius say too much. The children don't listen anymore. Your words are like a breeze brushing their ears."

"You're the father. You're supposed to discipline them. If you'd been stricter with them when they were young, they'd be more obedient now."

"Go ahead, blame it on me. It's always my fault anyway."

"I think our biggest mistake was to bring the children to America. If your factory hadn't gone bankrupt, we wouldn't have had to leave Hong Kong, and our children would be practicing filial piety like real Chinese."

"You know why no one wants to take us in? It's because you nag too much!"

"Say whatever you want. I'm deaf anyway. Haiii, I really don't understand how our children can be so heartless. Since they were young, I've been singing this song to them:

Father, Mother give me life,

They feed me, clothe me, carry me in their arms

They teach me, cultivate me,
Help me grow to be a good person,
Their love is as vast as the ocean,
As boundless as the sky.
How I long to requite their love!"

"Mmmm… You're right. We loved them more than our own lives. There was nothing we wouldn't do for them."

"Remember how we had to squeeze every penny for them to go to college? I couldn't even fly back to Beijing to see my mother. She parted for eternity before I had the chance to say goodbye. Oh, I want to cry every time I think of it. This is the kind of sacrifice we made for our children, and look at how they're repaying us."

"I remember when one of them got sick, I always got up several times at night to check on him. No matter how busy things were at the shop—"

"Now it's our turn to be sick. You with your heart disease and me with my arthritis. We can't stay in this apartment by ourselves anymore. They should move us in and take care of us. That's the only right thing to do, what Confucius calls the way of the Heavens. A nursing home is only for people who don't have children. We have three and they all have houses and cars and even a beach house."

"Do you think Cary will take us in?"

"She lives too far away. I heard the winters on the East Coast are very cold. It's so much more comfortable here in California."

"Mmmm…."

"Oh, did you watch the news last night? A man is suing a nursing home for beating up his mother. The poor old woman had bruises all over her face and body."

"Nobody can force me to live in a nursing home! I'd rather die first!"

"Here you go again. Every time you want your way you threaten to kill yourself. You should have died a thousand times by now."

"You think I don't have the guts?"

"You can threaten all you want. The children don't believe you anymore. Your words are like a breeze brushing their ears… Where are you going? Wait, what are you doing? Why are you swallowing so many pills?"

"I'm killing myself. What are you waiting for? Call an ambulance."

BOOK ONE

Confucius says, "Filial piety is the foundation of virtue and the root of civilization."

Chapter 1

Where on earth are my parents? Travelers with special needs get to board the plane first. Shouldn't they be the first to get off too? The flight from San Francisco has been disgorging passengers for the last half hour. Even the crew is coming out, heels clicking and carry-on bags in tow. Yet there's still no sign of my parents. Big Sister reported handing them over to the airline staff. This is a non-stop flight, so they couldn't have gotten off mid-air.

As I inquire at the counter, a flash of silver turns the corner. It's my mother's coiffure sparkling like a crown. Rolling out in a wheelchair, Mami cranes her crooked neck to look around. The moment her eyes land on me, she flaps her hand and cries, "Cary!" I smile. Her dark green velvet skirt and a matching top are just the right color to highlight the string of pearls around her neck. I called them the night before to tell them to layer on their warmest clothes. Don't worry about color coordination, I said to my mother. But Mami is Mami. I catch a glimpse of my reflection in the window and wonder who's the hobo in the baggy sweatshirt.

Baba struggles a few steps behind. Dressed in a gray three-piece suit with a red triangle peeking out of his breast pocket, vanilla mustache trimmed and starched, he looks as formal as a foreign ambassador presenting his credentials. My parents are old-fashioned travelers. Unlike today's frequent flyers who dress for comfort, they put on their best finery. To them, a plane ride is as major as a wedding or funeral, and they dress accordingly. I'm relieved to see a wrap piled on Mami's lap and a trench coat hanging on Baba's arm. Their California garb will have to do for now. Tomorrow I'm taking them to the Coat Factory for some real winter clothes.

I tip the attendant and take over the wheelchair. The sea of airport humanity parts as we roll down the hallway. Baba toddles along, oblivious to the attention he's drawing. Both men and women beam at us, faces crinkling and fingers itching to pinch the adorable cheeks. I feel like a proud mother hen showing off her younglings.

We make it to baggage claim after a few stops for Baba to catch his breath. He points to some luggage festooned with red ribbons. I dive into the crowd to retrieve it. But instead of me pulling it out, it's pulling me in. I'm on the edge of tumbling onto the carousel when a man grabs the other handle and together we haul the bag out. After thanking the helpful stranger, I stare at the bulging bag, wondering what on earth they packed in it? Every piece of their prized possessions? Then I remember. My parents aren't staying for a few weeks. They're staying the rest of their lives.

*

My home is in the Virginia suburbs of the nation's capital, in a small town called Mapleton. When giving directions to my address, I always tell people to look for the million-dollar home on Oak Street. You can't miss it, I say. Then I tell them my house is the one to the right. The directions never fail.

Next to the McMansion, my split level is a doll house. But every time I roll into the driveway, crumbling concrete and all, I feel like a queen entering her castle grounds. This is the place where I raised a son and daughter, finished one career and launched another, and nurtured a marriage that's been kept fresh by separation. While my architect husband flew around the world supervising projects in Shanghai, Tokyo, or the Virgin Islands, I fretted about the "other woman." Every time he came home, I felt on top of the world, having vanquished a gorgeous, sexy rival who might or might not exist. I kept him on his toes too, mentioning dinner with a colleague (had to work late) without specifying the gender.

A figure appears at the front door. The porch light gilds a long silhouette, still lean despite the thirty pounds he's put on since our college days at Berkeley. Steve approaches, hunching over to get a little closer to his in-laws' level. Mami buries her face in his belly button. Baba, who's an inch taller, stretches his arms high above his head to grip Steve's shoulders. And I, who've outgrown my forebears thanks to American milk, need only tiptoe to reach my husband's heart.

I'm always annoyed when Mami tells people I'm married to an "American." We're all Americans, I protest. Chinese American, Hispanic American, and Irish American are equally American. I have a hard time, though, coming up with a label for Steve. English, Irish, Scottish, Polish, German, even Native American, he's all of the above. I'm willing to settle for "White American," but the description isn't quite right either, for Steve is mostly pink.

Steve and I get the luggage into the house. Baba can still climb the staircase hands free, although at the top of the seven steps, he's panting as if he's run a mile. The three of us watch Mami negotiate each step with her left leg, the good one. Hand over hand on the banister, she pulls herself like a rock climber up a cliff, a grunt accompanying every step. My heart pinches. I want to swoop her in my arms and carry her up. Then I remember how heavy she was when I helped her out of the car. For every inch of height she's shrunk she's made it up in pounds, which seem to have all settled in her jelly bowl belly.

"Let me show you your room." My voice is shrill with excitement. I guide them to the bedroom on the left. Ta-ta! I wish I had a camera to capture their surprise.

"Oh no, you shouldn't give us the master bedroom," Baba says to Steve. "This is *your* room."

"That's okay, we have a nice room downstairs," Steve says. "It's difficult for you to run up and down."

Baba insists "you shouldn't" some more, and Steve counters

with "it's okay" in equal measure.

This game of ping pong can go on forever unless I butt in: "We're happy to do it for you, Baba."

(I'll explain to my husband later: When a Chinese parent says, "You shouldn't go to so much trouble for me," the reply he wants is, "To be able to serve you is my greatest honor.")

Mami surveys the room, looking serene as a saint. "Confucius say, if you have harmony in your heart you be happy anywhere," she says.

If Big Sister were here, her face would redden as if hives were breaking out. She has a severe allergy to Mami's "Confucius says," which explains why she can't take in our parents and I can.

I pull off the bedcover to show my parents the *pièce de résistance*: an electric blanket with two controls, his and hers. Whenever I called them, they always greeted me with the same complaint: "I couldn't sleep all night. Your Baba (Mami) put the temperature on too high (low)." Baba likes the blanket burning hot, perhaps due to his heart condition. Mami likes it much cooler, perhaps because she came from the northern city of Beijing.

"That's it, this is what we need!" Baba exclaims. Mami gives a demure, close-lipped smile. (Showing her teeth would be a praise her daughter doesn't deserve.)

My blanket solution works! What were my siblings griping about? They probably didn't know how to handle old folks. As I see it, the needs of the elderly are basic. After eighty some years of living, what desires and ambitions can they have left? Their remaining days are purely a matter of logistics. Three meals a day, prompt medical care (don't wait till the cold develops into pneumonia), activities to keep their bodies and minds sharp, and a good dose of greasy Chinese food once in a while. That's no sweat for me. After all, I once managed an office of thirty people, engineers at that, each with an ego so inflated that no two could fit in the same conference room.

The next stop is my parents' study/TV room. "I got you cable TV. You can get over a hundred channels," I say to Baba with a wink.

"Does it have *my* channel?" Baba winks back.

"Oh yes." More winks. My philosophy is that an old man should be encouraged to enjoy whatever he still can. Besides, if Mami doesn't object to him watching Playboy, why should I? It's all watch and no play anyway.

I herd my tour group into the basement. I called it the "cave" when the children occupied it. The entire level was dark, dank, and dingy, and Fred and Maggie wouldn't have had it otherwise. After they moved out, I fumigated the place and converted the rec room into my piano studio.

This is the largest room in the house, and I make no apology for my greed. After all, the baby grand is the biggest piece of furniture in the house. This is where I teach piano. A hutch of desk and bookcases on the other end make up my office. A dog bed lies in the middle of the room, leaving just enough space for me to roll out my yoga mat.

Mami fiddles with the skin-toned device plugged in her ear. I remind myself to speak louder. It's important they understand my rules.

"I teach from three to six in the afternoon. I also practice the piano from eight to ten in the morning. If you need anything, I'll do it for you between those hours...unless it's an emergency."

"There's nothing much we need," Baba and Mama trip over themselves to assure me.

"One more thing. Please speak English in front of Steve."

Although I feel bad about dictating rules to my parents, it has to be done. A household is by nature a monarchy. The queen knows what's best for her subjects. All she wants from them is cooperation and a bit of appreciation. My parents ran their own kingdoms once upon a time, but even monarchs have to retire.

"How many students you have?" Mami says.

"Twenty." Now, why did I say that? Fifteen is all I have and all I want. Mami raises her eyebrows at me. I ignore her. She's never understood why I quit a well-paying job with one of the top ten government contractors in the country. To pick up my musical career? In her opinion I shouldn't have majored in music in the first place. She sent me to piano lessons to develop my brain, which was supposed to be used for studying medicine (her first choice), law, accounting, anything but music.

"Hey Laozi, get up and say hello," I say to the brown heap on the dog bed.

Laozi lies on his side, his loose skin rippling from head to tail. He's a rescue Chinese shar-pei, endowed with a coat several sizes too large. Sometimes I want to peel it off him and shrink it in hot water. At the sound of his name, he raises his wrinkled face and sniffs around with a snout that looks as if someone had smashed it with a pan.

Everyone laughs. I have yet to meet a person who doesn't laugh at the sight of Laozi.

"Why do you call a dog Laozi?" Mami says, a little offended by the disrespect.

"Laozi is the philosopher who founded Taoism," I explain. "This dog is a Taoist, because he firmly believes that doing nothing is the best course in life."

"He's not a very good watch dog," Baba comments.

"That's not his job. He has higher functions to fulfill—to love and be loved," I say half-jokingly.

Mami looks around, searching for something. "Can I have pen and paper?" she says.

I pick up the items from my desk. (That look in her eyes

warns me Confucius is about to say something again.) Mami sits down on the piano bench and places the paper on her lap. She draws a Chinese character 孝.

"You know what is this?" she tests me.

"It's my brother's name," I say cheekily, reading it upside down. Of course I know she wants to discuss the concept and not her son. That's the beauty of Chinese names—you can christen your offspring anything you want as long as it's less than two characters. Xiao likes to grouse about his name, but he really shouldn't. It could be a lot worse. He could have been called Lucky Fortune, Bring Gold, or Study Medicine.

"Yes, it's your brother's name, and it also mean something *very* important." Mami has learned English by way of mimicry. Her English grammar is spotty, especially with regard to verb forms. "The word is *Xiao*—filial piety," she goes on. "Steve, you hear about filial piety?"

Steve squints as he often does when he gauges the straightness of a picture hanging on a wall. Then he'll get up, walk to the painting and level the frame. Cursed by a keen visual sensitivity, anything that isn't level, plumb, and square drives him crazy. On the upside, it makes him a good architect.

"Filial refers to a child's relationship with his parents," Steve begins. "Piety is religious devotion. A combination of the two transforms the parent-child relationship into a kind of religion. In other words, the child worships the parents."

Whether or not Mami understands the big words or hears them at all is irrelevant. Once she pushes the start button, the only direction is forward to the end. "Filial piety is most important virtue," Mami says. "There are ten big virtues and filial piety is number one. Now, let me explain this 孝." She points to the character on the paper. "Top part mean old, bottom part mean son. Son carry old father and mother on his back." Mami pats her crooked spine. "Can you carry me?" She tosses her chin to taunt her son-in-law while her eyes slide toward me.

"Don't worry, you not carry us for long," Mami says. "One to two years, and we kick the buck."

Bucket, I correct in my head. My mother's mangling of English idioms has the same effect on my skin as a sour note from a violin.

"I'm eighty-two years old. I never think I live this long. My father is fifty-five when he die, my mother seventy-eight. So, I can't have many more—one year most." She looks at her husband. "He's eighty-four now, but his parents live long time. He can have two."

"Only two?" Baba teases.

"Ming-Jen and Tak," Steve addresses his in-laws by their first names. "You're welcome in my home for as long as you live."

I circle an arm around my husband's waist. "Till death do us part" takes on a new dimension.

"You say it now," Mami says. "What happen when I have Alsi-heimer?"

I know what my mother is fishing for. Six months ago, Mami sobbed to me on the phone, "Your father tried to kill himself because your brother and sister want to put us in a nursing home. We're Chinese, we don't go to nursing home. We have to live with our children."

Actually Big Sister had already told me the story: Baba swallowed a bottle of vitamins in front of Mami. This wasn't the act of a person who really wanted to die. It was blackmail pure and simple. If I'd known they were willing to move across the country, I would have spared everyone the melodrama.

I reach out for my mother's hand and look into her shriveled raisin eyes. "I'll *never* put you in a nursing home. I give you my word."

A rush of emotions surges in my chest. I suddenly realize

this is my last chance. Mami may be right—a year, two or three is probably what they have left. This is my last chance to repay my debt to these people who've given me life and loved and cherished me since I was a bawling bundle of demands. Living on opposite ends of the continent, I haven't been able to do much for them.

I squeeze my mother's hand. "You'll never go hungry with me. See, I've got a lot of meat here," I say, patting my thigh.

Mami beams, looking both surprised and pleased. "You remember the story."

Of course, I remember. How can I forget the story about the Chinese boy who slices a piece of his thigh to feed his ailing mother? Night after night, I fell asleep listening to the music of Mami's voice and bursting with admiration for the boy. I want to offer myself to my mother too. And there's plenty to go around, for unlike the starving boy, my well-fed American thigh can serve up several meals.

Chapter 2

It's a pity he had to leave Hong Kong, Tak laments to himself. If he'd stayed, a pretty Filipino would be sleeping with him tonight, every night. If he'd stayed, a Filipino maid would be handing him his pills on a plate. She would service him the way she serviced his father in his last days. She'd slept in a cot next to the old man by night and tended to his every need by day. She fed him, massaged him, bedpanned him, bathed him, and wheeled him out to the park in nice weather. Though paralyzed on one side, legend had it that he could still raise his "little brother" when the pretty Filipino cleaned him.

Tak digs into the suitcase and pulls out his pill box. He grimaces at the multi-colored tablets and capsules. In America, you have to do everything yourself. Now, which pills is he supposed to take? The box is divided into seven columns, each subdivided into four compartments for different times of day. But it's 9 pm where he is and 6 pm where he came from. Never mind, he'll swallow them all. He tosses a handful into his mouth and throws his head back with a gulp of water. Years of pill swallowing have stretched his gullet. Like a python, he can swallow a cow whole.

Now for the next bedtime ritual. Tak sits down on the edge of the bed and presses two fingers on his wrist. He can almost hear the little animal thumping against the pressure. There, there it is again. Thump-thump thump-thump instead of a steady thump thump thump. Cary should take him to a cardiologist soon.

He had a triple bypass three years ago, but recently the irregular palpitations have returned. The doctors said his arteries are clogged again. Instead of another surgery he opted for medication. Death doesn't scare him, especially if it takes him away while he's under anesthesia. The problem is Ming-Jen. He's promised to take care of her till the end. He loves her with all his heart, even if it's a defective one. He would have settled for a beautiful and sexy wife, but as luck would have it, she turned out to be intelligent, competent, and virtuous as well. She's a Confucian disciple while he's just confused. Life without her is simply unimaginable. He'd much rather die first. On the other hand, she'll have no one to protect her after he goes. Who should die first, who should die last is a dilemma they can't sort out no matter how many times they discuss it.

Ming-Jen shuffles in from the bathroom, her face lacquered in cold cream. She's dressed in her flannel pajamas, smelling of shower and soap. Tak has been waiting for this moment. "I told you Cary wouldn't stick us in the basement," he gloats.

Ming-Jen maintains her right to silence as she lathers lotion on her hands. Tak knows his wife doesn't like to be wrong. Perhaps he shouldn't rub it in. "All the credit goes to you. You're the one who taught her *Xiao*. The parents are always the parents, and children always the children, no matter how old they are or how far they've climbed. Cary understands that." Steve's face floats up in Tak's mind. "I'm not sure about Steve, though. Did you notice how his nose twitched when he talked to us?"

Ming-Jen stops rubbing her arm and looks at Tak. Up till the mention of Steve, she hasn't heard or *seen* a word of what Tak said. When he's speaking to the wall, she can't read his lips. She still has her hearing aids on, but they're too selective to be reliable. Certain sound waves glide through the device with ease, while others, no matter how aggressive, can't force their way in. It all depends on the angle of the speaker's lips in relation to her ears, the prevailing wind, temperature, humidity, and most importantly the person under discussion.

"You have to be careful of Steve," she says. "He's much bigger than you are. If you pick a fight with him, he can knock you out with one punch. Not everyone is a soft shell crab like our other son-in-law."

Tak smiles at the memory. If Karen hadn't been there to shield her husband, he would have suffered much more than a pair of broken glasses.

"Steve is taller and heavier, but does he know how to fight? Don't forget I'm a *Wing Chun* master."

"I'm here only because of you," Ming-Jen carries on. Her policy is, if she can't hear, just keep talking. And tonight she has a lot to say. "If we'd held out a bit longer, Xiao would have offered to take us in. Chinese parents have always lived with their eldest son. This is the way it's been for thousands of years. A man and his son-in-law can't live under the same roof. It's like putting two male lions in the same territory. They have to fight to the finish. Haven't you learned your lesson from living with Karen? It didn't last six months."

Tak gets up to turn on the electric blanket, his side of it. His wife is muttering again. How does she expect him to hear her? Anyway, he knows what she's griping about. He's not going to waste another breath arguing about this. The problem isn't Xiao but Xiao's wife. She'd been a Red Guard who denounced her parents at a public meeting and paraded them in dunce hats. To people like her, whatever Confucius says is wrong, even if it's something as basic as "Honor your father and mother."

The electric blanket is scorching by the time he gets into bed. The prickly heat makes him shiver with pleasure. Ming-Jen climbs in on her side, slowly, carefully, trying as much as possible to avoid the painful spots in her.

She waits for the twinges to settle to three on a scale of ten. "I still think the five years we spent with Xiao were the best," she says in the dark. "I know it didn't end well. The Red Guard"—her nickname for Xiao's wife—"twisted everything I said and accused me of meddling in her family business.

Well, isn't *her* family business *my* family business? We're all one family!"

Tak isn't interested in talking about the Red Guard. The only person on his mind now is his father's maid. "Hey, do you remember the Filipina who took care of my father? She got pregnant and my mother had to send her back to the Philippines."

"What are you talking about? The Red Guard never went to the Philippines," Ming-Jen says. Tak can be terribly confused sometimes. "She's behaving better these days," Ming-Jen goes on, remembering the farewell dinner her daughter-in-law cooked in her honor. "Times change, people change. I heard her daughters are giving her a hard time. Maybe she's beginning to understand the Confucian saying, 'Do not do unto others what you don't want done to you.' If she doesn't want her children to be mean to her, she shouldn't be mean to us."

"You know what I think?" Tak says. "I think my father got her pregnant!"

"I'm willing to let bygones be bygones and give her another chance. When the time is right, I'll have a good talk with Xiao."

Tak rolls into the valley in the mattress and tickles his wife's ear with his mustache. "We haven't played in a long time," he coos.

"I'm too tired, and my knee is acting up," she moans. "It's like somebody stuck a looong needle under the knee cap and is whipping it around."

Tak sighs. His wife can paint graphic descriptions of her pain. Maybe it's just as well. The fire in his belly is still strong, but it's more like the burning sensation of a urinary tract infection, the frustration of wanting to pee and not being able to. His doctor in California has denied him Viagra because of his heart condition. Perhaps the doctors in Virginia will deliver a more agreeable second opinion. Cary must make him an appointment soon.

*

Steve buttons his pajama top. This is their first night in their son's old bedroom. Cary seems flustered, pulling out drawer after drawer to look for her nightgown and questioning him as though he has something to do with its disappearance. Sleeping in a strange room is the story of Steve's career. As long as the carpet doesn't stink of old cigarette smoke, he can overlook the crookedness of the ceiling, the view into a parking garage, the hide and seek with the light switches, and all the usual hotel room flaws. His eyes are closed anyway when he's asleep.

"I'd hate to have the name Filial Piety," Steve says, reminiscing about Ming-Jen's lecture.

"So does George. That's why he never uses his Chinese name," Cary says, taking a pause from her search.

"I much prefer your Chinese name. *Ka-Yi*. *Ka* for family and *Yi* for Righteousness." He punches the air to underscore the capital R. "And your English name Cary is as close as it gets to *Ka-Yi*."

"Very good. You get an A, Professor!" "Professor" has become his new nickname since he started teaching rather than practicing architecture. The old one was "Artichoke," their little girl's rendition of "architect."

"Here it is," Cary exclaims, waving her nightgown. "How about Karen? You remember her Chinese name?"

"She's *Ka-Ren,* and *Ren* stands for…" Steve knuckles his head to jolt his memory. Since flunking high school French, he'd figured language isn't his strength.

"Compassion," Cary says. "*Ren, Yi,* and *Xiao* are the major virtues of Confucianism."

"How did Xiao become George?"

"My parents couldn't find anything close to Xiao in English, so they named him after the King of England."

"You all have a lot to live up to," Steve says.

"We sure do. And tonight justice has been served," she declares. "They took care of me when I was a child and now I'm taking care of them."

Laozi moseys into the room and plunks himself in front of Cary. "Oh, you poor thing. You're confused, aren't you? You don't know why we're sleeping down here, and what on earth are those strangers doing in our house! Don't worry, sweetie—" she pats the round head—"you'll get used to living with them."

Steve chuckles to himself. Cary likes to project her emotions onto her dog. "Come here, Laozi," he says and bends to tickle the ridiculously tiny ears. At least now he can pronounce Laozi properly. It has taken him a while to get the Chinese "z," which involves rubbing the tip of the tongue against the front teeth to produce the "tz" buzz. He chuckles again, this time with disbelief. When he was growing up on a farm in Kansas, if anyone had told him he would one day live in a Chinese household where even the dog is Chinese, he would have said, "You gotta be kidding!"

Steve slips under the cover and throws his arm over his eyes to block off the light. Through a crack he watches his wife's back as she undresses. Her shoulders have always been broad, but the widening of the waistline is a new phenomenon. She now looks like her father not only in features but also in build. The two are like houses in the same development, with slightly different exterior options. He'll never dare to say it aloud, knowing how much Cary wants to favor her mom—ivory skin, almond eyes, cherry lips, and all that. Instead she's inherited her father's round walnut eyes, toast brown complexion, and generous mouth, which Cary likes to enlarge into a smile at the slightest provocation.

Watching her hang up her clothes, he wants to tell her she's fine as she is. Actually she's more than fine; she's the perfect partner for him. It's unthinkable that he once wanted to leave her for a business associate. He was lucky his contract ended before Cary found out. Cary is the ground on which he stands, the foundation of his buildings. No matter how far he travels, the earth under his feet is always there. He never knows when to stop once he gets rolling. Without Cary's sense of balance, harmony, and whatever else Confucius teaches, he would have kept on going until he plunged down a cliff.

Oh, there's something else he loves about Cary—she laughs at his jokes no matter how many times she's heard them. Without his sense of humor, she often says, she'd be as deadly serious as an airport security officer herding passengers into the X-ray booth. Perhaps that's why a person's spouse is called his "better half." Cary and he are indeed each other's better half.

A pair of icy feet tuck under his warm ones. "Thanks for taking in my parents, giving up your bedroom and all," Cary breathes into his ear. He turns to his side to return the embrace.

"You've always supported my shenanigans. It's only right I support yours." The truth is he feels guilty about constantly leaving her. After all the years of traveling, he was ready to settle into a local job. But when the college in Philadelphia invited him to help start a school for architecture, he couldn't say no. Cary was disappointed, though she didn't complain, which made Steve feel worse. Taking in her parents is the equivalent of swallowing an aspirin for his conscience. He won't feel so bad when he drives away tomorrow, because Cary won't be alone in an empty house.

Steve quips, "I tell people in my department I visit my girlfriend every weekend. You should see them turn green with envy. How can that old geezer have so much fun?"

"All right, old geezer, when are you going back to Philly?" the girlfriend says.

"Sunday afternoon and coming back Thursday for a long

weekend. This will be my schedule this semester."

"Will you be home for dinner?"

"Yeah." He can imagine Cary penning on her Thursday menu: BBQ. She knows the way to a Kansas farm boy's heart.

The arm around his chest tightens. "Whatever happens, you'll always be my number one priority," Cary says. "You married me, not my parents. If they get to be too much for you, just let me know. I'll find a solution."

In spite of his philosophy that heavy emotions are bad for your health, Steve feels a twinge in his heart. "We'll get along fine. I like your parents. They're good people, salt of the earth, as we say in the mid-West. And they've raised three wonderful children. Confucius says, they will be happy in their old age."

Chapter 3

I stand admiring my masterpiece in front of the bulletin board in my office. It's no Mona Lisa, nor would it ever find its way to an art gallery. Nonetheless it's my crowning achievement. The piece of scribbled-over scrap paper is the outcome of many hours of brain- and legwork. Two months after my parents moved in, I've completed all but one item on my List.

Visit Social Security—make sure checks are sent to the new account
Call Medicare—have M&B ready to ID themselves
Dr. Frye—general checkup for M&B
Acupuncturist—M only
Handicap parking sticker—Dr. Frye has to fill out application
Audiologist—B needs hearing aid. He's as deaf as M!
Shopping list:
Coats
Scarves
Hats
Gloves
Book case
Walking cane—let M pick out color
Boots
Senior Center—Tuesday is Chinese day.

My List is, on the surface, a simple "to-do" list. When you dig deeper, however, you'll discover two powerful undercurrents: American can-doism and Chinese must-doism. My American spirit refuses to recognize such a thing as an impossible mission. No job is too great as long as it can be broken into tiny pieces and chipped away bit by bit. At the same time, my Chinese psyche tells me we're flies trapped in a web of obligations. (Never mind that I've lived in the U.S. since age ten. Any fly can tell you, once you're caught in a spider's web, you can't escape.) We *must* perform our duties, which are as varied as the roles we play. As daughter, sister, wife, mother, aunt, niece, friend, teacher, student, neighbor, caregiver, dog owner.... Hold on, my head is spinning. Let me sit down. With so many things a person must do, I can't imagine how anyone can go through life list-less. World peace is at stake here. Mami says Confucius says, if everyone does his duties as he's supposed to, all bickering and finger-pointing will cease, and harmony will reign.

My children like to laugh at my lists. (They're not so amused at the chores list, which assigns one of their names to each task.) Laugh all you want, I say to them. Call me boring, square, retro, uncool, etc., etc. The List was what propelled me to management and got me to where I am today. "Cary has an elephant's memory," my superiors used to say. "She never forgets anything." Hah! Little did they know. I thought I would have to work till sixty-five before I could retire and devote more time to the piano. But shortly after my forty-seventh birthday, I received an email from Personnel offering golden handshakes to anyone interested. I made a quick calculation. The house was paid up (I refinanced every time interest rates nosedived), the children were paid up (though one still needed a subsidy every so often), car loans and grand piano loan had all been amortized. If Steve and I were careful and if I took on some students, we could get by comfortably. It turns out "comfortable" is an understatement. I'm now earning a fraction of my former income, and yet I'm wallowing in riches. Time, not US dollars, is the most valuable currency.

I pin my can-do, must-do to-do list back on the board. For the sake of world peace, I'll wake up Mami and Baba and get them ready for the last entry on the List: the senior center. Ooooh, what's going on? Did somebody turn up the thermostat? I feel water boiling up in me, bubbling over and splashing out of the top of my head.

"Laozi, did you feel that?" I say to the sleeping dog.

He stirs and looks at me, beady eyes peering out of the folds. They seem to say, "Be content with what you have."

The feeling is gone in a flash. I put the two words together, hot and flash. Oh no, it can't be happening to *me*!

*

I glance over at my parents and see they're as fascinated as I am. The scene is like a fabulous Chinese opera. In one corner of the auditorium, mahjong tiles clash like a symphony of cymbals and gongs. In another, people sit with quiet concentration at a table, dabbing paint at ceramic figures of rabbits, turtles, and busts of Buddha. In yet another, a teacher leads a group in the slow underwater motions of *tai chi*. Once in a while billiard balls snap a lively beat.

The mother of a student of mine told me about this place. It belongs to the county and runs separate programs for different ethnic groups: Chinese, Iranians, and Hispanics. Tuesday is Chinese day.

The director, a brawny drill sergeant looking man, takes us around. People wave and shout hello, greeting my parents as if they were old friends from Hong Kong. Their good cheer is infectious. Mami's smile squishes her eyes into slits and all that shows on her face is a row of teeth and implants. Baba's smile is a hint of one, which means he's not sure but wants to be polite. I'm confident he'll warm up after a while. The people he enjoys squabbling with fall into two categories: family members and "barbarians." But here, people are "civilized." They speak his language and share his experiences from the old country. What's not to like?

I fill in the pile of paperwork, pay the $1 lunch fee each, and say goodbye to my parents. Baba opens his mouth and stammers, "uh uh uh." Mami opens her mouth and shoots the question she asks every time I sneak out the front door. "Where are you going *this* time?"

"I'll be back to pick you up after lunch. One o'clock." I raise my index finger for visual effect.

"We'll take good care of them," the director says, signaling me to vamoose.

I bounce down the steps outside the building. My sneakers seem to have sprouted wings. The world looks brighter and fresher than on my way in. I take in a lungful of the mild, silky air. Walking across the lawn, I notice purple crocuses peeking out of the dull winter grass. The trees are reddish, as if a woman had kissed the branches and left smudges of lipstick. A flock of finches is chirping a chorus. I want to belt out with them, "Spring is here!" But I'll save it for home, the glorious empty house that will reverberate like a cathedral when I unleash my squeaky voice. I may even take off my clothes and stomp up and down the staircase. It's been two long months since I've done anything I want in my own house.

Mami is right. She *is* heavy, and so is Baba. And they're enjoying their piggyback ride so much they refuse to get down. We've been stuck together like a three-headed monster. When they're not home, it's because they're out with me. When I'm not home, their anxieties travel with me. They must count the seconds I'm gone, for the moment I walk in (deaf as they are, they can hear me tiptoeing around), one of them says, "You've been gone more than two hours!" Or whatever the case may be.

This is the first time I can leave them in a place where I won't have to fret about them, because they'll be too busy to fret about me. It's perfect!

*

"Uh uh uh," Tak sputters. The more he wants to say, "You can't leave us here," the more his jaws freeze.

"We'll take good care of them," the bearded man says to Cary. His eyebrows squirm. Tak notices Cary's eyebrows squirming in reply before she hurries away. What are they up to? What if Cary doesn't come back? Virginia is a foreign country, he doesn't know anyone here—

"Have you done *tai chi* before?" the man says.

The question, coming from a white man, is an insult. "*Tai chi* is too slow for me. I prefer *Wing Chun*." He flings out a backfist and is pleased at the *whoosh* it creates. "Why don't you give *tai chi* another try? Maybe you weren't ready for it before."

Not ready for it?! Is that a challenge? Tak throws off his tweed jacket, unbuttons his cuffs, and rolls up his shirt sleeves. Then he seats Ming-Jen at one of the long cafeteria tables and tells her to sit tight until he finishes the *tai chi* class.

The instructor is doing a "netting fish underwater" move. Tak genuflects to scoop up the fish. His knee screams in agony, but he forces himself to bend lower than the woman next to him. The next move, thank goodness, returns to standing position. While "grasping the sparrow's tail," he glances over at his wife. She's talking to another old woman, her lips twitching faster than a flea-infested monkey. In the early days of their marriage, Ming-Jen was a woman who measured her words in a teaspoon. It gradually grew into a tablespoon, soup spoon, bowl, pot, and bucket.

The instructor steps sideways and brings his arms up to "hug the moon." Tak follows suit. Ming-Jen disappears from his line of sight. His heart ticks a few extra tocks. Anything can happen to her the moment she leaves his watchful eyes. She can slip and fall, or suffer a stroke, or choke on her own spit.

"Ah-ya," a woman's voice clangs in his ears.

"So sorry, so sorry," Tak says, realizing he's stepped on his neighbor's toe. He quickly looks in his wife's direction to see if she's witnessed his gaffe. Her chair is empty. Where did she go? A vision of her lying on the floor flashes before his eyes.

He must go look for her.

"There you are," he says, finding her at the ceramics table. "I told you to sit there and wait for me."

"This looks like fun," she says. "You know how I loved to draw. If only I had the opportunity, I could have become a famous artist."

Tak winces at the jab. Whenever Ming-Jen says, "If only…," it means she regrets marrying him. If only she'd married a wealthy man, she wouldn't have had to leave her own family to babysit American brats, coming home every other weekend and working on holidays. She could have taken up drawing, singing, dancing, anything she wanted.

"You're too old for that now," he barks in anger. "Your hands tremble so much you can't even draw a straight line." Noticing the audience around him, he relaxes his tone. "Let's go sit down. I'll get you a cup of tea."

"It's not tea that I need. It's the bathroom."

"What, you want to go to your *bedroom*?"

"Where do you think it is?" She swivels her head around.

"What, are you dizzy? You need to lie down?"

One of the women at the table points to a double door. "The bathroom is out that door, to your left," she says.

"Oh, bathroom," Tak says. "Why didn't you say so?"

"I did. You're as deaf as I. And why aren't you wearing your new hearing aid? Your children paid $2,000 for it."

"I don't need it. The problem is you mutter. You should speak up."

You're deaf. You mutter. You're deaf. You mutter. They argue their way down the hall. At every step, the aluminum cane taps a hollow ring. Tak is glad Cary dragged Ming-Jen to the store to pick out a walking stick, and now she can't part with it. It has become her third leg.

Around noon, Tak tells Ming-Jen to hold his seat while he gets their lunch boxes. When he returns, he finds himself surrounded by women at his table. Tak is horrified at being the only male. Then he sees a man wandering around looking for a seat. Tak stares long and hard at him until his head turns and his eyes land on the empty chair across from Tak.

The man must have been as relieved as Tak. The two males quickly open a conversation with an immigrant to immigrant greeting. "How long have you been in America?" the man says.

"I've been here more than fifty years," Tak says, adding a decade to the truth. Among immigrants, who came first determines the pecking order. Tak always likes to be on top.

"Wah, that's a long time," the man says, duly impressed. "I've been here only ten years. I left Hong Kong after I retired. May I know what business you were in?"

"I was a manager at Macy's," Tak says proudly. No one can accuse him of lying. A floor salesman "manages" merchandise, and he's managed them all from women's shoes to men's underwear.

"Big company," the man says, impressed again.

"What business were you in?" Ming-Jen chimes in.

"I owned a garment factory in Hong Kong—the high-end fashion kind, not the basic jeans and T shirts. The mainland Chinese have taken over that market. They have plenty of labor, cheap and unskilled, which is fine for the low-end garments. We in Hong Kong have expensive taste!"

"What a coincidence," Ming-Jen said. "We were in the same—"

Tak kicks her foot under the table. Hong Kong is a small place, the garment industry even smaller. He doesn't want anyone to know his little pajama shop went bankrupt, and if his in-laws hadn't bailed him out, he would have gone to debtors' jail.

"I ran a convenience store," Tak says.

"Really? Where was it? Let's see if I've been your customer," the man says.

"I sold it a long time ago. You probably weren't born yet."

"Ha, ha, you compliment me. You think I look that young? I have to tell my wife when I get home."

"There's not a fleck of gray in your hair," Tak rubs it in. His message is as clear as shouting: You dyed your hair!

Unfortunately, Ming-Jen doesn't get it. "Your wife must be very young too. Why isn't she here today?"

"She has to stay home to wait for the plumber. My son is building an extension to his house. It's almost finished now. We can move in the moment the water is hooked up."

"You're living with your son?" Ming-Jen says. Her eyes shine with an unnatural light, as if they're beholding a divine apparition.

"My wife and I are nomads. We live a few months with a son, a few months with a daughter, and when we can't stand it anymore, we fly back to Hong Kong for a few months."

"You have a home in Hong Kong?" Ming-Jen says.

"We have an apartment at mid-levels."

Ming-Jen's body goes limp, as if she's about to fall on her knees and kowtow. She turns to Tak and says, "I've always wanted to live there."

Tak throws down his half-eaten sandwich. "I'm going to get more tea," he says. He can't stand this pompous ass anymore—his phony hair, high-end snobbery, and now his mid-levels apartment in Hong Kong. A native of Hong Kong, Tak understands the code words of his tribe. "Mid-levels" isn't for middle income; it's a status symbol for the upper crust. He's never coming back again. Ever.

Chapter 4

I bang on my parents' door and shout, "Time to get up. We're leaving in an hour." It's Tuesday again, Chinese day at the senior center.

Silence. I jiggle the knob. It's stuck. I press my ear on the door. It opens and I almost fall into Mami.

"We're not going to the center today. Baba is sick."

I peer down at my father. Although his eyes are closed, his forehead is awake with knots and wrinkles.

"How are you feeling?" I say with concern.

Baba's eyes open a crack. Slowly he lifts his arm and points a finger at his chest. "Pain," he whispers.

"Chest pain? You have chest pain?"

Baba nods. His hand sweeps down his entire left side. Sirens scream in my head. I've read somewhere pain shooting from the chest spells Heart Attack.

"I'll call an ambulance!"

Baba opens his eyes wide and waves no, no, no. "It's not so bad," he says. "I just need to rest."

I calm down, remembering what Karen once told me. "Chest pain" is his excuse for getting out of anything, mostly so he can stay home and watch porn flicks. I wish he would say it outright. My fear is that one day the heart attack will be real and I'll think he's crying wolf again.

"You shouldn't go to the senior center then." (Aha, do I see a quiver of a smile?) I turn to my mother, "You can still go. Hurry up and change. We're leaving soon." Turning back to Baba, I repeat my threat, "Let me know if you feel worse. I'll call 911."

He waves no, no, no again. I chuckle the moment I'm out of

the room. It's no wonder they call old age "second childhood." He's an eight-year-old faking sickness so he can play hooky. I'll let him off this time, since he's not the one who desperately needs an outlet for his jabber.

While I'm reading the papers in the kitchen, shuffling footsteps approach. Mami must be ready for breakfast. Wait a minute, another set of footsteps pound dangerously behind her. I run out to see who's after my mother.

"He won't let me go," Mami says. She's wearing the bottom of her pant suit and a pajama top that's half unbuttoned. The sight is shocking, because my mother never leaves her room before she's perfectly groomed and color-coordinated.

"How can she go by herself?" Baba shouts. "Look at the way she walks." Baba mimics by inching one foot in front of the other. He crooks his neck to pretend he has osteoporosis.

I want to laugh at his clowning.

"She's going to fall and break her bones and lie in bed for weeks! I'll have to take care of her! She's not going anywhere!"

He's not funny anymore. "There are volunteers at the center," I reason. "They'll help her get around."

"Will they catch her when she falls?" Baba shouts, a vein popping up in his temple.

All right, I've humored him enough. "Listen, you don't have to go if you don't want to. But Mami has to go out and see people. If she stays home all the time, she'll get Alzheimer's!"

"No, I don't want Alsi-heimer," Mami says, shuddering. "My mother was senile before she died. She didn't recognize anyone and peed and pooed all over herself. Oh, I'm so afraid I'll get it too one day."

"Go finish changing then," I say, pleased that my ploy is working. Actually it's not a ploy. I read somewhere the best prevention for dementia is to stay active.

Mami heads for the bedroom. Baba remains standing,

eyeballs rolling back and forth like marbles under the puffy lids. (His chest pain is obviously gone). I slip underground before he hatches another scheme to hold Mami hostage. While putting on my socks and sneakers, I hear voices reverberating on the floorboards above. Actually it's only one voice, as the other is too soft to be heard. I tell myself not to run up and intervene. The shouts sound like the last gasps of a person about to capitulate. Baba will come around for me. A glimpse in the mirror reminds me of our special connection. I'm practically his clone. The only genetic material Mami seems to have given me is the X chromosome.

"Don't look so sad," I say to Laozi gazing up at me. He offers his hippo snout for a kiss, to which I oblige. I grab a bunch of his skin and give him a facelift. As always, Laozi suffers my laughter in good humor. There, I feel better already. "Everything is going to be all right," I assure my best friend.

After checking my List and the day's teaching schedule, I venture back up. Mami teeters at the top of the staircase, her head lolling on her chest. She props it up with one hand to keep it from dropping to the floor.

"I'm going to faint," Mami moans.

I cloak my arms around my fragile mother and bring her to the sofa.

Baba appears, clutching the strap of a handbag. By the disgusted look on his face, he could be hanging on to the neck of a dead chicken. "She leaves her handbag wherever she goes. If I hadn't been there, she would have lost hundreds of handbags!"

"Leave her handbag at home then!" I counter. Uh oh, something is boiling up in me. I feel a noose of heat close in on my neck.

"It's no use. She's just a stupid old woman who doesn't know anything. How can she go anywhere on her own? Look what's in her handbag." He digs his hand into the leather bag and fishes out a card case. "See, these are all her cards. ID, Medicare, AARP. If she loses them she'll have no identity!" He throws the pouch on the floor. Little pieces of paper fly out. "And here, this is her wallet. See this cash? She's going to lose it!" Another thump and coins spill on the floor.

He pulls out a picture holder and brandishes it. "As soon as you step out the door, I'm going to flush your parents down the toilet!" he yells.

Reaching out, Mami cries, "Don't! This is their parting gift to me! This is the only thing I have of them!"

What happens next can only be called an "experience." I'm floating on the ceiling and gazing down. I see Mami slumped on the sofa and also another woman who looks a lot like me (except she has more gray hairs than I and flabby jowls). Her fists are clenched, and her neck pulses as she screeches, "Give me the picture! Goddammit, give it to me right now!" What a voice. The whole house shakes.

Baba scampers into his bedroom. The shrieking woman goes after him. "You're driving me crazy! Mami is going to the senior center and I don't want to hear another peep from you! Now give me the picture!" She waves her fist dangerously close to Baba's face. He cowers in a corner, an arm raised in self-defense.

The woman snatches the picture from Baba's hand, twirls around and walks away. The next moment, I find myself back down on earth, standing among a litter of coins and cards. My head feels empty. I look up the ceiling to see if my brains are still up there. Apparently not, and I have no idea where they've gone. The autopilot in me says, get down on all fours. Where there is debris, there's cleaning up to be done. Slowly, deliberately, I pick up each nickel and dime and drop it in the wallet. My fingertips tingle as blood gushes back into my deadened limbs.

I hand Mami the handbag with its original contents. "Let's

go," I say and clasp a firm grip on my mother's elbow.

I drive in silence, still feeling a bit like a Boeing 747 flying without a pilot.

"You have to apologize," a stern voice beside me says.

I look at my mother. Did I hear right?

"Filial piety is the root of civilization. If filial piety isn't pursued from beginning to end, disasters are sure to follow," Mami lectures. What comes next is worse than a slap on my face: "You have to apologize to your father."

Chapter 5

When the front door slams, Tak is still cowering in his bedroom. He gets up tentatively and looks out the window. Cary is marching to the car while Ming-Jen totters behind her. How he wants to run out and support Ming-Jen with his arm. But he has vowed never to go to the senior center again, or anywhere for that matter. He's going to spend the rest of his life in his room.

How dare Cary yell at him? Cary, his little Cary who used to light up his heart. Now she's his excuse to sink into the cozy dark hole where he's always wanted to stay forever. He'd gone there several times before, but each time his family badgered him into crawling back out. They just wouldn't let him enjoy his misery in peace.

Tak stretches his eyes until the car carrying his beloved Ming-Jen disappears. He then pulls down all the shades in his room and spreads out the fingers of one hand before him. The five digits are clearly visible. Dissatisfied, he goes into his study and looks around. His eyes land on a cardboard box under his desk. He drags it out and dumps the contents on the floor. Finding scissors and scotch tape, he goes back to the bedroom.

With every piece of cardboard he puts up, the darkness thickens. When both windows are covered, Tak conducts his finger test again. Good enough, he concludes. Even the most timid ghost will find the lighting acceptable. He turns on the bedside lamp and opens the night-table drawer. He giggles at the sight of the goodies. He fingers through the medicine bottles, like a child agonizing over which flavor of lollipop to pick. Other people drink alcohol to drown their sorrows. Unfortunately for him, alcohol, even as little as half a bottle of beer, makes him nauseous. He has to resort to a different medicine for his heartaches—medicine. His drawer is like a mini pharmacy. Uppers and downers, stimulants and suppressants, anything to suit his mood. Right now, he wants something to knock him out, so he can sleep through the day, through the *plink plonk plunk* of Cary's students, through Ming-Jen turning on the lights to look for something, through the pain of living.

He picks up a bottle. The Oxycontin left over from his heart surgery is prescribed and therefore should be reserved for special occasions. For now, over-the-counter will do. He narrows his choice down to two—Sudafed or Benadryl. Since the former is controlled and the latter isn't, he pours out three Benadryls and gulps them down. Aah, he smacks his lips. Now, there's nothing more to do than let the darkness digest him in its belly. He turns off the lamp and snuggles under his heated blanket.

The window rattles, and a gust ruffles his few strands of hair. Laozi barks from the basement. Then the *woof woof* turns into a hair-raising *woo-ooo-ooo*. Tak opens his eyes. Staring at him from the foot of the bed is a frail figure with a wide flat head that resembles a mushroom cap. "There you are, Mushroom," he says. "I knew you would find me sooner or later. I've fallen into the hole again. I hope you're satisfied. Go ahead and laugh."

The figure doesn't laugh; he just stands. Tak squints at the ghost for a closer look. Born three days apart, he and Mushroom had been neighbors and best friends since they could crawl. They were as close as twins, though the distribution of resources in the womb seemed rather lopsided. While all the brains went to Mushroom, the muscles went to Tak. Their mothers always wished they could put the two boys in the same pot, stir them until they were evenly blended, and then divvy up the mixture in equal portions. This was their recipe for two perfect sons.

"Make yourself at home," Tak says to the ghost. "There's tea in the kitchen." He's relieved his childhood friend has stepped into the open. Mushroom is always lurking behind a corner, waiting for the chance to stick his foot out and trip Tak up. It's a prank they used to play on one another. Nowadays, however, the ambush is only one way. Fair enough, Tak thinks, considering what he did to Mushroom.

Years ago, when the workers in Tak's pajama shop left him for another company, people told him he could replace the workers and rebuild. He knew better though. The only way to escape Mushroom's vengeance was to leave town. But he'd forgotten ghosts could fly anywhere without a plane ticket or passport. Mushroom caught up with him in America and continued to destroy everything Tak created. Tak's bad luck became so notorious that no businessman in the Chinese community wanted to partner with him.

Tak burrows deeper into the blanket. Remembering something, he sticks his head back out: "Let me remind you about our agreement. You can do what you like with me. I know I deserve it. But if you touch a hair of Ming-Jen or anyone else in my family, I'll chop off your head myself."

Mushroom cracks a loopy smile. He's the same gawky twenty-four-year-old, hopelessly clueless about women and such things. While Tak has aged into a worldly old man, Mushroom's mortal clock stopped more than half a century ago.

*

They waited anxiously. He and Mushroom had stolen into the basement and hidden behind the crates. Sitting cross-legged on the floor, Tak listened to every sound, the clack-clack-clack of military boots, the soft patter of cloth shoes, and voices of men, some of whom he knew. Before the war, his father had come here once a week to get supplies for the family store. Tak had always accompanied him. He knew the building layout as well as that of his own home.

Finally he heard the sound he'd been waiting for, the screech of the rusty grill sliding across the entrance of the building. The turbaned watchman, an Indian named Ah Singh, would sit by the gate all night, his hockey stick leaning against the wall. Tak would normally exchange pleasantries with him, but tonight he would use a different exit—the window.

Tak waited a while longer. When he was sure the only sound was the pumping of his heart, he stood up and stretched out the kinks in his legs. Although he couldn't see his companion he could feel his breath close by. Mushroom had an annoying habit of breathing through his mouth when he was nervous. "It's time," Tak hissed.

Together they groped their way to the mountain of rice. Ah, rice. The aroma wafting through the gunny sacks made Tak woozy. He steadied himself and reached for the sack on top.

"Come here," Tak whispered to his friend. His hands grabbed the fuzzy outline of a shoulder. The sharpness of the bone jolted him. In three years of Japanese occupation, Hong Kong had become a population of skeletons. The war had cut off supply lines, and Hong Kong was too small to produce its own food. Whatever food there was was reserved for the Japanese and their running dogs. Tak had to punch extra holes in his belt to keep his pants from falling.

Bracing his legs, he heaved an eighty-pound sack onto Mushroom's back. A thud sounded. Tak reached out for his friend and found only air. A soft heap lay at the tip of his shoes.

"It's too heavy for me," Mushroom whimpered.

"Don't be such a sissy. When carrying heavy things, you have to use your legs." This was his first lesson from carrying merchandise around his family store. "Get up. Let me teach you." A sob escaped from Mushroom. Tak wanted to pick him up and wring his spindly neck. He'd gotten into many fistfights on behalf of Mushroom, though never with Mushroom. It would be as cruel as torturing a puppy.

"The old and young in your family depend on you," Tak growled.

His words took immediate effect. Mushroom scrambled up. Tak grabbed the bony shoulder. "Spread your legs a little," he whispered into Mushroom's ear. "Now tighten your muscles from your tummy all the way down to your calves." He pressed his hand on his friend's midriff. The thin belly caved in. Tak thought he could feel the vertebrae. "All right, I'm going to give you a forty-pound bag. You're ready now?"

"Give me the eighty pound," Mushroom said, his voice no longer a boy's.

"You sure?"

"Go ahead. I'm not afraid to die."

"Spit it out and say it again, you idiot," Tak says, furious his friend should mention the unlucky word. "Here it comes."

Tak tightened his muscles and hoisted. The sack stayed. Mushroom doubled over, but he didn't collapse.

"Can you walk?"

Mushroom shuffled a few steps. "You're sure you're all right?" Tak says.

A grunt was all that Mushroom could muster.

*

At this point in his reminiscence, Tak always pauses to ponder the what-ifs and should-haves. For example, before loading the sack onto Mushroom's back, he should have stopped to think for a second, just a second. If he had done that, he would have remembered. In the best of times, Mushroom had to hold a bag of sugar to coax the scale to read a hundred pounds. In the worst of times, he couldn't have weighed more than eighty. In that second's pause, Tak would have remembered that Mushroom was all brains. Give him the hardest math problem and he could solve it in his head. But give him a hammer and he would drop it on his toes. His arms and legs were as smooth as a girl's. In that second's pause, Tak's sensible self would have taken charge. He would have loaded Mushroom with a forty-pound bag instead; he would have shut up about the old and young in Mushroom's family, he would have, should have.

Tak ran from shadow to shadow. The load on his back was heavy, but the iron pumping he'd done to impress girls came in handy. Mushroom, on the other hand, was never interested in girls. He staggered somewhere behind, Tak could hear him. The three-quarter moon played hide and seek among the clouds, sometimes shining on them like a search light, other times smothering them in darkness. After a few blocks, Tak glanced back. The street was empty. Where was Mushroom? Tak ducked behind a building to wait for his friend. His heart boomed like a tom-tom in his ears. He wished it weren't so loud. Two more blocks and they would be out of the heavily patrolled Central District. After that, they would follow the safe route they had staked out.

A bizarre-looking creature emerged from the shadows. It looked like a tortoise crossing the street in a drunken zigzag. The shell slipped off. Mushroom stood up, his soft flesh exposed. Tak waved to him frantically, his mouth miming a shout, "Leave it! Leave it!" Mushroom picked up the corners of the sack and began to drag it.

Tak wanted to rush out of hiding, but the burden on his back put a brake on him. He couldn't set it down. The sack of rice was his family's lifeline. Letting go of it meant watching his little sister and grandfather die. Life had been leaking fast out of the youngest and oldest in the family. Without replenishment there was no hope for them.

A light flashed on Mushroom's face. And it wasn't moonlight.

Three soldiers rushed out. "Halt!" they yelled in their stilted Cantonese. Tak crouched close to the ground, making himself as small as possible. A flurry of ideas scattered in his head like a flock of frightened birds. He would walk out as carefree as a man taking an evening stroll and offer the soldiers cigarettes. He would creep up from behind, grab a rifle from a soldier and bayonet them all. He would wave to the soldiers and taunt them to chase him. He would hurl himself against the soldier who had raised his sword high up in the air.

The next part he can bear to remember only in reverse. One night before the war, when they were boys looking for fun, he and Mushroom stole into the school auditorium. They got their hands on the movie projector, which was still loaded with a film. Fiddling with the controls, they played it in reverse by mistake. How they'd laughed at the sight of people sprinting backwards, a body flying out of the water onto the diving board, a man spooning food out of his mouth, two boys unwinding their punches from each other. They played the scenes backward over and over until their bellies cramped with laughter.

Tak shifts his brain into reverse. Mushroom's head leaps up from the ground and settles back between his shoulders. The Japanese soldiers run backward into the dark, their little legs pumping like Charlie Chaplin's in a silent movie. A giant wind sucks at Tak's back, pulling him into the building, out onto the streets through the front entrance, and into the convenience store owned by his family. The film ends with Tak sitting at the counter dealing cards to Mushroom, surrounded by empty shelves. They should have kept on playing cards all night.

Tak feels the Benadryl flood his body. About time. The Benadryl has been rather slow today. Perhaps he should get up and take two more...if only his legs didn't feel...so...heavy...

Chapter 6

A thick cloud of Tiger Balm billows out as I open the door to my parents' bedroom. Tiger Balm, which Baba uses for everything from headaches and backaches to heartaches, smells of menthol in small dabs. In huge quantities it smells like a rat pickled in formaldehyde.

I step back to let Mami lead the way into the disaster zone. The rest of us file in according to age hierarchy: Karen, George, me, and Laozi. "You don't have to come," I mouth to Steve, who rubs his nose to hide his relief. We leave the door ajar to let the light in and the foul air out.

Since our blowup more than a month ago, Baba has holed up in his darkened room like a mole. I've bought him chocolates and girlie magazines as peace offerings (so embarrassing to see the male cashier snicker while ringing them up). However, there's one thing I refuse to do—apologize. Mind you, I'm not one of those hard-headed people who can't spit out the little word "sorry." If I know I've done a person wrong, I'd ask for forgiveness until I'm begged to stop. But if I know I'm in the right, nothing can force me to compromise, regardless of who it is and what calamities might befall.

"How are you feeling, Baba?" Karen queries the motionless body in the bed. Her voice rings with the authority of a high schoolmistress, which she happens to be. And she got plenty of practice as a child, when she ruled over a school of two students named George and Cary.

Baba points to his heart and shakes his head to indicate, "Not well." His eyes linger lovingly on his eldest daughter. Tears well up, but he blinks them back stoically.

My insides shrivel with envy and disgust. This besotted gaze was once directed at me, when I was the visitor from afar and

Karen was the terrible daughter who lived close by. Now our roles are reversed.

"Has he seen a cardiologist?" Big Sister asks me.

"I was going to make an appointment, and then this came up," I say sheepishly.

Big Sister pierces me with a laser beam. I feel like a student hauled to the principal's office to explain my tardiness. Then I remember we're all grownups now. She can't treat me like a kid anymore. I blast back with my own laser gun, and she turns away. Her profile is just like Mami's, the eyes, nose, and mouth as elegant as a porcelain doll's. Her skin, too, is like Mami's, smooth as silk and taut as permanent press. Six years older than I, she's a fifty-five who's the new forty-five, which means some people have mistaken her for my Little Sister. I hate her.

"Has he had any blood work done since he came here?" Big Sister carries on the interrogation.

"They've both had comprehensive physicals. Blood tests, EKG, X ray, stool sample, the whole works. Everything checked out fine," I declare with defiance.

"Has he been back to the doctor's since, you know, the 'incident'?" Karen pursues. The "incident" is our shorthand for the blowup that triggered our family crisis.

Lowering my voice to spare the patient the grave diagnosis, I report, "Yes, and the doctor thinks he has depression."

Karen nods an all-knowing nod. "He's been depressed all his life," she whispers back. "It's not your fault." Her hand finds mine and squeezes.

Right, you know everything, I say in my head. Before the doctor said so, you already knew Baba had depression. You've known all along what's wrong with our father. You were just keeping it to yourself. Never mind that I devoted the last three months of my life to making our parents happy. The moment I slip up, you and George gallop in like officials of the Inquisition.

Grill me all you want, put me on the rack, water board me. Just don't patronize me.

George kneels by the bed, holding Baba's hand and sobbing as if the old man were wheezing his last breaths. Two huge drops leak from the corners of Baba's eyes. George pulls out his handkerchief and tenderly dabs at the pasty face. "I wanted to come earlier," he chokes, "but I was on a business trip. Please get well soon, Baba."

Of the three of us, the boy is the crybaby. This behavior may be caused by all the estrogen around him, first from two sisters and now three daughters. All that's needed to open his tear glands is the sight of another person crying. Our parents worried how he would fend for himself in the world. When he opened a bank, they fretted over the day he would blubber in front of his staff and clients. It wasn't a matter of if, but when. Yet his little bank continues to grow. It's not so little anymore, with branches shooting up in every part of California.

After a mutually long and passionate gaze, George wobbles up—his knees aren't what they used to be. He's put on a few pounds and is looking more like Baba. When his face was long and slender, he was Mami's son.

He checks the mug on the night table. "The tea has gone cold. Let me get you a fresh cup," he says to the patient.

Baba hangs out his tongue like a man stranded in the desert. If the cup weren't half full, one would think he hasn't had a drop for days.

"I'll get it," I say, glad for any excuse to leave the room. Laozi shadows me as if to give me moral support. How I wish he could speak. He sees everything that goes on in this house. He can give my siblings an eyewitness account of all the things I do for my parents.

When I return, Mami is huddled with my siblings like a quarterback strategizing the next play. However, she doesn't seem to know she's not supposed to broadcast her words to the opposition. Or more likely she's too deaf to realize she's shouting: "Baba will be fine when he goes back to California. This place isn't right for him. The weather is too cold, and Cary has a stinky temper." My siblings dart glances at me standing behind her. Mami carries on, "I don't know what came over her. She flew at Baba like a mad hen. You've got to move us back."

I'm stunned...shocked...like the time I stumbled on Mami naked in bed with Baba. At eight or nine, I had no idea what she was doing, only something "yukky" was going on. I quickly stepped back and closed the door. I feel I should do the same now. Part of me tells me I should pretend not to have heard (in her mind she was whispering after all). But the other part says, "You can't let her get away with this!"

"WHERE ARE YOU GOING TO LIVE?" I shout into Mami's ear. She turns around, startled. I unleash my lips on her so she can read me loud and clear. "You've used up your welcome in every home. Who's going to take you next?"

"I'll live on the streets then. A person who follows the Way is at peace anywhere. In all my life, I've never shouted at my parents. My only fault is I've failed to raise my children to practice the virtues—"

"All right, all right." Karen inserts both hands to split us apart. "We'll talk about this later." She gives me a wink and nod that tells me she's got a plan.

Well, if you do, let me know before you fly home tomorrow, I'm tempted to say. I always toe the line. After all, I was trained to be handmaid to Princess Karen. Fanning the princess on a hot day, holding up the train of the royal bedsheet dress, leading away the horse of the knight (George)—those were the handmaid's chores. Tell me what needs to be done, and I'll humbly comply.

*

We arrive at Happy Family, Virginia's premier Chinese restaurant. At two in the afternoon the crowds that usually spill onto the sidewalk have gone home, probably for a nap after the dim sum binge. The place looks as desolate as the aftermath of a carnage. The scene reminds me of the battle of Gettysburg, where I took the children for a civil war lesson years ago. The dishes littering the tables are wounded soldiers moaning for help. The steamers stacked four, five high are the dead waiting to be buried. The air is rank with rotting flesh. I don't know why I feel this way. Maybe it's because war is on my mind.

Sitting across from Baba at the round table, my eyes bump into his by accident. He shoots me an icy look that says, "I don't need you anymore." I dish it right back to him: "That's what you think. They're flying home tomorrow. Whatcha gonna do then?"

Though pale from the lack of sunlight, he's far from wasting away. In fact, he may have put on weight. When I lie awake at night (feeling hot and agitated), I often hear him rattling around upstairs. The next morning, the leftovers in the fridge are gone, and dirty dishes are scattered around the TV room.

Actually, I'm not mad at him anymore. He's the way he is because he has depression, which is an illness like a cold or cancer. You can't blame the patient for getting sick. But Mami is a different story. I shift my gaze to her. A smile beatifies her face; a halo glows over her head. I've always thought of my mother as a saint—kind, honorable and sincere. (She loved to quote Confucius as saying "Sincerity is the basis of all virtues," meaning, we shouldn't lie to her.) My opinion of her has changed as of an hour ago. She's a devil with a forked tongue. Only yesterday, she told me she wanted to stay in my home: "Of course it's more convenient for a daughter to take care of me." Today, she tells my siblings I'm too dangerous to live with.

"Sister, are you still serving dim sum?" George says to the waitress.

"Brother, the carts stop coming out at two. Tell me what you want, and I'll bring them out."

George orders the usual *har gao, shiu mai,* and *char siu bao.*

"Don't forget the chicken feet," Karen says.

I glance at Steve next to me. Karen catches my expression.

"Sorry, you probably don't like chicken feet," she says to Steve.

"It depends on whether they've been manicured," Steve replies deadpan.

Karen looks stumped.

"He doesn't care for them," I explain. "You can order them. Just keep them on your side of the table." Frankly, I have a yen for them too, those juicy, gummy toes, but I'm afraid Steve will never kiss me again. He says they remind him of the chickens on his parents' farm, with their long nails scrabbling in the dirt they pooped on. Since he started hanging out with me, my husband has acquired a taste for funguses, thousand year old eggs, and other Chinese delicacies, but chicken claws will forever pose a cultural gulf between us.

After food and drinks are ordered, the smiles vanish and serious hustling resumes. Karen works on Baba, George on Mami, and Mami on George, which leaves Steve and me playing footsies under the table. I nudge his sneaker with mine.

"They're gabbing about things you're not interested in," I assure my husband, whose understanding of Cantonese is limited to a few graphic cusswords. "I'll let you know when something important comes up." I try my best to shield my husband from my family dramas. It's only fair since his contact with his own family is only a phone call now and then. I'm one of those lucky people who don't have to put up with in-laws.

"I love this place," Steve says. "It's so classic. I wish I could bring my students here. You can't find a better example of how *not* to decorate a restaurant."

"Really?" I say, not sure what I'm questioning. My eyes are on Steve, but my satellite dish is pointed at the signals coming from Karen's mouth:

"You know, Baba, it's quite common for an older person to feel sad. Sometimes the reason is your body has stopped producing certain hormones. Or your body doesn't absorb vitamins as well as before. This can cause a chemical imbalance, which can make you feel weak, tired and...*sad*."

This is the closest Karen can come to using the word "depression." We tiptoe around this term because it's a mental illness. Most Chinese equate "mentally ill" with "crazy" and therefore unspeakable where it concerns a family member. We divide the world into two categories, sane and insane, and the shades in between don't exist.

"Just look at the color of this carpet," I hear Steve's voice. "What color would you call it?"

"I'm not sad," Baba says to Karen. "I just don't feel like doing anything. I'm too old."

"Green," I blurt the first thing that comes to my mind.

Karen: "But you're still alive. As long as you can breathe, you have to live."

Steve: "It was green once upon a time. Now it's the color of rotten lettuce. Parts of it are brown and watery, and the rest is yellowish green, like snot."

In our previous discussions of Chinese esthetics, I'd told him we go to restaurants to eat, not to look at the décor. (A Chinese can squat by the roadside, slurping a bowl of noodles while rats scurry in the sewer close by, and still be in paradise as long as the noodles taste good.) This time I let it go because I'm too busy eavesdropping. Karen is spouting about vitamin B12 deficiency, anemia, and supplements. She's a biologist by training. Just as a priest has a spiritual solution to every problem, her approach is physiological. My stomach sinks. If vitamins are all she has in her plan, the battle is lost.

"The gem is over there," Steve says as he points to the rows of pink strips glued to the wall. Only people who read Chinese can order from this menu of delicacies. "Are they serving bull's 'whip' today?"

"No," I say without looking at the strips. In normal times, I would have said, "The bull saw the cook coming and ran away." But today, bantering about the Chinese appetite for reproductive organs isn't on my agenda.

George is jawing with Mami about an apartment building close to his home, a luxury condo with doorman and receptionist. "I'll hire somebody to cook and clean for you," he says.

So...you think a housekeeper can replace me, I fume to myself. You expect a housekeeper to monitor our parents' health, take them to the right specialist as needed, fix their TV when they mess up the settings, treat them to restaurants and movies (and give them a synopsis beforehand), and labor like an indentured servant without pay or weekends off? Even if you're close by, you can't do much since you work twelve-hour days and travel frequently on business. Your Red Guard wife (excuse me, this is Mami's name for her, not mine) regards them as people's enemy number one. And what's the price tag on this deluxe care package? You have two girls in college and one to go. Can you afford it, and more importantly, will your wife agree?

"How's the food? Would you like anything else?" asks the restaurant owner, a Vietnamese Chinese woman around my age.

"Everything is excellent," George says. "When I go back to California, I'll tell my friends the dim sum in Virginia is better than San Francisco Chinatown's."

We're all smiles again.

"You flatter us. You're here on a visit?" the woman asks with a broad grin.

"I'm here to see my parents. These two are my sisters." I gesture with my eyes that he's forgetting somebody. "And that's my brother-in-law. Hey, bro—" George switches to English— "how are you doing over there?"

"What a big happy family," the woman says. As her eyes land on the old folks, her spine goes limp and her face melts into a pool of dimples and folds. She leans forward as if wanting to tickle them under the chin. Little does she know these two darlings, with a flick of their hands, can destroy your life as you know it.

"Can you tell me please, where is the bathroom?" Mami says with the sweetness she saves for the public.

"It's over there. Let me take you," the woman says.

Baba gets up to go with them. Thank goodness for their overactive bladders. Finally I have a moment to rally my forces.

"I have a proposal to make," I say once our parents turn their backs. "Baba should see a psychiatrist for his depression." I hold my breath, waiting for lightning to strike. George lowers his head, as if ashamed to hear his sister utter such sacrilege. Karen looks at me like a mother at a precocious child who uses big words she doesn't quite understand.

"He's eighty-four years old. Isn't it a bit late to change who he is?" Karen says.

You don't know everything in the past, present, and future, I retort in my head. If you did, you wouldn't have married the hippie, only to divorce him after a year. You wouldn't have gone to med school, only to quit after a semester. And you would have noticed your son was trying out drugs before it became an addiction.

For the sake of harmony, I give a clichéd answer, "Better late than never. There's no harm in trying."

"You'll never get him to go. He's got too much pride," George says, speaking like a man.

"Just give me a chance," I'm close to begging. "Three months is all I'm asking for. If by the end of July he doesn't get better, you can take him back. He's all yours." My siblings, who seemed so sure of themselves a minute ago, show signs of wavering. The prospect of taking possession of Baba, with the added bonus of Mami, would make anyone think twice.

"I'm just worried it's too much work for you," Big Sister says.

"I don't mind the work, but I need support from both of you. In the past, our parents have used 'divide and conquer' to put us down. When they complained about you, Karen, and you too, George, I believed them—"

"What did they say about me?" George says with alarm.

"It doesn't matter," Karen holds him back. "Let Cary finish."

"We can't let them jerk us around anymore. We have to face them with a *united front*. Let's agree on a plan and stick to it, at least for three months."

Silence. I can almost see the smoke curling out of my siblings' ears as they try to cook up an answer. Karen is the first to speak. "If Baba is willing to go, he may actually get something out of it. Who knows? What do you think, George?"

"If that's what both of you want," he shrugs. Deflecting Karen's gaze, he turns to Steve, "What do you think, bro?"

"Me?" Steve says, startled at being included in the decision-making. "I always think whatever Cary thinks. She's my four star general." He mocks a salute in my direction.

"Four stars only? Mine has five," George quips.

"The fifth star is awarded only during wartime," Steve notes. "There are no more than five of them in the army. They're MacArthur, Eisenhower..." He goes on listing them all.

Frankly, I want to say, I don't care whether I'm a four or five star general. All I want is to play princess for once. It's about time Karen calls me "My lady," George kisses my hand and I get to issue a royal edict. From the way the discussion is going, I think my siblings will grant me my wish.

Chapter 7

Ming-Jen marches into the room. Considering her mousy steps, "march" may be too strong a word. However, considering the determination in her heart, her gait meets the military connotation in spirit. She "marches" to the window and gives the shade a firm tug. It rolls up with a snap. The noon sun burns through the cardboard squares, diffusing the room with a muted glow. Tak utters "mmm" in protest. Ming-Jen shoves back her husband's leg and plunks herself on the edge of the bed.

"Wake up. We're going back to California," she says.

Tak's eyes pop open. "Xiao has found an apartment for us," she goes on. "We have to give him some time to get the place ready. He said in a month or two he'll send for us. Come on, get up. This isn't the time to play sick."

Tak's legs stir under the cover.

"You have to eat well and get strong. There's a lot of work ahead. You can't expect me to do all the packing."

She stands up to give Tak room. A dry, scaly foot pokes out of the blanket, then the other.

"You go wash your face and brush your teeth. I'll get lunch on the table. Guess what we're having today? Long life noodles. You like that, don't you?"

As soon as she enters the kitchen, Laozi walks up to her and says, "Ar ar ar." She can't help smiling at the wrinkly face, so ugly that it's beautiful. He truly looks like a Laozi, which means Wise Old One. She never cared for pets before, but this one is different. He's practically human, the way he talks and communicates with his eyes.

"You know it's lunch time, don't you?" She opens the

pantry and tosses him a saltine, then another.

At her request, Cary has made noodle soup for lunch, Tak's favorite food. Ming-Jen wants to make sure her husband has a happy stomach today. In English they say "the way to a man's heart is through his stomach." In Chinese they say "the people regard food as heaven." When the children first broached the psychiatrist idea with her, she'd thought it was ridiculous. Depression is a white man's disease, so how can her husband have contracted it? Her children, however, refused to listen. They were going to do things their way, with or without her permission. In which case, she'd better be smart about it. She may not have a fancy degree, but no psychiatrist understands her family's psychology better than she.

She turns the switch on the stove and bends to see if the flame is on. Cary has told her to listen for the click. Ming-Jen prefers to look. It's a bit of trial and error. By rotating the knob back and forth, a ring of fire eventually appears.

While the soup is warming, she decides a sprinkle of green onions will add color and fragrance. She takes out a bag of the herb from the fridge. Although she's lived here three months now, this is still an unfamiliar kitchen to her. Cary is the boss here, and not a good one at that. Her knives are blunt and the chopping board is plastic instead of solid wood. With these primitive tools she can only cut the scallions into crude disks instead of the finely minced bits they should be.

When she turns around, the broth has frothed up the lid and splashed all over the stovetop. A pungent odor stings her nostrils. She lifts the pot and discovers the fire is out. She quickly turns off the gas.

At the table Ming-Jen takes the seat next to Tak. For the purpose of listening, which she does with her eyes, sitting across is preferable. In this case, however, talking is more important. She wants to be able to lean over and drill her words into Tak's good ear.

Tak mumbles something. Ming-Jen guesses he must be asking about the others. "Cary is having lunch with a friend. You know how she likes to go out with her friends." A tang of vinegar makes her mouth pucker. "And Steve is never home. It's just us," she sighs.

She notices how pale her husband is. Even the age spots on his face have faded to gray. She decides not to waste more time. "Cary has changed. She was such a sweet, good-natured child. I've always said of all my babies, she was the easiest to take care of. Even at a month old, she slept from sunset to sunrise. Look at her now. She even dared to yell at you. No matter what a parent does, it's no excuse for a child to behave with disrespect."

She shakes her head to show her disappointment. "Listen to me, Tak, this isn't the right home for us. The best place is an apartment close to Xiao. After a few months there, he'll see how helpless we are and take us into his home. He has to. He's the eldest son."

"When is he sending us the plane tickets?"

"In any major move there must be meticulous planning. Xiao has every intention to move us back, but our two girls have laid down one condition. They want you to see a doctor—just for a check up. You know, you're almost eighty-five. It's best to catch a problem early."

"I had a checkup recently. The doctor said I was fine."

"Your daughters want you to see a doctor for your brain. They say there's a very good hospital in DC that specializes in Alsi-heimer. You know, of people over eighty-five, half have Alsi-heimer." She shudders as she always does at the mention of the dreaded disease. She may not remember what she had for lunch, but she'll never forget the statistics that Cary has drilled into her head.

"You think I have Alzheimer's?"

"Noooo, this is just to humor our daughters." Ming-Jen grasps his hand in earnest. "Listen to me, Tak. When dealing with our children, we have to speak with one mouth. When they're naughty, we have to punish them together. Otherwise they won't know right from wrong. This is how I see it. You know how stubborn your daughters are. If no one gives in, the situation will turn into a stalemate. Sometimes to attack you have to retreat. Let them win this round. Go to your appointment. Let the doctor check you out. There's nothing to be afraid of."

"What appointment?"

"Well, it's not till next week. There's no harm in getting a few tests. Afterwards you can come home and go back to bed. Xiao will send for us soon."

Tak is silent. Time for her to pull out her most potent argument. She plows right in. "Maybe the psychiatrist will give you the medicine you want. You know, the medicine *all* the other doctors won't let you have."

"Oh, *that* one." Tak's lips crinkle into a crooked smile, then a pout. "All right, I'll do it for you," he huffs to indicate he's doing her a great favor.

Ming-Jen refrains from clapping her hands. A little warning flags in her head. What do the commercials say? Anybody experiencing an erection for more than three hours should contact the doctor immediately. *Ayah, what have I done to myself?*

*

As Ming-Jen lies down for her afternoon nap, she contemplates another most important virtue—*Zhong*, loyalty. For a woman, *Zhong* means that when her husband falls into the sea, she jumps in with him. If she's a strong swimmer, she'll pull him to shore. If not, they'll sink together.

Ming-Jen thinks of the occasions she had to dive in to save her husband. Every time she feels like sinking to the bottom with him, a last minute burst of energy always propels both of them to the surface. After all, it's her duty. A woman should serve her husband even if he happens to be a dog, or pig, or horse. Perhaps she shouldn't have married him in the first place, but once the deed was done, her obligations to him were non-negotiable. Loyalty is her soul, the source of her strength to carry on.

The first time she set eyes on Tak was at the convenience store down the street from Auntie's apartment in Hong Kong. The abundance of goods packed into the little space was dizzying. She'd had to sidle between the narrow aisles to get in. Then the goods were right up against her face, so close they made her eyes cross. Every household item was there, from the mundane toilet paper and soap to the exotic medicinal herbs and jewelry boxes. There was even a shelf for clothing. Ming-Jen caught sight of a pile of bras. She guessed that was what they were. She'd seen pictures of women who wore them and had been shocked by their outrageous shapes. Virtuous women hid theirs under stiff cotton undershirts.

She was bending over the glass case to examine a pretty lacquer box when a bass voice said, "Shall I take it out for you, Miss?" She straightened up and turned around. Her nose almost brushed his. The blood rose to her hairline. She took a step backward and stammered, "No, no, I didn't come here to buy. I came here with my Aunt."

The man looked across the store where a woman was browsing the shelves. "So you're Mrs. Ho's niece. No wonder you look like her and talk like her. You must be from out of province."

Ming-Jen hated the local term for anyone from north of Kwangtung province. Hong Kong people sounded as if they, the Cantonese, were the center of China. In Beijing, though, the Cantonese were regarded as southern barbarians.

"I'm from the nation's capital, Beijing." She refused to say

Peking, the harsh Cantonese pronunciation of her city.

"Are you running from the communists?"

"I'm not running from anyone," Ming-Jen replied, surprised at her bluntness. He started it first, although there was no need to stoop to his level. She blushed as her eyes fell on the knots of muscles on his calves. The man was wearing shorts! She felt an urge to escape. The high collar of her *chipao* was choking her. There wasn't enough oxygen in the cramped space for the two of them. She whipped her braid around and tugged at the brushy ends. It always had a calming effect on her, as it gave her an excuse to lower her eyes.

"You must have just arrived, or I would have seen you before. You can't walk around my neighborhood without my noticing. I'm here all day. I was born in the store, and that was twenty-six years ago. Ha ha ha. The storekeeper over there is my father. Everyone calls me Tak."

Tak means virtue, Ming-Jen noted. She had no idea about his character, although he certainly lacked the virtue of propriety.

"I came two weeks ago," she felt obliged to respond. Her father had taught her to treat everyone, from the highest to the lowest, with good manners.

"Are you going to settle down in Hong Kong?"

"No," she said firmly. "I'm just visiting. My parents are still in Beijing."

"Still in Peking! Aren't they afraid of the communists?"

"My father is a patriot. He'll never leave China." Her eyes felt hot at the mention of her father.

"Isn't he afraid the communists would put him in jail?"

Anger was her first reaction. How could this mere stranger express the greatest fear in her heart in such a brash manner? Then discipline took hold of her. She would show him an example of civilized behavior.

"My father is a learned man. All his life he has followed the path of compassion and loyalty. Every government since the Manchu dynasty has found use for his talents. I expect this government will do the same."

The man stared at her with his round, savage eyes, opaque with incomprehension. It was as if she'd spoken in a foreign language. Ming-Jen walked away with satisfaction. She'd put the oaf in his proper place.

"I saw you talking to Tak," Auntie said on their way home. "What did he say to you?"

"He asked if I were settling in Hong Kong."

"What did you say?"

Ming-Jen sensed anxiety in her aunt's voice. Was she worried that Ming-Jen and her siblings were staying forever? "I told him no. I was going back to my parents in Beijing."

Auntie was silent. Ming-Jen stole a sidelong glance at her father's elder sister. Auntie's husband, a capitalist and engineer trained in the U.S., had shipped his textile factory to Hong Kong at the first communist victory in the northeast. When Beijing fell, Ming-Jen and her two younger siblings were sent to visit their relatives in Hong Kong. At the train station, Father told her to obey Auntie in "ten thousand things."

"You have to know," Auntie said, "during your stay here I'm responsible for your safety. You have to be careful of Tak. He's not in your class. His father is the owner of the store, a crude man with little education. Your father is a scholar, a mandarin. There's nothing more important to him than learning and virtuous behavior." Aunt leaned closer to Ming-Jen. "Tak is known for running around with loose women. His mother is frantic about it. She's been knocking on the door of every matchmaker, trying to find a decent wife for him. You don't want to get close to this kind of man."

"I understand," Ming-Jen said obediently. This rule would

be a pleasure to comply with. At this point in her life, all she wanted was a letter from her Baba saying it was safe to return. Even if the most educated, most superior man in the whole of Hong Kong sought her hand, she would turn him down. Avoiding a storekeeper's son would require no sacrifice on her part.

News from Beijing finally came—a letter from her eldest brother. The Communist Party had recognized his contribution to the student movement and accepted his application for party membership. Father was also active in the revolution, having "volunteered" to go to reeducation camp. "Don't worry, Father is treated well," her brother wrote. "The Communist Party is like our mother. She is kind to her children, although she is also strict in disciplining them. It is for their good. Long live the Communist Party!"

She tried not to worry. In Confucius' teachings, fraternal respect was second only to filial piety. She adored her eldest brother, the lad who had taught her brush painting. He would never lie to her. Then again, if the government was as benign as he described, why hadn't he arranged for her return?

She discovered why when a cousin who had escaped from Beijing knocked on Auntie's door. The young man had hung on to a float and paddled across shark-infested water from the mainland to Hong Kong.

"Where are you staying now?" Auntie asked as Ming-Jen and her siblings gathered around the visitor in the living room. He was related to Ming-Jen's mother and thus no blood relation of Auntie's.

"I'm staying with my brother," he said.

"Good," Auntie said.

Ming-Jen understood the meaning of that one little word. Lately Auntie had been lamenting her apartment had been turned into a refugee camp.

"Do you have news of my brother?" Auntie said.

The man clutched a clump of his unkempt hair. Ming-Jen noticed he was no longer the bright-eyed, round-cheeked cousin she'd last seen a year ago. They were around the same age, yet lines marked his face and his eyes were weary.

"Ah," he moaned. "Before I left I went to his home to say goodbye." He turned to Ming-Jen. "Your mother told me the Communist Party had asked him to write an essay to denounce Confucianism. He refused and they shipped him to the Siberian border for reeducation."

A long silence ensued. Ming-Jen felt her heart sink to the floor. However, she would never disobey Father's last command: Be strong, and set an example for your younger brother and sister.

That night, pockets of whispering buzzed behind closed doors. Ming-Jen huddled with her brother and sister, weeping on each other's shoulder. They knew their father had received a life sentence, as he would never, ever denounce Confucius. Auntie must have drawn the same conclusion. While passing by Auntie's bedroom, Ming-Jen heard her murmur to Uncle, "The boy can help you at the factory. The girls are a burden. We'll have to marry them off as soon as possible. I have an idea for the older one…"

The next day Auntie took Ming-Jen to the convenience store. Auntie's rule was fresh on Ming-Jen's mind. She was determined to avoid the dangerous man called Tak. Auntie led her to the clothing section. Ming-Jen was too stunned to react when Auntie picked up a bra and eyeballed Ming-Jen's chest. "This should fit you," she declared. "It seems you'll be staying in Hong Kong for a while. You have to do what the locals do. Hong Kong is a modern city and you have to dress like a modern woman." Auntie looked her up and down. "Your *chipao* is from the Manchu dynasty. We'll have to do something about it."

She brought two bras to the counter. Ming-Jen traipsed a few steps behind to distance herself from the scandalous merchandise. Tak was wiping the dust off a plastic doll, dabbing the eyes gently as if the doll had feelings. In spite of herself Ming-Jen felt a tickle in her heart.

"Good morning, Tak," Auntie said cheerfully. "You're busy tidying the place again. I always say your father is lucky to have a good son like you."

Tak twisted the legs of the doll into a sitting position and placed it on the shelf. "Good morning, Mrs. Ho. What would you like today?"

"I have a whole list of things to get," Auntie said, waving a little piece of paper. "But I have to run to the hairdresser's. My niece, Ming-Jen, I think you've met her, will pick them up for me. Can you help her find the items?"

Ming-Jen stared at her aunt with surprise that turned into panic. She was going to be left alone with this dangerous man and the bras! For sure he'd know they were for her!

"No problem," Tak said. "You go have your hair done. I'll take care of your little miss here."

Ming-Jen stood like a mannequin while Tak darted in and out of the aisles and deposited one item after another on the counter. A bar of soap, two soup spoons, a towel, and a dozen clothes pins. He added them up on the abacus. Ming-Jen looked away as he counted the two bras.

"Haven't seen you around in a while. I thought you went back to Peking," Tak said.

"I'm still here," Ming-Jen said, feeling silly for stating the obvious.

"How's your father? Has he found a job with the government?"

Ming-Jen was surprised that he remembered. She couldn't help blurting, "He's been sent to reeducation camp."

"That's unfortunate," Tak said. "I guess you won't be going home any time soon."

Ming-Jen swooped up her package and darted off before her emotions overflowed.

From then on, Auntie sent her to the corner store every day. There was always something she needed urgently—a handkerchief, toothpicks, shoe polish, a spool of thread, rubber bands, hairpins. The number of household items was endless. Tak was always there and always had so many questions. At first she replied as briefly as possible, always with her eyes downcast. Then by and by, she found herself behaving like one of those women she despised—leaning on the counter and chatting the day away with the storekeeper.

Perhaps it was because he was attentive, hanging on to her every word, curious about her past, allowing her the chance to reminisce about the heady smell of ink and scrolls in Father's study, the quiet evenings of embroidering by Mother's side. As a mandarin's daughter, every moment of her life was spent on cultivating goodness and beauty, both within and without. From the moment she stepped out of her bedroom, she would be groomed to perfection—every hair in place, every single button on her chipao securely fastened. Grooming the inside took longer, usually the rest of the day. Under the supervision of various tutors and sometimes Father himself, she and her sisters studied the classics in the morning and practiced calligraphy and painting in the afternoon.

Tak could have been anyone with a pair of ears. A huge void had opened in her and Tak happened to be there. All her life she'd known only goodness and beauty. Now evil and ugliness surrounded her. How was she to go on? She wished Father would enlighten her with his words of wisdom.

Summer ripened to autumn. She watched the moon grow into a juicy round melon. The Moon Festival was coming up, and the expectation filled her with longing and dread. On the fifteenth day of the eighth lunar month, the moon was the largest of the year. This full moon, more than any other, symbolized wholeness, unity, and family. Her moon had been broken into many pieces.

"I'm going out with my friends to view the moon. You want to join us?" Tak said to her a few days before the festival.

She looked at him and heard herself say, "Yes." Just like that. Not "Where are you going?" or "Who's going to be there?" or "I have to check with my aunt." She already knew Auntie would say what she'd been saying all summer. "Tak is a good son to his father. A filial son can't be a bad husband. Whoever marries him will be a lucky woman. The moment she enters the family, she'll be the boss woman of a store." Since Ming-Jen's stay in Hong Kong became permanent, Auntie's reading of Tak's moral compass had swung a hundred and eighty degrees.

Victoria Peak twinkled with lanterns that night. Ming-Jen held one shaped in the form of a rabbit, while Tak carried an airplane. They'd fallen behind the rest of the group. As they walked side by side Tak's hand brushed hers. She recoiled at the accident, and then realized it was no accident. His hand sought out hers, clenching it in a tight, hungry clasp. She tried to wriggle free. Finally, like a trapped animal exhausted from struggling, her hand relaxed. His clasp loosened to an embrace, a caress. She laced her fingers between his and curled them over his knuckles.

After such an intimate act with a man, what else could she do but marry him?

Chapter 8

"Welcome to the Hilton," a disheveled old woman yells in my ear. "Check in is over there! Turn right and then left and then right. Waaay over there. Yes it is, waaay over there." Her arms flail in every direction.

I herd my parents away from the crazy woman. Sorry to use that word. The woman is just old and her brain has degenerated the same way other organs do. Still, crazy is crazy, no matter the cause, and her belligerence is scary.

"Hi, how may I help you?" the woman behind the counter beams. *This* is the real receptionist of the Neuro-Psychiatry Department.

I introduce Baba, the patient, and Mami, who has come along for the ride, literally. I had to put her in a wheelchair, as the hospital is as big as an airport. The receptionist hands me a clipboard with papers to fill out.

I seat my parents as far from the others as possible. Aside from the loud greeter, there are two other patients: an old woman rocking a doll in her arms and an old man flipping through a magazine and spewing passionate commentaries on every page. My parents look uncomfortable with this company. Baba sits on the edge of his chair, as if getting ready to run if someone attacks. Mami inspects the folded hands on her lap, as still as a possum playing dead. It's a shame this is their first impression. Getting Baba here was hard enough. Already, I can hear him hollering, "I'm never going back to that madhouse!"

After the volume of paperwork is completed, a tall woman in a white lab coat approaches. On Karen's advice, I'd asked for a female psychiatrist, because my macho father will never expose his weakness to another male. The receptionist suggested Dr. Litchmann. Since then, I'd conjured up the image of a stocky, mannish woman sporting a headful of mad scientist's hair. But the person swaying toward me in half heels is slender and lithe, and her short chocolate hair frames a face that reminds me of the actress in *My Fair Lady*. What's her name? I can see her face, but the name draws a blank. Oh my God, what's happening to *my* memory?

"Hello, I'm Dr. Lichtmann. I'm very pleased to meet you all," the woman says in a British accent that rings as pure as the notes plucked from a harp.

Audrey Hepburn! The name lights up like a neon sign. I'm relieved my brain is intact, even if it's on the slow side. "I'm Cary...his daughter...He's my father...Oh, and he's the patient."

As the doctor stoops to shake Baba's hand, he looks her up and down, from the dimpled smile to the long shapely legs below the lab coat. Mami also puts out her hand, eager to greet this lovely young woman.

"Mr. Chan, my assistant will be with you shortly," Dr. Lichtmann says. "He'll put you through a series of tests on your cognitive skills. In the meantime, I'll have a chat with your daughter and your wife. While you're waiting, please feel free to get yourself a cup of coffee or tea." She points at the kettle on the table. Her inflection on the word "tea" sounds absolutely delicious.

I cross the threshold into the doctor's room: one small step that feels like a giant leap. This is my first psychiatric experience, and so far it bears no resemblance to what I've seen in movies—couch for the patient, overstuffed chair for the doctor, warm colors, and plush carpet—all that is absent. Bare is the only word I can use to describe this room—bare of furniture except for an examination table and several metal folding chairs, and bare in color except for white.

Mami does her giant leap behind me. We both feel like aliens on the moon. Dr. Lichtmann invites us to the cold, hard chairs while she grabs one for herself.

"Can you tell me what your father is here for?" the doctor asks.

I sit up eagerly, feeling like a student who has done his homework. I whip out the notebook that contains the highlights of my presentation.

"My parents came from California to live with me in January," I say loudly so Mami can hear. I begin with laying down the bare facts: the reason for the move, my parents' health status, and so on. Then comes the highlight—the "incident" that brought us here. My account is as detached as it can be, full of he said, she said, and I said. Some adjectives are unavoidable, such as "furious" to describe my emotional state, "unreasonable" for Baba, and "upset" for Mami. I stay away from "depressed." After all, any diagnosis should come from the doctor.

Dr. Lichtmann takes plenty of notes, her pen jiggling and wiggling like Laozi's tail when he's expecting a treat. "Can you tell me about your father's background? Where he was born, where he grew up, what he did for a living, and so on? Whatever you know."

Got it. I flip to the page about Baba's history. Karen and I have put it together during a marathon phone call. "My father was born in Hong Kong. He was the third child out of seven. His family ran a convenience store. Then the Japanese invaded, and times were hard for everyone during the occupation. The entire population suffered from food shortage. My father's youngest sister died of TB. His childhood friend was beheaded for stealing a sack of rice.

"After the war, my father took over the family store. The department stores soon squeezed out the mom and pop businesses, and Baba went into the garment industry." I have a few personal snapshots of this part since I was born by then: the cheerful clatter of sewing machines at the shop, the gasoline smell of new fabric, and the doting aunties who fished out candies from their pockets.

"In 1967, my parents decided to emigrate to the U.S. because the revolution in China was heating up. Although Hong Kong was a British colony, it's just next door to China. My father sold his shop—"

"He go bankrupt," Mami interrupts.

I stare at her lips as she repeats her statement. No, I didn't hear wrong.

"His workers leave because they get more pay somewhere else. One day, they all gone. No worker no work. He lose everything!"

I may hear it but I can't believe it. This means my parents have been lying to me, my siblings, and the rest of the world. "Baba sell his shop for good money," is the mantra Mami has been chanting up till now. This pot of "good money" stashed away somewhere was the source of my trust in Baba's ability to provide for the family. I slept very well as a child because of it. It shouldn't matter now, as I don't need his financial support anymore. So why am I feeling as if the ground under my feet has collapsed and I'm falling into a sinkhole?

Dr. Lichtmann's pen is waiting for me to go on. I remind myself my head isn't the one scheduled for shrinking today. It doesn't matter how I feel.

"Anyway, my father took the family to the U.S. to start over. He opened a laundromat and later a Chinese take-out, but they both went under after a few years. It was bad timing, bad luck—"

"No bad luck," Mami interrupts again. "Your father give up easy. He don't fight like a man—"

"You're the one who told me it was bad luck," I snap. "Bad luck the laundry machine caught fire, bad luck the cook got sick. You always say, 'Your Baba born on bad luck day.'" When you hear something often enough as a child, it becomes an unalterable truth.

"Other people have bad luck too. Other people stand up and fight." Mami puts up her dukes like John Wayne. "Confucius say, if you fall, you get up, try again. That's how you learn to walk."

I concede defeat to Dr. Lichtmann. "Apparently I don't know anything about my father. Maybe he has a wife hidden somewhere and an entire family of five children and two dogs that I haven't met."

"He has girlfriend in Paris."

No, Mami can't be saying this.

"He go to Paris every year for fashion show. What is reason? He make pajamas. You hear of fashion show for pajamas?"

"He was planning to diversify his line," I say to the doctor in Baba's defense. "Besides, his main buyer was headquartered in Paris. He had to pay his respects to them once a year."

"I know about his girlfriend," Mami carries on. "Other Hong Kong people go to Paris too. They come back and tell me. They say Tak has fun in Paris."

"That doesn't prove anything!" I shout, this time not for the sake of her hearing. "They're just rumors! The only way anyone knows for sure is if he sees Baba…" Baba what? I can't finish my sentence.

"We can discuss this later," the good doctor comes to my rescue. "What I'd like to know is, has Mr. Chan showed this kind of anti-social behavior before—hiding out in his room for days and weeks?"

I want to kiss her hand and thank her for changing the subject. If Mami has evidence of Baba's French connection, she can keep it to herself. A horde of half-breed half-siblings roaming around Paris? This is a scene right out of a horror movie.

Back to the doctor's question. "I remember the time he got the flu, he went to my grandparents' home to recuperate. I was *told* it was because he didn't want his children to catch it." I want to make sure the doctor understands I'm neither a pathological liar nor psychotic. I'm only telling what I was *told*.

"My husband is spoiled. He's mama boy. When something go bad, he run home to mama. Close curtains and sleep all day."

Nothing she says surprises me anymore. While the doctor scribbles away, I try to digest all the new information Mami has shoved down my throat. I hate to admit it, but her revelations do shed light on Baba's character. My sibs and I have always thought of him as quirky, the oddball who makes people laugh and tear their hair out at the same time. There's probably a law of nature that says out of a certain number of people created, one will be out of whack. My father is the one in our family, and we accept it as the way it is.

Now I see Baba differently. He's a tragic hero with a fatal flaw. Because of his lack of willpower to tough it out, all his enterprises have fallen flat. He's the figure skater who loses heart after falling on a triple lutz, the politician who throws in the towel after losing one race, or the man who slashes his other three tires because he has one flat. The question is why? What's the root cause of his weakness?

There's a knock on the door. A middle-aged man with a pony tail pokes his head in. "I'm through with Mr. Chan. Do you want him to wait outside?"

"We're almost finished." Turning to Mami and me, the doctor says, "Is there anything else you'd like to tell me?"

I glance down at my notes and see three points I haven't touched on yet. But then, Mami would probably tell me I'm wrong again. "Nothing important," I reply.

"He's okay in California," Mami says. "He like California. Weather is nice and we have two children there. Here we have only one."

"It's not as simple as that," I protest, angry at yet another strike out of the blue.

"We'll discuss that later," the doctor says and beckons the assistant to usher Baba in.

Baba hesitates at the door. Seeing the doctor, he quickly slaps on a smiley face. I can imagine the emotional turmoil that must be going on inside him. My poor father, the beat-up boxer who has suffered only defeats in life. I feel an urge to run up and envelope him in a mother bear hug. I'm sure of it now—a horrible experience must have traumatized him in his childhood. Maybe he was sexually molested. The secret must have sat on his chest and kept him down all these years. That was why he couldn't haul himself up every time he fell. Finally, the shrink will dig the secret out of the darkest depths of his soul. No longer will he torment himself and others around him. He'll become a different person, contented and happy to enjoy the remaining days of his life.

"Mr. Chan, please have a seat," the doctor chimes in her crystal voice.

"The results are not bad," the assistant said, handing over a folder.

"Let's see." The doctor pores over the sheets. "You named the objects without a problem, except for 'lawnmower.'"

"That's because he never owned one," I point out to make sure my father isn't disadvantaged by a culturally skewed test. "He's always lived in apartments."

"Your memory is slightly below average," the doctor reads from the chart. Looking up, she explains to me, "He was given three words to remember. Five minutes later, he was asked what the three words were, and he could remember only one. And he has a problem repeating 'no ifs, ands, or buts about it.' That's usually a sign of memory loss."

I say in my head, "No ifs, ands, or buts about it." Good, I still have my marbles. I'm tempted to ask the doctor what three words Baba got. Let's see how many I'll remember.

"Overall, you did well, Mr. Chan," the doctor says, leaning forward, her finely carved knees almost touching Baba's. "I'd like to examine you now. Can you get up on the table?"

I see Baba do a mental one-two-three and spring up on the table. He's putting on his best performance for the beautiful doctor. His legs dangle happily while she listens to his chest, peeks into his ears, and tells him to say "Aaah."

"Now hold my hands and squeeze," the doctor says.

Baba is more than happy to oblige. He takes her hands and holds them tightly.

"You can let go now, Mr. Chan...Mr. Chan!"

Mr. Chan wakes up from his reverie. His whiskers twitch like a rat's at the smell of garbage. He's having a great time. The next game is even more interesting. She grips his fists and pushes down with her weight. He pushes back to resist her. They switch positions and he's the one on top.

"Now, pull me toward you as hard as you can." Dr. Lichtmann braces her legs and offers him her hands.

Baba doesn't hesitate to obey. He's very good that way. Whenever a doctor tells him to do something, he'll follow instructions to a T. His whiskers come alive and mischief twinkles in his eyes. I want to warn the doctor, but it's too late. Baba pulls as instructed—as hard as he can—and the doctor goes flying into his arms.

His hands clasp her waist. She pushes herself up and gives her lab coat a stern tug. Her cheeks are as red as stop lights. "It seems there's nothing wrong with your nervous system, Mr. Chan," she says, slightly out of breath.

"What's going on?" Mami says to me in Chinese. She pokes a finger into her ear, desperately dialing up the volume of her hearing aid.

"The doctor said he passed the test," I explain.

Chapter 9

Ming-Jen comes out of the shower to find a colorful display of men's wear on her bed. Tak is standing over the array, mixing and matching the tops and bottoms. He places the white pants above the Hawaiian shirt of red and turquoise flowers, then the brown pants above the beige polo shirt he just bought at Macy's. With an approving nod, he smoothes out a crease on the Hawaiian outfit and hangs it on the closet handle.

"You're seeing the doctor this afternoon?" Ming-Jen says. "Girlfriend" is on the tip of her tongue.

His head jerks with irritation. He grunts an unintelligible reply and walks out of the room.

Ming-Jen stares after him. This isn't how it's supposed to work out. According to her plan, Tak was supposed to throw a tantrum and absolutely refuse to go back to the psychiatrist. He was supposed to crawl back into bed. He was supposed to demand to move into the luxury apartment Xiao has found for them. Instead, he's been going to see the psychiatrist once a week for three weeks now. Before leaving, he preens in front of the mirror, combing back the few hairs on his head and trimming the tufts sticking out of his nose.

When he comes home, instead of burrowing in bed, he sits at his desk poring over a thick book called *The Happiness Handbook*.

That's ridiculous, Ming-Jen mutters to herself. American happiness isn't the same as Chinese happiness. Americans care only about the individual, whereas Chinese sacrifice themselves for the family. Confucius never talks about individual happiness. His philosophy is all about relationships between people. That's why 仁, the character for compassion, is a combination of two elements: person and two. Two is more important than one. A parent sacrifices for his child, and later on, the child sacrifices for his parent. This is where true happiness lies.

Tak now wants to chase a different kind of happiness. He thinks the pretty young doctor can satisfy his craving. "If *she* can make him happy," Ming-Jen screams in her head, "then the fifty-eight years I've spent with this man, all the blood and tears I've shed for him, have been for nothing!" In a rush of anger, she grabs a corner of the Hawaiian shirt and crumples it. For good measure, she spits on the white pants. Exhausted, she toddles to her chair in the corner and collapses into it.

It's all Cary's fault. On the surface her youngest daughter is doing everything that's required of filial piety. When people at the senior center tell her how lucky she is to be living with a daughter—always accompanied by a sigh that none of their daughters want to live with them—Ming-Jen only smiles vaguely without agreeing or disagreeing. It's true Cary is performing deeds of *Xiao*, but the deeds are meaningless if the most important ingredient is missing: reverence.

Cary's disrespect is most appalling. She even dares to usurp her mother's role. All these years, Ming-Jen has kept her husband safe from harm. Through her willpower and cunning, she's always pulled him back from the brink. This time will be no different, if only Cary hadn't barged in and elbowed her aside. Cary, once the baby in her arms, the little girl who couldn't wipe her own bottom, is now telling *her* what to do.

"Lunch is ready!" Cary's head springs out of the doorframe, then disappears.

Ming-Jen blows a stream of dismay through her nose. No manners at all. A proper Chinese would stand erect in front of her, announce lunch, and stoop to help her out of the chair. This daughter of hers is as uncivilized as an American. When they first arrived in this country, Ming-Jen had every intention to coach her in classical Chinese as she had her older children.

However, the moment Ming-Jen got a job she was hurled into the rapids of American life, and all her plans got washed away. She spent more time taking care of other people's children than her own.

Ming-Jen pushes herself out of the chair. Perhaps it's time to teach Cary a few basic Chinese traditions.

Ming-Jen takes her usual seat at the table. Laozi deposits himself by her side, his large tongue drooling with hope. Cary has forbidden anyone to feed Laozi at the table, all the more reason for Ming-Jen to deliberately "drop" food on the floor. It's become a ritual at every meal, she letting a piece of meat fall and then chiding herself for being clumsy. Today, however, she's going to disappoint her best friend.

"Laozi stinks," Ming-Jen says to Cary in Chinese. "You should give him a bath." Getting no response other than a shrug, she presses on, "He has a terrible dog smell."

"Well, he *is* a dog," Cary says cheekily. "Steve is here. Can you speak English?"

"When you wash Laozi? Today? Tomorrow?" Ming-Jen says, raising her voice.

"I don't know. Whenever I have time," Cary says with another shrug.

Ming-Jen can't stand the flatness on her daughter's face. It's an "I'm sick and tired of you but I'm trying very hard not to show it" kind of face. Ming-Jen's heart hardens. When necessary for her children's good, she'd never hesitated to take the stick to their hide. Cary is the only child she spared. Her belief had been that once the older children set a good example, the younger ones would follow. These days, however, there's no good example from anyone. It's time to reestablish her role as Mother.

"When? Tell me what day you wash Laozi."

"What are you so agitated about?" Cary says.

"He's your dog. It's your duty to wash him."

Ming-Jen feels something touching her knee. A furry paw rests on her lap and a pair of shiny eyes looks up at her, promising love and devotion forever. She steels herself against Laozi's wiles.

"Go away," she chides and nudges him away with her slipper. He lets out a piercing howl as if he's been stabbed in the guts.

"You kicked him!" Cary cries.

"Don't complain so much. Think positive and you'll be happy," Tak advises. "There is a positive side to every situation. You just have to look for it."

"You're absolutely right, Baba," Cary says. "Whether you're happy or not is all in the mind."

"There are many kinds of distorted thinking," Tak goes on. "One is the 'should' statement. If you always think you should do this and you should do that, life is no fun anymore."

"That's wonderful, Baba. You've learned so much from *The Happiness Handbook*." Cary reaches across the table to squeeze his hand. "I'm *very* proud of you."

Wonderful? How is he wonderful? Ming-Jen sneers. He can get out of bed, eat, talk, watch TV, and even read a book. Listening to all the fuss, you'd think he's won the Nobel Prize.

"Laozi, come over here." Steve snaps his fingers.

Laozi shortcuts under the table to get to the other side. Steve slides his hand behind the little ear and massages it in circles while cooing sweet nothings.

A Confucian saying comes to Ming-Jen's mind. *Nowadays to be 'filial' means simply to be capable of providing nourishment. But even dogs and horses get their nourishment from us. Without the feeling of reverence, what difference is there?* If only Confucius were here to see this. Not only is Laozi well fed, he's getting more love and respect than I am.

"Look at your husband," Ming-Jen says in Chinese. "He talks to the dog more than he ever talks to me. Since I came here, he hasn't said more than ten sentences to me."

Cary glares at her. They both glance at Steve, who's munching his sandwich, oblivious to the criticism. A devilish idea comes to Ming-Jen. She's going to repeat what she just said in English. After all, speaking English in front of Steve is one of Cary's house rules.

"St—"

"Don't you dare," Cary warns.

It's Ming-Jen's turn to shrug. "When are you going to wash the dog?" she says, half gloating and half taunting. She knows where to get Cary now. Her daughter's weak spot is sitting right at the table, an easy target that stands out head and shoulders above everyone.

"All right, all right, I'll do it tomorrow!" Cary surrenders.

Chapter 10

I look up from the glossy pages of *Southern Living* and see Dr. Lichtmann hurtling toward me, lab coat flapping.

"The nurse just took your mother's blood pressure and found it's very high. She should go to the Emergency Room right now. If she doesn't get treatment soon, she can have a stroke."

I spring to my feet. The double door opens and the nurse wheels Mami out, her head drooping like a rose bud wilting before it has bloomed. A pang of remorse hits me in the stomach. When Mami complained of a headache in the morning, I ignored her, thinking it was her excuse to weasel out of the appointment.

Karen and I, after hours of psychoanalyzing our mother's outbursts, had come to the conclusion that Mami suffered from depression too. However, Mami never bought our ploy to get her to the shrink (the business of checking for Alzheimer's), because it was the same ploy she'd used to get Baba there. I finally proposed a joint session with Baba. "Don't you want to know what he talks to the doctor about?" I asked. She opened wide and swallowed the bait.

"What about my father?" I say to the doctor.

"I haven't told him yet. I wanted to talk to you first. He's still in my office."

"Can you keep him there until things calm down?"

The doctor's eyes meet mine on the same page, the same line. She understands my father quite well by now. He's going to pop a vein if he knows Mami is anywhere near danger.

"He can wait here in the reception," the doctor says. "We'll keep an eye on him."

At the ER, Mami is rolled into a room, where a male nurse wraps a cuff around her baggy arm. I watch the cuff inflate and deflate, trying to remember how the instrument works. I used it once upon a time in high school biology. The terms systolic and diastolic have stayed in my head, but the rest has been filed away in a place so safe I've forgotten where it is.

The nurse writes on the chart. "What is it?" I ask.

"190 over 112."

"Is that high?"

"Yes, it is," he says cheerfully.

Before I can ask more questions, Mami is whisked to the next station in the assembly line. More nurses, more machines, and more numbers. Finally, we end up in a private room, where the nurse hands me a backside-open gown. She instructs me to undress Mami down to her birthday suit. I glance up at the ceiling to avert my eyes from Mami's breasts and quickly hold up the gown for a curtain.

A young woman in a lab coat walks in and introduces herself as Dr. So and So. "Your mother's blood pressure is very high. Is she taking medication for hypertension?" the doctor asks, her big words in a little girl's voice.

"She's been on medication for the last twenty years." I rattle off the drug name and dosage, feeling rather impressed with myself. "I took her to the doctor's for a cold last week, and her vitals were fine. I don't know why her blood pressure spiked suddenly."

"She may have forgotten a dose, or there may be a change in her body. Too much stress can also cause an increase."

Oh my God, stress! Of course Mami is stressed out today. I've dragged her into this pressure cooker for quick happiness—talk to a stranger, pop a pill, read a book—and now she's about to implode.

"I'm going to give her medicine through an IV," the doctor goes on. "Our immediate goal is to get her blood pressure down. Then you'll have to follow up with her family doctor.

Hypertension is very dangerous. You have to monitor her blood pressure closely."

I hear reproach in her voice.

Out goes the doctor and in comes another new face. Like the other nurses, she's dressed in a flowery tunic and a pair of blue pants. She's also wearing a black headscarf that covers every strand of hair.

"Hello, my name is Soraya. I'm your nurse this morning." Turning to her patient, she says, "Mama, how are you doing?"

Mami struggles to give a little smile.

"We have to put an IV in you. It will be just a little stick, OK?"

Soraya pulls on a pair of thin rubber gloves, then snaps off the tip on the index finger. She presses her naked finger on the inside of Mami's elbow. A bluish thread suggests a vein. The nurse pokes it some more and gives up. She goes for the other arm, but the situation is the same there. I'm getting nervous. Soraya's face is deadpan. She ties a rubber tube tightly on Mami's right arm and tells her to make a fist.

Soraya tears open a little packet. A needle half a finger long appears. "*You're going to feel a little stick*," Soraya sings.

The tip disappears into Mami's tofu flesh. Mami squeezes her eyes shut. I fix my gaze on the buried needle as it wiggles around…and around. Soraya presses a cotton ball on the point of entry and aborts.

"I'm sorry, you have little veins," she says. "Did you have anything to drink this morning?"

"I had tea," Mami says weakly.

"Next time you should drink lots of water. Let me try again."

I have time to think one thought—Mami didn't plan on landing in the emergency room—before the nurse chirps out her warning again, "*You're going to feel a little stick*."

I hold Mami's other hand. It clenches tighter and tighter with every movement of the needle. The nurse straightens up and pulls her shoulders back. Mission aborted again.

"I'll try it once more," she says. "If I still can't get it, I'll get somebody else... *You're going to feel a little stick.*"

This time I turn away from the needle. Perhaps my watching jinxes the nurse's touch. I devote my energy on Mami's free hand, stroking it, patting it, and squeezing it back. My hand expresses everything I want to say to my mother but doesn't seem to find the occasion to say it. Thanks for everything you've done for me. You were a good mother. I love you.

Soraya gets up. "Please give her some water. Paper cups are over there." She points to the stack on the counter and disappears.

While I'm plying Mami with water, a new nurse walks in. Her name is Cindy, blond, rosy-cheeked, and looking too young to have drawn much blood. I tell myself to keep an open mind. For all I know, Cindy may be the world's leading expert on small veins.

"*Let me take a look at the teeny veins,*" she croons at Mami in a kindergarten teacher voice. She picks up the right arm, sees the bruises there, and goes for the left. After digging around the limp flesh, she says gravely to me. "Your mother has small veins, and on top of that they've grown stiff with age." The needle has gone in by the time she finishes her sentence. "You see how the needle is chasing the vein? It can't get through the thick wall." Switching to her other persona, she says, "*I'm sorry, sweetie. Yes, yes, I know it hurts. Bear with me, sweetie.*"

The needle is out. "You see what I mean?" she says to me. "Let me give it another try... *Okay, sweetie, squeeze your hand real tight now.*"

I think maybe I should go away. My presence is making all these wonderful nurses nervous.

"I have to go to the bathroom," Mami says, wiggling to get out of bed. Cindy has just left after promising to send somebody else.

"I'm not sure if you're supposed to get up. Let me get the nurse."

"I have to go *now*."

I can see from Mami's expression that "now" means "this instant." I grab a bedpan and shove it between her legs.

"Can you lift up your—?"

Too late. The dribble has started. I push the pan as far up as possible. A sharp smell of ammonia stings my nostrils—we had asparagus for lunch. I open my mouth and gulp a deep breath.

"I love going out with you," Mami says, sounding much lighter. "You always know where the bathroom is."

After cleaning up, I go back to my seat next to Mami. The huge clock on the wall says we've been here for an hour. I begin to worry about Baba, but I can't leave now as the next nurse can arrive any minute.

Her yellow face is reassuring and even more so the name pinned to her chest. Jennifer Zhou. The last name is Chinese, and the broad face and high cheekbones indicate northern origins.

"Where are you from?" I ask. I'm seldom as forward with a total stranger, but in a place where you have to strip the moment you walk in, coyness is out of place.

"I'm from Beijing."

"Really? My mother is from Beijing too."

After I shout the information to Mami, she breaks out in Mandarin, wanting to know which street the nurse lived on, how old she is, married or not, and if not, does she have a boyfriend.

I'm confident this nurse from the same hometown as Mami is going to succeed. She has to.

The needle goes straight down into the vein. While the other nurses attacked from the side, Jennifer Zhou goes for an aerial strike. It's a direct hit. I can see it. This has to be it.

We wait. The syringe is empty. The nurse shakes her head and clucks her tongue. She takes her position and attacks again... and misses again.

When the fourth nurse walks in, the atmosphere in the room is as somber as a funeral parlor. We skip the introductions. What use is a friendly nurse if she can't draw blood? The African American nurse wearing the name tag "Chantella" completes the racial spectrum. From black to white and the colors in between, Mami has experienced them all. If this nurse fails, the next one will have to hail from another planet.

Snap goes the rubber gloves. *Zeeep*, the foil packet tears open. *Vrooom*, the nurse's chair rolls forward. The needle punctures the skin without a sound. I can no longer think of the black and blue surface as my mother's flesh, alive with nerve endings. It has become a dead object, like a sponge or pin cushion. And I've stopped looking at Mami's face.

The needle tunnels straight ahead. All eyes stare unblinking at the same spot, all hearts murmur the same prayer. A dark red fluid seeps into the tube.

*

I find myself wandering in the hospital maze. I can ask for directions, but I'm quite happy to take my time, like a diver ascending slowly from the deep. Mami is resting comfortably, with life-saving medications dripping into her vein. It's now 3 pm. For sure, I won't be able to complete my to-do list for the day. Grocery, laundry, and lessons will have to be postponed. I should feel peeved and anxious, yet surprisingly I feel nothing. So what if I eat cereal without milk tomorrow morning and put on a dirty sweatshirt? So what if I have to call the parents to reschedule? My students will shout, "Yay, no piano lessons today!"

I find the hallway back to Dr. Lichtmann's office. Baba must be sitting patiently at the reception, looking around with a benign smile and minding his own business. He's a master at keeping a lid on his angst in public, all the more to save for his daughter later. I've been gone almost two hours. That's a lot of angst waiting to explode in my face.

You may think I'm stalling but I really need to go to the bathroom. While washing my hands in front of the bathroom mirror, a familiar boiling feeling rises in me. Here comes another hot flash, I warn myself and brace for sweat to pour out. Something pours. To my astonishment, it's coming out of my eyes. I think it's called tears.

"Why did I think I have the strength to do this?" I say to the puffy-eyed woman in the mirror. "To watch my mother suffer and eventually die. Who on earth gave me the idea that I and I alone can see her through? Nobody ever told me about the body fluids and odors. Nobody ever told me I have to stand by and watch people take turns torturing my mother." More water pours out of my eyes.

A voice startles me: "So now you know. What are you going to do about it?" I look around to see who the speaker is. The restroom is empty except for myself and the puffy-eyed woman staring at me.

I blow my nose into the rough paper towel. "The three-month deadline is coming up," I reply. "Theoretically speaking, I can let my parents go."

The woman jumps out of the mirror. "You're a wimp! You fall apart after one trip to the ER. What about the piece of flesh you were going to give your mother?"

I snap back, "I said 'theoretically speaking,' which means I *can* if I wanted to, but it doesn't mean I *will*. Don't you understand English?"

She shakes her finger at me. "Now, now, don't get mad. You better pull yourself together. Your father is waiting. Look at you, your nose is all red."

"Stop nagging me. Your nose is red too!"

I splash cold water on my face and walk away without another look in the mirror.

*

"What took you so long!?" Baba shouts the moment I enter. "What happened to Mami!? You should have told me immediately! How can you leave me here!?"

"Mami's blood pressure was a little high—"

"I know! The doctor told me. Where is she now!?"

"She's OK. Her blood pressure has dropped. You better calm down or you'll end up at the ER too." I rub his back to smooth out the hackles.

The receptionist beckons to me. I go to the desk and am told that Dr. Lichtmann wants to talk to me in her office. Baba sulks but knows he can't contradict the doctor's order.

"Come in," a carillon voice chimes. "How's your mother doing?"

I take a seat in Dr. Lichtmann's office, a cubbyhole lined with medical tomes. "They're giving her medicine through an IV. When I left her, her blood pressure had come down to a safe level."

"Good, I'm glad to hear that. I'd like to give you an update on your father. He's tolerating the Prozac well, and at this point there's no reason to change the dosage. He says he feels lighter and has been able to get himself up and perform daily functions. He enjoys reading the self-help books I recommended. And he says he's now committed to staying at your home."

I look blankly at the doctor. I know I should say something like, "That's wonderful! Thanks very much for helping him reach this decision." But I can't because another part of me wants to exclaim, "Oh my God, I have to take care of him the rest of his life or mine, whichever ends first." So I keep my mouth shut.

"He also says he's worried about your mother. It's unfortunate I didn't get to examine her today."

"Yes, I'm sorry too. She's been very agitated lately. I was hoping she'll get some relief from talking things out."

"It's quite common for a person to share a spouse's mental illness. We call it codependence. But today, controlling her blood pressure takes priority over other problems."

The way she pronounces "prioritee" reminds me of the Queen of England.

"Once she stabilizes you can call to make another appointment," the doctor goes on. "As for your father, I'd like to refer him to one of the psychologists in our unit. Treatment for depression requires a two-pronged approach. Medication is one, and the other is cognitive therapy. At the initial stage, your father should see the psychologist once a week for therapy."

"The psychologist is a man or woman?" I want to clarify this question before going any further.

"It's a woman, and she's top-notch, the best in our unit. I'm sure your father will enjoy working with her."

A twinkle in her eyes tells me this psychologist isn't bad-looking.

"I'll see him once a month to monitor his medication," the doctor continues. "Later on, we can space the appointments to once every three months."

She hands me a sheaf of papers. "Please take this to the front desk. The receptionist will give you the next appointment."

I get up promptly from my chair. I'm never one to waste a doctor's time with babbling. There's something in a doctor's office that compels me to speak quickly and sparsely.

"How are you holding up?" Dr. Lichtmann says.

The question pulls me back down. I open my mouth and close it again, looking for words to describe my state. I finally settle on the profound words, "I'm fine."

The doctor's eyes scan my face as if searching for abnormality. Can she see that I've been crying? Are there traces of salt on my cheeks?

A little smile comes to the perky Audrey Hepburn lips. "Cary, you're doing a great job taking care of your parents. Please remember to take care of yourself."

BOOK TWO

Confucius says, "Our body, skin, and hair are all received from our parents; we dare not injure them. This is the first priority in filial duty."

Chapter 11

Is seven years a short or a long time? Laozi ponders the question as he lies on his bed, his chin resting between his paws. Early afternoon is the best time for him, when Cary is out running errands and before her students arrive. The house is quiet and the studio is all his. There's nobody to disturb his contemplation of life's mysteries.

He imagines asking a seven-year-old that question. The answer is obvious: the seven-year-old would say seven years is a long time, because they're equivalent to his entire life. As the child lives longer and longer, though, every year will feel shorter and shorter. When he reaches eighty, he will no doubt say that seven years is a short time because it represents less than ten percent of his life. It's simple arithmetic.

Moods also determine the length of a day, Laozi muses. A happy day flies by, which is a pity as you want it to last forever. Misery, on the other hand, drags on. His time at the vet's always feels longer than it should, a testimony to the relativity of time. Thus although the seconds tick at the same pace for everyone, each person lives by his own inner clock.

Satisfied with his philosophical reflections, Laozi looks out at the backyard. A wintry mix laces the bare branches with a white lining, making the trees look as old as the people in the house. Cary and Steve are faded versions of themselves, with gray streaks in their hair, and in Steve's case, what's left of it. Tak and Ming-Jen, who came already gray seven winters ago, have faded into a state of semi-translucence. Their skins are so fragile you can almost see through them. And the older they grow, the stronger their scent. It's a complex aroma that reminds Laozi of the soup bones he buries in the backyard. He can smell those two from one end of the house to the other.

Throughout the seven years, Laozi has witnessed all the goings-on in the household. He's privy to every conversation, to hidden feelings only his nose can detect, and to thoughts expressed only to him in confidence. They trust him because they know he won't think any less of them. Why should he? A human has to do what a human does.

He knows what the last seven years means to each one. For Tak, the seven years at Cary's have blown by with the whoosh of a race car. He's been rushing to the next new cure for heart disease, low testosterone, low energy, insomnia, and every other problem that prevents him from functioning like a twenty-six-year-old. Subscriptions to six health magazines keep him informed of the latest elixirs. He studies the articles closely, high-lighting sentences in yellow and jotting notes on the side. Every day, at least one package slips through the mail slot—horny goat weed, ginseng, glucosamine, Omega 3, and so on.

For Ming-Jen, the seven years have been a vacuum. Although her days have been packed with activities—senior center, doctors' appointments, exercise classes, art classes, psychotherapy, and so on, they mean nothing to her. As far as Ming-Jen is concerned, her life is over. She says to Laozi many times a day, "My responsibilities are over. Nobody needs me anymore. I'm just sitting here waiting to die." The only time she comes to life is when her parents come to visit. She brews them tea, and together they sit down and chat about old times. Laozi plays along, sitting by her side as she entertains her guests. He knows they're just in her mind, for he can neither see nor smell them.

For Cary, the seven years have been a tumultuous period that gradually settled down to stasis. Since her hot flashes and panic attacks stopped, time has ticked on as steadily as a metronome. Her body now smells different, not better or worse, but different. She once said to Laozi while rubbing his tummy, "Every stage in life is like a season, each with its own beauty. Am I glad I don't have to deal with that bloody mess again!" Her hot flashes with her parents have tapered down as well. Flames still flare up now and then, but she has devised methods to keep them from exploding into a wildfire. When Tak smolders, she disappears into the basement and plays a three-movement Sonata, long enough for the embers to cool. With Ming-Jen, her approach is the opposite. Cary smothers the fire at once, before Ming-Jen can escalate a mundane issue (such as Laozi's hygiene) into moral questions of right and wrong, good and evil, and ultimately, filial piety.

For Steve, the seven years have been a period when time is irrelevant. He behaves like a person in love, forgetting to eat, sleep, and walk Laozi, an oversight he lived to regret when he stepped on the damp spot outside his study. He's been consumed by his book, which he calls the "magnum opus." Laozi has heard him say to Cary, "I can die in peace after I finish my book. Everything I ever learned in forty some years of architecture is in here." Between writing his book and replying to the never-ending emails from his students, he's been too busy to notice time passing by.

Laozi rolls on his side with a laborious *oomph*. For him, the passage of seven years is significant, seven years in a dog's life being equivalent to forty-nine in a human's after all. During this period, Laozi has aged from a man in his prime to a centenarian wobbling with his walker. His fur coat has grown dull and even more wrinkled, his milky eyes see only shadows, and his hearing is too weak to catch the dinner call. His nose, however, still works fine. It hasn't failed, so far, to lead him up the staircase to the dining room at meal time.

*

"Come on, Laozi, you can make it," I cheer him on. Poor Laozi has to pause after every step to catch his breath, and with tremendous willpower, launches himself onward to the next.

When Laozi has taken his place at Mami's feet, the gathering is complete. Dinner can start.

"Do you know what today is?" I ask everyone at the table.

Mami blinks anxiously. Baba straightens his spine as if rising to a challenge.

"No ifs, buts, and..." he says, then hits his forehead. "I always forget the last one."

"It's oh nine," Mami says.

She always gets this part of the test right. While the date and month change all the time, the year stays the same for a long time.

"That's the year," I say, exchanging a mirthful glance with Steve. "I mean the month and date."

"It's January," Baba weighs in.

"I *know* it's January," Mami says. "Look at the snow outside....But how come it's so warm?"

"That's because we have the heat on high, very high!" I point out. Here I am, barefoot and short sleeved at the height of winter and still sweating. My parents, on the other hand, are bundled in sweaters and woolen socks and still shivering.

"The date is...the thirteenth?" Baba says.

"It's the eighteenth. Today is January 18th. It's the day you came to live with us." I finally give away the answer to the multimillion-dollar question.

"How time flies," Mami says. "I live here one year already!"

"The older you get the more confused you are," Baba chides. "We've been here three years."

"You've been here seven years!" I blurt.

Two cries of "What?" ring out. Both Baba and Mami are busy dialing up their hearing aids to make sure they didn't hear wrong.

"Seven years," I repeat. For visual aid I raise all fingers on one hand and two on the other.

"One year, seven years, is the same to me," Mami says. "My responsibilities are over. I sit here and wait to die."

"How can it be seven years?" Baba says, his brows furrowed with perplexity.

"You arrived in the year 2002," Steve, the mathematician, says. "That's oh two. It's now oh nine. Nine minus two is—" He raises nine fingers, then takes away two. "Seven."

As everyone oohs and aahs at the magical number, Laozi paws my knee. He senses the festive mood and wants to be a part of it.

"*Later,*" I say to him. "You'll get leftovers *later.*"

"Why are you home today?" Mami says to Steve.

"My job at the college is finished," Steve says. Speaking from one corner of his mouth, he mumbles to me, "I've told her a dozen times already."

"You're home every day now," Mami goes on. "Oh, that's terrible. You get tired of seeing us? Chinese say old people stay home all the time, they stink up the house. You stay home too much, you get old too. See, you have no hair on top. Soon you get arthritis like me. You feel pain here, here and there…"

I turn to Steve. "Don't mind what she says. It's just her morphine speaking. That stuff frees her from all inhibition. She'll say anything that comes to her mind."

"When are you giving me some from her stash?" Steve jibes.

I elbow him. If anyone should sample the drug, it's me. The temptation is there every time I put the drop on Mami's tongue. The tiny dose has done wonders for her. She's tried many other painkillers, but stopped because of the deadly side effects. Morphine, on the other hand, kills her pain without killing her, with the added benefit of a high.

"Look at Baba," the morphine dribbles on. "He used to get mad at me because I can't hear. Now look at him. He's more deafer than me. Right, Baba?"

Baba, suddenly realizing he's being spoken to, says, "What did you say?"

"You, too, Cary," the morphine goes on. "One day you deaf like me. People laugh and talk and you don't know what going on. One day you have arthritis like me. You have so much pain you cry." The words gush out, as uncontrollable as her bladder.

She's gone too far now. The morphine is no excuse to get even with me.

"You don't have to curse me. Even if I have all your problems I won't behave like you," I fling it right back.

Steve kicks me under the table, mouthing, "It's her morphine speaking."

I speak loudly for everyone to hear, "I think she's using it as an excuse to get away with murder. Morphine or not, she has no right to jab me as though I'm a voodoo doll. If somebody hurts you, you should let him know. Otherwise, he'll keep on jabbing."

I've picked up a few tips from the *Happiness Handbook* too.

"How do I behave?" Mami says.

"You're whining and complaining all the time. I won't do that to my children."

"You never listen to me. I say you should study medicine, be a doctor. But no, you study *mewsic*!" Mami blabbers like a child who hasn't quite got the hang of the finer motors of his tongue. The words spill out in clumps, like overcooked pasta stuck together. "If you be doctor, you make lots of money now. You have *big* house. People come visit more. They don't have to sleep on sofa." Mami waves at the sofa bed in the living room.

"There's nothing wrong with my house!" I yell. "Karen and George don't visit because they can't stand your whining."

Steve clenches my elbow, trying to hold me back. Nothing doing. If my mother can say anything she wants, so can I.

"Mami!" I declare. "You're never satisfied with your children. You ask me to do ten things, I do only eight, and you go around telling everyone I'm not there for you. You want me to stay home and listen to you moan and groan all day long. Even then, I'm sure you'll badmouth me for something else."

Laozi swipes at my knee with his overgrown claws. I feel a sting, but nothing can stop me now.

"You're the worst mother in the world!" I burst out.

Mami clucks her tongue. "Where you get bad temper from? Not from me. You get it from Baba."

"He has a bad temper because you're always beating up on him!"

Mami clucks her tongue again. "I can't hear. I'm deaf."

Dinner ends in collective deaf muteness. Mami heads for the bedroom and Baba the TV. I decide to leave the dishes till later. Right now, I'd like a glass of wine, or two.

*

Laozi watches everyone scatter from the table. *Where are my leftovers?* He knew there was going to be trouble when he smelled the skunky odor coming out of Cary. He'd scratched her to stop her from saying what she didn't mean, but she was as out of control as a mad dog. Too bad for him, because when humans are furious at each other, they punish him. Although it's totally irrational, that's the way it is.

Laozi lingers at the table, smelling the juicy morsels clinging to the plates. His duty is to pre-wash them with his dishrag tongue, but he can't do it without Cary handing him the dishes. Well, Cary will come back later when she's in a better mood. He'll hang around for a while.

Laozi pokes his smashed nose into Tak's room. Tak reclines in his chair, watching TV. Laozi sniffs once, concludes there's no food there, and leaves. He pushes through the crack in the bedroom door. It's dark inside. He puts his nose to the ground and traces Ming-Jen's track. Standing on her side of the bed, he uses his large wet snout to nudge at the heap in the bed. The heap stirs. A hand reaches out and pats his head.

He licks Ming-Jen's fingers, which tastes of salt—tear salt, not sweat salt. He can tell the difference. "Roo roo roo," he croons softly. "Don't cry, Ming-Jen. Cary didn't mean what she said. She loves you very much. You should hear her on the phone with Karen. She's always trying to find ways to make you happy. She gets mad at you because you love to be miserable. If she didn't love you, she wouldn't care."

"Laozi, you're a good boy," Ming-Jen says.

A treat usually follows this remark, but not this time. He waits a while and finally gives up. With a sigh, he wobbles down the steps. His nose informs him that something delectable is happening. He hurries down, at the risk of breaking his neck, and swivels a sharp left toward Steve's study.

"Woof woof, you're having a wine and cheese party!" Laozi cheers. There hasn't been one in a long time. Before the older couple moved in, Cary and Steve used to relax on the couch and listen to music on weekends. They sipped and nibbled and talked about this and that. How Laozi misses those tasty days.

"Here you are," Cary says, throwing him a piece of cheese.

"More, please," he says.

"No more!" Cary barks. "No!"

Laozi backs down. Patience is the key. In a while Cary's "no" will soften into "Oh all right. One last piece." He curls up at Steve's side. As expected, a long arm reaches down, finds the sensitive spot behind his ear, and scratches absent-mindedly and oh, so divinely. Laozi congratulates himself for training his humans well.

"Here's to surviving seven years of my parents," Cary says,

clinking glasses with Steve. She guzzles half the glass.

"I wish your mom would stop asking me the same question every time she sees me. 'Steve, why are you home today?' I've been working from home for weeks now, and she still doesn't get it. Sometimes she makes me feel unwelcome in my own home." His fingers stop for a moment. Laozi wiggles his head to urge him on.

"No, no, she doesn't mean it that way. I think she feels obliged to talk to you, to show that she likes you. You're her favorite son-in-law. I've never heard her say a bad word about you." Laozi notices Cary doesn't even blink at the blatant lie. Ming-Jen is an equal opportunity critic of her in-laws. He's heard her say, "Steve is a barbarian. He doesn't show respect for his elders."

"I don't really care what she thinks of me," Steve says. "I'm just worried about you. You've been looking rather tired. You've got bags under your eyes."

Ouch, Steve! Laozi pulls his head back to shoot Steve a warning look. You just stepped on Cary's tail. Having seen how she frets in front of the mirror over the pouches and wrinkles on her face, he knows this is a sensitive part of her anatomy.

"Of course I'm tired," Cary yelps. "I've been carrying those two on my back for the last seven years, and you were gone most of the time."

Her words drop with a boom, then silence. Uh oh, Laozi thinks. This wine and cheese party isn't going well.

"I'm glad your book is out," Cary goes on, not so explosive now. "You've fulfilled your dream and all that, but I wish you could spend some time with me too."

"I thought you were busy with your parents," Steve says, a snarl in his tone. "If there's anything you want me to do, you have to tell me. I can't read your mind."

"I don't need you to do anything for my parents, but you

can give me some emotional support."

"I try to take you out to dinner, just the two of us. But you always bring your parents along for a double date. I really don't know what you want of me."

Cary waves "forget it," downs her wine, and sticks out her glass for seconds.

"I'll tell you what I'm thinking," Cary says. "I think I'm the black sheep of the family. Mami is always bragging about Karen because she has a Ph.D. George is a fat-cat businessman. I only have a bachelor's in *mewsic* and making hardly anything off my students. It must be a real let-down for her to be living in my *humble abode*."

Laozi places a paw on Cary's lap. "No, no," he says, "you've got it all wrong. Your mother loves you the most. She complains about you because you're the closest to her."

"You've had enough already, Laozi. Go away!"

Laozi puts his paw down, but he's not going away. "Listen, Cary, your mother complains about you because you've done more than enough for her. She doesn't dare to complain about her other children because she can't afford to offend them. She wants them to do more for her. Don't you get it?" He stamps his feet. Human behavior is so agitating. They waste time barking, and the more they bark, the more rabid they get at each other. If they'd only sniff one another in the right places, love or hate would be revealed in an instant.

"Laozi, don't be such a nuisance," Cary says. "Oh all right, you can have one last piece." She cuts off a chunk and holds it out. Snout trembling, Laozi eases the cheese from Cary's fingers with his teeth.

The party is over. Cary carries the leftovers upstairs. Laozi follows, hoping for another last piece for his labors.

She starts clearing the dining table, scraping remnants of the plates into one and stacking them on top of each other.

Laozi fidgets impatiently. His due has been a long time coming tonight. Suddenly she stops what she's doing, frowns, grumbles "Oh all right," and walks away.

Laozi is at her heels as she enters her parents' bedroom. Ming-Jen is lying still, too still to be asleep.

"Are you okay?" Cary says blandly, looking down at her mother.

Ming-Jen whimpers. "All my life I've tried to do right by my children. I don't know why, none of them has good feelings toward me."

Cary sits on the bed and holds her mother's hand. "I'm sorry I said what I said. You're a good mother, and we all love you very much. We just want you to be happy."

"I'm a huge burden to you. One day the burden will be too much for you, and then, what will happen to us?"

"I will never abandon you. You're my mother. How can I ever abandon you? When I was a child, no matter how terrible I was, did you ever think of abandoning me? Of course not. It's the same now. I will never abandon you and Baba. I promise."

"Roo roo roo," Laozi joins in, happy to see his humans reconcile. After they hug and kiss, he can mop up the dishes at last.

Chapter 12

I close my eyes and imagine walking in a park at night, hand in hand with my lover. Whoever he is he isn't Steve. His touch is tender, his fingers fine and sensitive, and his frame is much slighter than Steve's. A face floats up—a nest of hair swept back in dreamy waves, a pair of sad eyes, a pointed chin—it's Frederic Chopin!

I'm in the middle of a Chopin Nocturne when the stomping starts. It's only a few minutes past eight. Why is Baba up so early? I prefer my parents asleep. The moment one or both are awake, a vague feeling of guilt gnaws at me. Isn't there something I should be doing to make them young again?

Don't type the notes, is my advice to my students. Yet here I am turning a romantic Chopin Nocturne into elevator music. I always tell my students that if they play with their hearts, even the tedious task of learning the notes will be fun. While other teachers give out stars, I grade each lesson with little sticky hearts. For playing the right notes, a student gets one heart. For emoting well, even if the notes aren't perfect, the reward is two hearts. For doing both well, three hearts will be bursting with pride—the child's, the parent's, and the teacher's. Perhaps for this reason, my students have been winning little gold-plated cups at local competitions.

I get to the *da capo*, my chance to repeat the passage and play it right this time. The melody flows out of my fingers, not as quarter notes or half notes, not as *forte* or *piano*, but as a river of feelings, tripping over stones, falling over boulders, lingering, rushing with the contours of the terrain. My eyelids flutter with ecstasy.

A flicker catches my attention. I ignore it. My love affair with the consumptive composer is unstoppable now. Another flicker. There's no mistake this time. My fingers still caressing the keyboard, I gaze up at the ceiling. Liquid oozes out of the plaster, collects into a pearl, and holds on until gravity proves irresistible. Plop it goes on the carpet.

I sprint up the staircase. Baba is on all fours in the bathroom. "What are you doing?" I shout.

"I can't get up."

I notice the floor is wet and the toilet is full to the brim. Putting two and two together, I recognize what kind of water it is. No matter. I have to get him up. I take off my slippers and step barefoot into the cesspool. Baba's head is wedged between the toilet and sink. I circle my arms around Baba's midriff and yank. He's as set as a block of concrete. I contemplate giving it another try, but painful experience has taught me that aging isn't reserved for my parents. My back isn't what it used to be.

"I'm going to get Steve!" I yell into Baba's ear.

I run down the steps into Steve's study. "My dad fell. I can't get him up."

Steve rushes into the bathroom and, with a mighty tug, hauls Baba to his feet. I put down the toilet lid for Baba to sit on.

"Why is the floor wet?" Steve says.

"I flushed the toilet and water came out," Baba says, wheezing.

I say to Steve, "Don't worry, I'll take care of it. Thanks for getting him up." I give him a grateful pat on the shoulder and send him back downstairs. I never like to bother Steve with my parents' affairs. In fact, I try to keep the two parties apart as much as possible. I think of the staircase as a DMZ, a buffer against conflicts. Now that Steve is always home, it's all the more important to enforce the separation.

Baba is still sitting on the toilet, his pajama pants drenched in eau de toilet.

"You're all wet," I say. "You better change before you catch a cold. What were you doing on the floor anyway?"

"I was trying to wipe it dry," he says gruffly.

I want to pursue, "How did the toilet get clogged?" But the answer is everywhere—bits and pieces of toilet paper matted to the floor. I warn myself not to show any emotions that he can misconstrue as anger. He's had a major breakthrough recently. After studying the *Happiness Handbook* all these years, he tells me he's actually feeling moments of joy and contentment once in a while. I don't want to set him off again and send him back to the shrink.

*

Tak mimics Cary's clenched-teeth tone, "You better change before you catch a cold."

What Cary really meant was, I hope you catch a cold and die! Tak flings his soaking pants on the floor.

"What's the matter?" Ming-Jen says, raising her head off the pillow.

"Nothing. Go back to sleep," Tak orders.

He's mad. Cary doesn't have to say anything. The color of her face shouts louder than her words. It's darker than usual, as if she's standing in the shadow of a storm cloud. She despises him because he has no money. He's here to live off her and her precious husband. Has she forgotten whose money it was that sent her to the best private school in Hong Kong? Whose money it was that brought her to the U.S.? Where would she be without him? She wouldn't even have been born!

Tak's chest caves with despair. He should have known the toilet was clogged. Why did he keep on flushing? Why does he have to ruin everything he puts his hands on?

Wait a minute, he catches himself. To err is to be human, the *Happiness Handbook* says. We have to forgive one another because there's no telling who's going to screw up next.

Besides, he's ninety years old. A man who's lived that long is beyond rebuke. His faults deserve to be overlooked, his virtues, however minor, lauded to great heights. His few remaining days on earth should be his best. It's his children's duty to see to it. Cary should have said to him sweetly, "It's not your fault, Baba. There must be something wrong with the toilet. I'll get a plumber to fix it."

Or she could have said, also sweetly, "Don't worry, Baba. I'm happy to clean up after you. It's my duty to serve you and I do it with great pleasure."

At his age he should have a pretty maid by his side, wiping his behind and spooning food in his mouth. The thought brings a brief smile to his lips.

*

I suit up for a toxic waste cleanup: rain boots that protect me to the shins, heavy-duty rubber gloves, a surgical mask to filter out the smell, and a ski cap to hold my hair in place. The equipment at hand consists of a mop, bucket, broom and dustpan, and bottles of Lysol and Clorox, both advanced formula.

As I stand at the bathroom door, debating which corner to tackle first, a chapter in the *Happiness Handbook* comes to me. Entitled "Shoulding Yourself," it describes people who make odious chores more odious by telling themselves they have no choice. This is negative thinking that generates resentment. Reframing the statement can provide a positive motivation and thus turn the task into a constructive experience. In this case, I can say, "I *choose* to clean up my father's mess because… hmmm….because I love him?"

Love? Is there anything to love at this time and place? I thrust the mop into the filthy water. To hell with the *Happiness Handbook*. I read it only to help lift Baba out of depression. People like him need to sugarcoat their reality. To a normal person like myself, a chore is a chore and nothing but a chore.

"Don't you have *any* love for your father?" a voice asks.

"Don't bother me now," I answer with an angry jab of the mop.

The voice persists: "Your heart must be made of stone if you can't even love your father."

"If you're trying to guilt-trip me, you succeed," I say. "Of course, I love my father. But there are times when he's simply not lovable, and right now is one of them."

"You were buddies once upon a time," the voice reminds me.

I chuckle at the word "buddies." I never thought of Baba in that term.

Yes, we were buddies once, hanging out many a Saturday night when Karen and George were away in college and Mami was babysitting the doctor's brats. Baba and I treated ourselves to TV dinners in front of the TV. Afterwards, we hit the community center and painted it red.

The moment Baba and I walked into the center, the *ping pong* stopped. The two teenage boys laid down their paddles and retreated to the sideline.

"Please don't let us interrupt your game," Baba said in his formal Chinese-British English.

The pimply boy said with a toss of his bangs, "It's all yours."

I remember him well. Usually I played a friendly game, but when the boy boasted he'd never been beaten by a girl, I had to show him. The game ended at 11-3. Since then he had walked away every time I walked in.

Baba and I each took an end of the table and whipped out our paddles. Instead of the handshake blade that most Americans used, we preferred the penhold, which was held by curling two fingers around the handle. According to Baba, a *ping pong* champ in his youth, the penhold gave better control.

The rubber on our paddles was also state of the art, a turbo version that combined speed and precision.

Baba nodded "ready" and I sent the ball to his side. *Pinkity pong, ping pong.* We warmed up with a good-natured rally. After a while, Baba lobbed the ball over in a high curve. I rushed up and slammed it down with the full force of my body, the way Baba had taught me. He picked up the ball a hair's breadth from the floor and returned it with a topspin. I refrained from attacking it head on (which would have launched the ball into space), waited for the twirl to weaken, and counter-spun it back.

"One, two, three, four," a lone voice counted the volleys. More voices joined in. I took my eyes off the ball for a split second and noticed that a small group had gathered.

The cheering crowd drove me on. I kept whamming the soft volleys Baba sent over, and Baba kept picking them up from under the table. Backhand or forehand was the same to him. The counting swelled in unison like crowds at a football stadium. I felt obliged to add variety to the entertainment. I cocked my paddle back in a murderous gesture and, at the last minute, changed the kill to a kiss. The ball touched the net and teetered over. Baba lunged to the rescue. With his short arms he had to sprawl on the table to reach the ball. The long shot he sent back took me by surprise. I stumbled back and struck out blindly. The ball flew in an elliptical arc to the other side and bounced off the edge. The crowd roared.

And so the counting went on. At a hundred and thirty two, sweat was pouring into my eyes. The salt stung. I wished the rally would end. Through the mist of tears I could make out Baba's blurry figure on the other end. He was centered steadfast as a boulder. Every time he flicked his wrist I hopped around like a kangaroo. I suddenly realized he could have ended the rally at the count of three. His attacks had been all sound and no fury. Their sole purpose was to give me the chance to wow the crowd with my flashy slams.

"Aw," a unified cry rang out. Baba's volley fell wide of the table.

I stared at my father. He hit his head with the paddle to punish himself for the stupid mistake. Then he winked, and I understood. My heart throbbed faster than it already did. My father loved me. I loved him too, with my whole heart and soul....

"Are you finished?" Baba's voice brings me back to the present.

I straighten up to take stock of what more needs to be done. The little green tiles are sparkling clean, and some of them are already drying. The bathroom smells of lemon, thanks to the scented Lysol. The *Happiness Handbook* is right, and I haven't been lying to my students: love does make everything better.

*

"Are you finished?" Tak says.

Cary looks around and mumbles something into her mask. Tak cups his ear to indicate he can't hear.

Cary pulls down her mask. Her muzzle is red and the elastic band has cut a crease across each cheek, giving her a fierce warrior look. "I'm done with the bathroom, but I still have to wash the mat," she shouts, pointing to the sorry heap in the bucket.

"I've had it with you!" Tak shouts back. "You've been mad at me all morning. I can't put up with your temper anymore!"

"What did I say?" Cary says, eyes wide with bewilderment. Tak can tell she's faking it. She understands very well what he means.

"You don't have to say anything. I can see it in your face. Don't you think I'm so stupid I can't see what's going on? You blame me for ruining your house. The real problem is your toilet. Look at the hole in your toilet. I've never seen such a small hole. How can anything get through it? It's entirely the fault of *your* toilet!"

For a minute Tak thinks Cary is going to laugh. The next minute her lips press together as if she's going to cry. Then she does something that disarms him. She gazes straight into his eyes. "Baba, I'm not mad at you," she says evenly. "The person who's mad at you is you. You're mad at yourself for flooding the bathroom. But it was an honest mistake. You didn't do it deliberately. There's no need—"

Tak can't stand it anymore. Cary's screaming is easy to handle—he'll match her scream for scream. Gentle reasoning, however, is intimidating, because he'll have to reason back. He escapes into his study and sinks deep into his lazy boy chair, hoping his checkered shirt will blend into the checkered upholstery. No such luck. Cary stands over him, her eyes pinning him down.

"There's no need to be mad at yourself," Cary says. "Remember what the *Happiness Handbook* says? Forgive, forgive, forgive, is the key to happiness."

"Okay, I forgive you," Tak says. He'll say anything to get Cary to leave him alone.

"I don't mean me. I mean you. The person you should forgive is yourself. You should read the *Happiness Handbook* again." She pulls the paperback off the shelf and flips to a page. "Remember the Ten Forms of Distorted Thinking?" Cary holds open the book for her father. "Here they are. See here, 'Magnification'—you exaggerate your shortcomings and minimize your strengths. Then there's 'Overgeneralization'—you make one mistake and you think you're a loser."

Tak perks up. Ah yes, he's on familiar territory. He's read the *Happiness Handbook* cover to cover many times, discussed it with the therapist, and done the exercises at the back of each chapter. No one can challenge him on this topic. Jutting out his chin, he says, "Do you know why I'm making your life difficult?"

Cary stares at him, speechless. Tak is tickled he can still teach his daughter a thing or two.

"To make you a better person!" he declares. "It says so in Chapter 4. When a person is nasty to you, you have to thank him for it. He's teaching you to forgive."

Cary smiles and gives him the cuddly look that she reserves for Laozi. "Baba, you're a wonderful father," she says, adding, "the *best father* in the world."

"Really? You mean it? You're not saying it to humor me?"

"Of course I mean it. Why would I lie to you?"

Tak feels the sun bursting through the clouds in his heart. Can it be true? Can he have finally done something right?

*

I carry the mop and bucket to the basement. Now, why did I call him "best father in the world?" What criteria do I use to compare him with all the fathers in the history of mankind? I wasn't aiming to flatter him either, so there was really no reason to use the superlative. A good father would have sufficed.

As I throw the bathmat into the laundry machine, I remember what Mami used to say to me, "You're my favorite child." Even as a six- or seven-year old, I knew there was something wrong with her statement, because she'd said the same to Karen and George. How could she have several favorites? It was only when I became a mother that I understood this: A mother's heart is large enough to love every child the most.

I pour in a large cup of detergent, enough to cleanse the machine as well as the mat. If multiple superlatives can coexist, I muse, then it's possible to have many "best fathers" in the world. Perhaps every father who has done his best is a best father.

The phone rings twice and stops. Steve must have gotten to it. I wait for him to shout, "Cary, telephone!" Nine out of ten calls are for me—from my students' parents wanting to reschedule and doctors' offices calling about appointments and lab results. In fact, I've been waiting all morning for the rheumatologist to report on Mami's blood test.

Steve's voice travels from his study into the laundry room. His mutterings of yeses and okays give me no clue as to who the caller is. I catch myself wondering if it's a woman. A colleague? A former student? Anybody I know? Then all is quiet. A tall, lean shadow appears at the doorway.

"The doctor just called," he says.

"You should have let me talk to him," I say, annoyed that Steve didn't pass the phone to me.

"He says the biopsy came back. I have cancer in my colon."

Chapter 13

I reach over to hug my passenger. As always my heart stops at the sight of the sun of my life, my son named Fred after Frederic Chopin. I'll never understand how two plain people like Steve and me could produce such exquisite progeny. You would think a hybrid is a combination of two varieties. In which case, Fred would have my flat nose and Steve's thin lips, my short torso and Steve's long legs, or some such configuration. As it turns out, his features are sculpted to perfect proportion with one another. He looks nothing like Steve or me, combined or stand-alone. You would also think that Steve and I, who are of average intelligence, would produce more of the same. As it turns out, Fred's intelligence is just *more*. My conclusion is, therefore, that a hybrid isn't a mishmash of genes but a transformation into an improved species.

"Snazzy sunglasses," Fred comments on the aviator shades I use for driving.

"These? Got them for ten bucks at the drugstore. After going through four cataract surgeries with your grandparents, I learned what damage the sun can do to my eyes. You should get a pair too, and sunscreen—" I cut myself off. That's enough nagging for five minutes.

We exchange news that isn't news, as we've already shared it during our periodic phone calls. Sharing it again in person, however, makes the events three-dimensional and real. We sigh with relief that the doctors cut off Steve's tumor at an early stage and no further treatment is needed. He'll be home from the hospital in a day or two. We chuckle over my recent piano recital at a church where I covered up a memory lapse by repeating the same phrase over and over, like a car circling in a roundabout, until I found the right exit. We celebrate Fred's coffee shop, which turned a modest profit last month for the first time in two years. Fred listens as I recount his grandparents' health (I try not to go into the gory details), and I listen as Fred talks about his girlfriend's new job.

Although nodding as if I'm absorbing every word, I couldn't care less about Annette's working hours and commute. The Big Question has been on the tip of my tongue ever since Annette gave up a Wall Street job to live with Fred in Boston, and that was two years ago. I've bitten my tongue too many times already. Once more, and I'll bleed. Fred is thirty-two years old; at his age I was a mother of two.

"When are you two getting married?" There, it's finally out.

"I don't know." A hitch of the shoulders, a twitch of the muscle around the mouth, a wiggle of the ears, none of which escapes my attention even while driving. "We don't see any reason to," Fred says, "unless we start a family. That won't be for a while. You know that."

"I know, I know. But your circumstances have changed. You used to be a full-time engineer for a company—" I omit highly paid—"you had health insurance. Now you have to buy your own policy. If you and Annette are legally hitched, her company policy will cover you."

"You want me to marry her for her health insurance?" Fred looks at me as if I've just told him to rob a bank.

"Sure, why not? You love each other, don't you? That's the key to any relationship. The rest is just practical stuff, like how to save some money so you can rent a larger apartment."

Fred is quiet. I can see the "larger apartment" resonating in his head. He's always wanted a second bedroom for an office. But I also know when to shut up. Nowadays, I have a reliable guide on how to maintain harmony with my children. All I have to do is peer into the Mami mirror. The writing on it reads: Do not do unto your children what you don't want your mother to do unto you.

I tell myself not to worry. Fred lives his life according to plans—master plan, plan A, plan B, and so on. (I wonder where he got that from.) His first five-year plan after obtaining an MSc was to make money and save money. Actually this phase kicked off ahead of schedule. An established engineering firm hired him as a student intern and offered him a job before he finished his degree. This five-year plan lasted seven years, which only meant the foundation for the second phase was all the stronger. He's now his own boss, master of his own destiny, at the beck and call of anyone who comes into his shop and pays two dollars for a cup of coffee.

As we exit the car, I catch a full frontal view of my son. Our eyes meet and we beam at each other across the roof of the car. Oh, how I love this boy. No matter what he does for a living or whether he gives me grandchildren or not, my love is immutable. We're bound together by muscles, tendons, and nerves. Only a mother can love a child so viscerally. It strikes me that my mother must love me the same way (even if she expresses it differently). Suddenly I feel I'm standing between two mirrors, reflecting image within image of myself, my son, and my mother, telescoping endlessly into eternity. I hang onto the car to steady myself.

"Are you okay, Mom?"

"Yeah, yeah, I'm fine. I'm just worried Maggie may have called," I say, making a big show of looking at my watch.

"Why can't she fly into Dulles? Now you have to go to National to pick her up." Fred speaks like a righteous older brother.

"Same reason as you. That's the cheapest ticket on the market. Now, let me see. You spend some time with your grandparents while I pick up Maggie. Then we'll go to the hospital together to see your dad."

"I hope we're not more trouble than help for you," Fred

says as I open the front door.

"Oh, don't be silly." When words can't express the emotions in the human heart, fewer is better.

The door opens to the welcoming committee on top of the steps. "Fred, you're here!" cry Mami and Baba, or to Fred, Gunggung and Popo. Laozi joins the chorus with a joyful howl.

*

The molasses pace of the airport traffic gives me plenty of time to study my daughter as she stands on the curb like a daydreaming child. She looks a little bored but not anxious at all, because she's confident her mommy will show up. Her name is Maggie, short for Anna Magdalena Bach, the second wife of J.S. Bach and a musician in her own right.

I feel like I'm spying on my daughter, watching her while undercover. Then again, what mother won't flip through a diary left lying around? I study Maggie with shameless abandon. Her golden brown hair tumbles in a torrent past her shoulders, spraying with the wind although there's no wind on that balmy spring day. Under the blue sweater, a shocking pink top collides with a green mini-skirt. Her long, slender legs are bare except for a pair of flip-flops.

The colors are all wrong. And yet, on Maggie's body, they look as right as blue sky against green fields. I wish the skirt could be two or three inches longer and I wish Maggie wouldn't wear flip-flops everywhere. She may well trip, or lose one or both. I'm already biting my tongue before we say hello. I also notice that I'm not the only student of Maggie's appearance. Almost everyone who passes by swivels in her direction, like a paper clip to a magnet.

Maggie is living proof of one of my pet theories: a person isn't shaped by parents but by siblings. I've seen it in a number of families, such as the one that raised me and the one I raised. One child spawns the opposite in another. When one is talkative, the other is quiet, one extrovert the other introvert, anxious easygoing, responsible irresponsible, tidy sloppy, and so on. The child doesn't make a conscious decision to foil his older sibling. He's only following the instinct to avoid competition and promote diversity.

If Fred were a professionally landscaped garden, Maggie is a field of wildflowers. You know what plant is going to sprout where in Fred's yard. The hostas and impatiens sit cool in the shade, azalea bushes bloom in part sun, and roses bask in the full strength of solar power. In Maggie's garden, a riot rainbow of poppies, black-eyed susans, lupines, chicory, and daisies sprout willy nilly. I've also noticed wildflowers aren't necessarily wild. Every spring public works crews dig up the wildflower patches along the highway, which means strictly speaking, you can't call them wild.

Without following any blueprint, Maggie drifted west, waitressing from town to town, and finally settled on soil that suited her temperament. She now has a steady boyfriend and a steady job as a graphic artist. She majored in Fine Art in college because it was easy for her. Steve had hoped she would apply her artistic talent to the field of architecture, but Maggie would have nothing to do with math and science. This daughter of mine has never been a good student, a defect that I blame myself for. (If I'd been home to supervise her homework, etc., etc.). Like all parents of art students, Steve and I worried about her earning a decent living. But nowadays, we're happy to point a finger at each other and say: "I *told* you not to worry." Our daughter is an artist and not starving.

Perhaps the wildflower is more cultivated than she lets on. It goes to show that just because a person is a multiplication of your cells doesn't mean you know her.

Maggie runs toward me, waving to catch my attention. I pull up at the curb.

"Blossom," I greet with Maggie's nickname. Every time I look at my beautiful daughter, a flower comes to mind. The kind depends on circumstances and moods, and today, at the moment I pull back from the full-bodied squeeze, Maggie's face radiates like a sunflower. Before planting a kiss, I brush aside a stray hair from my little girl's face and loop it behind her ear.

"How do you like living in Seattle?" I ask the moment we're out of the airport tangle.

Maggie's earrings tinkle. Glancing sideways, I see a miniature chandelier dangling from my daughter's ear. "Oh I love it," Maggie said. "The city is *awesome*, and people there are friendly and *cool*."

I cringe at my daughter's "awesome" vocabulary. She's a twenty-eight-year-old who talks, behaves, and looks like a high school sophomore. I've noticed that young people take longer to grow up these days, getting married later and having children later. All they have to do is look at their grandparents and realize they have plenty of time.

"Guess what?" Maggie begins with the rhetorical question that usually leads to a shocking announcement.

I brace myself.

"Fred and I have been talking about this. We want you and dad to live with us when you grow old. Six months with Fred and six months with me."

I was right. What she said was outrageous, although I never imagined it could be pleasant. Of course, I'm not going to take it seriously. It's just a childish whim, such as that time she promised to bring me on her honeymoon before she knew what a honeymoon was. "That's very sweet of the two of you. What's your future husband going to say?" I tease.

"Darin says he won't mind. Anyway, if he does, I won't marry him." She tosses him off with a jingle.

"You talked to Darin already! Wow, you mean business." I add jokingly, "You can tell him I promise not to nag him. I'll save all the nagging for you."

"Nah, you're not the nagging type, Mom. Well, let's say you've been much better since we left home. I just know you're not going to be like Popo. She nags because she's bored. You'll always be busy with something. You'll play the piano, go to concerts, run around with your friends. You won't have time to nag me."

"Wait a minute. When I'm ninety years old, I won't be able to do all those things. I'd be like Popo, sitting at home, waiting to die, and watching your every move. Maggie, when are you coming home? Maggie put on something decent. Maggie—"

"What do you mean, put on something decent? What's wrong with the way I dress?"

"Nothing, Blossom, I'm not talking about the present. I mean years from now, when I'm so old I don't know what I'm talking about." And can't hold my tongue. "I'll be talking gibberish. You'll want to kick me out after a week."

"No, I won't...Mom, are you saying you don't want to live with me?"

"No, no, I don't mean it that way. You've been listening to Popo go on and on about filial piety, but your dad and I don't expect it of you. We only want you to lead a good life and live out your passion, whatever it is. That's all we ask of you."

"I think what you're doing for Gunggung and Popo is really cool. I want to do the same for you."

"I—am—touched." I lay a hand on my heart to show how touched. I want to tell her things aren't always *cool* between her grandparents and me. In fact it can get pretty hot. Maggie's impression is based on her visits, each lasting no more than a week. Living together is a different kind of trip—it's climbing Mount Everest. The air gets thinner the higher you go, and the weight of your backpack gets heavier and heavier. There are times when you want to throw everything down and take a helicopter home.

"We'll talk about it later," I say. Much later.

*

"Gentle," I warn as Maggie sprints up the steps and lifts her grandmother off her feet.

Popo pulls away for a thorough inspection. Her eyes peer out of her forehead as she can no longer straighten her sclerotic neck. "Good, good, you look fat," she says, patting the high Asian cheekbones.

"You look fat too, Popo!" Maggie returns the compliment.

I'm glad my daughter doesn't take offense. She's learned that in the famine-ridden country her grandmother came from, calling a person "fat" is the highest honor.

"What pretty colors. You look...how you say...*awesome*!"

Maggie squeals, "Oh Popo, you look awesome too. I love your bracelet." She reaches for the jade on the knotted wrist.

"You have pretty earrings too," Popo says, fingering the chandelier. "Who buy it for you? Not your mommy. She don't like pretty things."

My mother darts me a reproachful look.

"I bought them myself," Maggie says.

"You have money?"

"Of course. I have a good job now."

"Job? Noooo," Mami says, straightening her neck as far as her vertebrae allow. "You're too young to work. You have to go to school, study medicine, be doctor, and come back take care of Popo."

Uh oh, she's going to get it. Nobody tells Maggie what to study.

Maggie giggles. "No medical school will take me. My grades aren't good enough."

"Why not good enough? You always have straight A."

"No, Popo, I'm just a B-average student."

"B is good," Mami says, nodding with emphasis. "Study all the time, you get no fun. Young people should have fun."

I'm flabbergasted. B is good? Is it possible those words came out of my mother's mouth? The mother who thought A was a pass mark, anything less a failure? Actually I'm doubly shocked by my daughter. If I as much as hinted at what she should study, she would scream at me and call me a tiger mom. I'm glad my daughter and mother get along so well, but why can't they be as nice to me?

Guffaws belch out of Baba's study, the boys-up-to-no-good kind. I go in to save my son from the old man's corrupting influence. Fred glances up at me and quickly hands the magazine back to Baba, who slips it into the stack of medical journals on his desk. They can hide the Playboy magazine, but they can't hide the playboy in their smirks.

"We should be going to the hospital soon," I remind my son of the purpose of his trip.

"Any time," Fred says, rubbing his nose to hide the grin.

Baba's face is one big giggle. This is the expression of pure delight he shows only to his grandchildren.

I run into Laozi in the hallway. He's been puttering from room to room so he won't miss out on any excitement. He looks at me, little eyes laughing under the rolls of skin. "You like having Fred and Maggie around, don't you?" I say, rubbing his head. "So do I, so do I."

It dawns on me why people have children—to have grandchildren! Someday my turn will come. I'll sneak my grandchildren candies and cookies and whatever their parents forbid, and they'll think I'm the awesomest grandma. When my dementia drives my children nuts, my grandchildren will think I'm funny and cool. That's why people call grandchildren "life's desserts." My main course is coming to an end, but chocolate cake is waiting. I wish my children would hurry up!

Chapter 14

Steve steps on the gas, the sunroof rolled back to give the car a convertible feel. A starry dome whizzes overhead. He feels sixteen again, joy-riding in his dad's pickup truck with his buddies while their parents sleep. They would have a wild time in the woods, drinking beer and shooting jackrabbits.

"You're going 70," Cary says. "Don't you think you should take it easy? You haven't driven for a while."

Steve does what a man is compelled to do when his wife tells him to slow down—he speeds up.

Tonight was his first night out in a long time. Hobnobbing with a bunch of business cronies is as wild as it gets these days. There was a lot of shop talk and boasting of wonderful vacations and golf exploits. Nobody once mentioned the word "bowel" or any body part in that region. For that and that alone, Steve is ecstatic. Since his surgery a month back, his life has rotated between the GI doctor's office and home. In either place, there's only one thing on people's minds, and it's not the war on terrorism, banking crisis, or crime rate. At dinner these days, whenever the inevitable subject arises, Cary and her parents switch to English to allow him to participate. They think his new condition qualifies him to join their bowel-gazing club.

"Come on, Steve, what's the rush?" Cary says edgily.

The speedometer needle drops down one mark, a token concession but not surrender. "I thought you were in a hurry to get home," he says. During the party, Cary had glanced at her watch every so often. And just as he was telling a joke to an attractive quantity surveyor, Cary barged in and raised her brows to signal, "Time to go."

"I'm not in a hurry," Cary says. "Why would I be?"

"Aren't you eager to see what you'll find when you get back? A house on fire or another flood?"

"I thought about asking Rosa to stay with them," she replies, taking his joke seriously. "But we were going to be gone just a few hours. I can't get them a sitter every time I go out."

"If you're worried about going away for a few hours, what are you going to do when we visit *my* folks in Kansas?" These are his very own blood relations whom he hasn't seen in years.

"That's in September. I have three months to make arrangements. Rosa may be able to come at night when she's done with housecleaning. I'll see if one of her sisters can cover during the day."

"I thought they didn't like Rosa," Steve says. They don't like anybody, he almost adds.

"They don't like her Guatemalan cooking. I'll have to stir fry some dishes and freeze them."

"You know what will happen the day before we leave? One of them will get 'sick,' like last time." He frees both hands from the wheel and scratches out the quotation marks with his fingers.

"Karen and I have talked about it. She thinks before the trip I should take them to the therapist and have her tell them they can survive the week without me. I'll also take them to the doctor and have him tell them they're not about to drop dead yet. I can also…"

Oh, c'mon Cary, stop obsessing over your parents. Since he started working at home, he's spent more time with Cary than during any period in their marriage. Yet he's never felt as lonely. Her body is there, but her mind is elsewhere plotting every gruesome detail of her parents' bodily functions. She doesn't even laugh at his jokes anymore. Is she turning into an airport security guard? She once said to him, "When I get too serious, you should tickle me until I laugh."

He can't do that while driving, but he can tickle her verbally.

"You know why there are no architects in heaven?" he says. It's a fresh joke he picked up at the party.

"No idea," Cary shrugs.

"That's because Jesus is a carpenter." Silence. Steve peeks at his passenger, who's looking glumly out the window. Maybe she doesn't get it.

"Carpenters and architects hate each other's guts. The architect comes up with impossible designs, and the carpenter has to carry them out."

"I see," Cary replies, still staring out the window.

"Here's another one," Steve says, unwilling to give up. "When you say, 'It's a nice day!' what does an engineer say?" His audience shrugs again. "He says, it's 70 degrees Fahrenheit, 25 degrees Celsius, and 298 degrees Kelvin."

"Hmm" is the only response.

Still not giving up, Steve pulls out one that's less technical, "You know the definition of a bank?" Without giving her a chance to shrug, he answers, "It's a place that lends you money if you can prove you don't need it."

"Yeah, yeah, I've heard it before."

All right, I've had it, Steve shouts in his head. The Cary of yesteryear would laugh at his jokes no matter how many times she's heard them before. He understands he's no Woody Allen or Steve Martin, and his jokes are at best third rate. Cary laughs at them because she wants to make him happy. And now she doesn't care. She's so busy taking care of those two that she barely notices his existence.

*

The moment the car turns into the street, Steve exclaims tongue-in-cheek, "Oh look, the house is still standing."

"Don't speak too soon," Cary says grimly, not acknowledging his humor.

They get out of the car. Cary is all competence, click-clacking up the sidewalk and keys jingling in her hands. Steve dawdles behind, mindful of the gash on his belly. The lights in his bedroom glow through the shades. Uh oh, did he forget to turn them off? He looks further and sees light in another window—his study. Not again! Is Tak snooping around his room, opening his drawers and leafing through his drawings? He won't let Cary stand in his way this time.

He flings open the front door, almost bumping into Cary. Three figures strike an odd tableau: Mami beckoning from the top of the staircase, Cary standing frozen in the middle, and Baba looking up and grinning from the bottom. His pants are rolled up to the knees. His legs move with the sluggishness of a person wading in a pond. Watery notes ripple.

"Heh, heh, heh," Baba chuckles. "Mami forgot to turn off the tap."

Cary looks up at Steve, a hand over her mouth. "Seems like they flooded the house again," she says in a cheerful voice that doesn't match her expression. To Baba, she says flatly, "Why don't you go back up? I'll take care of this."

"This is the fourth time," Steve declares, splaying out his fingers.

"Don't worry, I'll clean it up in no time. You go on to bed," Cary says, still cheerful.

A twinge twists his insides, the kind that requires immediate attention. Steve goes down the steps, passing Tak on his way up. The hair on Steve's arms stands on end as they squeeze past each other. *Push him down the staircase*, a little voice says. Relishing the wicked thought, Steve sits on a step and takes off his socks and shoes before sloshing through the pool. This stretch of hallway is the lowest point in the house. When it rains indoors, the water always collects in this oval pond.

Sitting safely on the toilet, Steve is more resolved than ever to spill his guts. He'll have it out with Cary. She says he's the most important person in her life, and if her parents get to be too much, she'll think of a "solution." He never thought he would have to ask her to deliver on her promise. Throughout their marriage, they've never interfered with each other's projects. Cary says each person is an independent circle, and marriage is when two circles intersect—no doubt more profound advice from the Happy Handbook or whatever it's called. Although he finds her psychobabble silly, this analogy appeals to him because he can visualize it.

These days, he feels like a circle lost in a maze of orbits. He's constantly dodging this way and that to avoid collision. Cary knows her way around this universe. She and her parents spin in sync around each other, crisscrossing, touching and grating. Although sparks fly sometimes, the damage is only fender-bender. Let's face it: he's the UFO that nobody wants to deal with.

Perhaps it's time for a business trip. His contacts at the firm will be happy to send him to some faraway construction site where nobody wants to go. Wait a minute. He sits up straight. Why should he run away from home? He's traveled enough already. According to his travel log, his number of days on the road already adds up to fourteen years, two months, and twenty-one days, representing forty-eight percent of his career. In the past year he's been content to stay put and design home renovations for Washington lobbyists and widows. Is it a sign of old age that he's become a homebody? If it were, so be it.

"Woof woof," Laozi barks.

"Shut up!" Cary yells. "What do you want? I have nothing for you, Laozi! You're so demanding! Always asking for more, more, and more! I've had it with you! Go back to bed and stay there!"

Good God, Steve thinks, Cary has cracked. He can picture her baring her fangs and frothing at the mouth. Laozi is the least demanding one in the family. Other than a few minutes of begging at the table, he's too old to do anything except sleep. Steve can think of other household members who are much more difficult to please.

He cinches the belt around his trimmed waist. Surgery has snipped off ten excess pounds. While the effect flatters his figure, the change to the face in the mirror isn't as welcome. That face has been long and narrow to start with, and now it appears pinched like a rat's. He twitches his nose to accentuate the resemblance. He's fed up with scurrying about in the dark. This rat is coming out of hiding.

Throwing back his shoulders, he jerks open the door. Cary snaps one last attachment onto the carpet cleaner. The potbellied creature with its snake of tubes and wands is ready for operation.

"We have to talk," he says.

"I know, but let me finish cleaning this up. You go ahead and read your emails. I'll be there soon."

"We have to talk now, this very minute, not in a while, not after you finish—"

"O*kay*. I know what now means."

*

Steve swivels around his office chair and plunks himself down. "We can't go on like this," he says. The heat in his ears reminds him of why he hates "heart to heart" talks.

When two people tell all to each other, their relationship is bound to change, and it's a tossup between better and worse. He's always shunned such risky behavior, but today he has to get it out regardless of the consequences.

Cary pulls up a chair. "I know, I know, this is bad," she says. "Next time we go out, we'll hire a sitter for them. This won't happen again, I promise."

"You can go out for a walk and your mother can burn down the house."

"I've forbidden her to use the stove. But you're right, absolutely right. They need more help than they're getting now. It's time to hire a full-time sitter. I'll call Karen and George. They said they would chip in."

"You want to turn our home into a nursing home?" He's finally going full steam. "It's crowded enough already in this house. Every time I go upstairs, one of your parents follows me around. Your mom asks me the same questions over and over, and I have to yell out the answers. Your dad gives me a dirty look, as if I'm the one overstaying his welcome."

"I know, I know exactly what you mean," Cary says, stroking his arm.

"And now you want to hire a full-time caregiver? A stranger is going to eat here and sleep here? Sometimes I walk into the house and I don't know whose house this is anymore."

"What are you talking about? You're the master of the house. Don't you forget that!"

Her stroking has turned into kneading, but he deliberately hardens his muscles. He isn't going to roll over and beg for a tummy rub. His IQ is a few points higher than Laozi's.

"I want them to move," he says.

Cary sits still, as if allowing the five words to drip into her brain one at a time. With a blink, she's all motion again. "Let's talk about it tomorrow. It's been a long day. Come on, let's go to bed. You must be tired." She gets up, beckoning to Steve to follow.

"I want to talk about it *now*." Steve folds his arms to emphasize.

"I'll talk to George and Karen tomorrow. I promise. I'll call them tomorrow and we'll come up with a game plan."

"I know what they're going to say. If they could take in your parents, they would have done it a long time ago."

"They both have their reasons—" Cary starts to defend

her siblings.

"Your parents can go to a retirement home."

"Steve, don't you know my parents by now? Chinese parents have to live with their children until they die. They're not going to any retirement home."

"Why not? It was good enough for my mom. She took care of my dad until he died. She lived by herself for almost twenty years, and when she couldn't anymore, she checked herself into a home. My sister offered to take her in, but Mom refused. She said in a daughter's house, she would be known as so-and-so's mom. She wanted to be known as herself."

Cary shakes her head. "You Americans are too independent for your own good."

"And you Chinese are too dependent for *your* own good."

"I guess you didn't know what you were getting into when you married a Chinese, huh?"

Steve holds his tongue. He seems to have developed an allergy to all things Chinese. Even the smell of dim sum, which he used to enjoy, flips his stomach. Sometimes he even dreams in Chinese, which is most irritating because he can't understand what's being said. He's a foreign devil in his own dream.

"You haven't answered my question yet," he says to Cary.

"Steve, this isn't something I can decide on my own. I told you, I'm going to call Karen and George tomorrow."

"Don't hide behind your siblings. I want a simple answer to a simple question. Your parents are getting too much for you to handle. Are you willing to let them go?"

"It's really not that bad. I know you must be sick of listening to my complaints. It's just me venting. I haven't reached the end of the rope yet. There are plenty of resources I haven't tapped into. The county runs a senior daycare center. It's like a children's daycare—eight hours a day, with nap time, activities and meals provided, even transportation—"

"Listen, *I* have reached the end of my rope. And look at yourself, Cary. You're so stressed you don't even know you're stressed. You got sick twice already this year."

"It was just a little cold," she protests.

"Listen to me, Cary. I can't do it anymore. I just can't. It's either me or them."

Without replying, Cary's eyes wander off toward something on the wall that seems to have caught her interest. She studies it for a long time.

Steve looks away to give her privacy. It's cruel to watch another struggle. Cary the American has promised to love and cherish her husband above all else. Cary the Chinese has promised to serve her parents above all else. In Steve's mind there's no right or wrong about the two cultural choices. She just can't have them both.

Cary lowers her eyes. Whatever she found interesting on the wall has landed on the floor. "I always say you come first," she says mechanically, as if reciting lines she'd learned by heart yet not necessarily from the heart. "You're my partner in life. My parents are not. But give me some time to find an arrangement we can all live with."

"We're going away in September," Steve says, the fever in his ears cooling. "They definitely can't stay here by themselves for a week. Maybe we can put them in one of the homes around here. What are they called? Sunrise? Sunset?"

"Something like that. It's only for a week?" She finally looks at him.

"They can start with that. If it works out, they can stay longer."

An exchange of glances shows their mutual understanding of how long "longer" is. Then their eyes slide apart to find different objects to fixate on—the screensaver image of the Grand Canyon and the spine of the telephone directory on the shelf. They're like two people standing side by side at the bus stop, so close and yet so distant.

"You're not really abandoning them," Steve says, breaking the silence. "If you find a home close by, you can still take them to the doctor's and whatever else you do with them. Knowing you," Steve chuckles to lighten the mood, "you'll be running to see them every time they call."

"Yeah," Cary says, stone-faced. "I better go clean up the mess." She gets up and trudges off.

Steve notices her square shoulders are hunched and her neck bent, the posture of a Chinese peasant toting a pole with a heavy bucket on each end. He knows what, or more like who, is in each bucket.

Chapter 15

Did I forget to look? Where the hell did the truck come from? How can I not have seen it coming?

I get out of the car, the grind of metal upon metal still clanging in my head. My legs feel rubbery, my heart is stuck in my throat, but I will show nothing, say nothing that may incriminate me. The right rear of my little Honda is like a crumpled piece of tin foil. I want to cry but I *will not* cry.

The nose of the truck suffers not a scratch. I fish a notebook and pen out of my purse and exchange insurance information with the driver. Several laborers peer down at me from the truck.

Unsure what to do next, I say, "I think we should report this to the police."

The driver snarls, "Go ahead, call the police. You came out in front of me." His hand sweeps the arc of my left turn out of the strip mall. Anyone can see he has the right of way.

I look back at the Fresh Foods and Mapleton Drugs in the mall. This is where I go for groceries and medicines several times a week. I can exit this parking lot in my sleep. Have I been sleeping?

Without a leg to stand on, I flop into my car and call for a tow truck. Then I call Steve to tell him what happened. After assuring him I'm fine, there's nothing else to do but turn the AC on high and wait.

Reliving the accident, I realize how lucky I am to have swung in front of a truck. If it had been a smaller vehicle, or, heavens forbid, a motorcycle, somebody could have been seriously hurt. Oh my God, I'd never forgive myself. Harmless as I look, I've been living a dangerous life. In my hands, a car is an unguided missile.

It's been almost two months since Steve delivered the ultimatum—move my parents, or else he moves out. I know I should write up a to-do list—consult the Area Agency on Aging, search online for nursing homes in the area, call the friend whose mother is in a nursing home, and so on—but the thought of abandoning my parents has blown all the fuses in my brain. I drag my carcass around like a sleepwalker. Most people won't notice anything different about me. My eyes are open and my answers to questions quite proper, though a bit curt. I continue to dole out hearts to students, cook for the family, and drive—ah, that's the giveaway that all isn't well with me.

I'm furious at Steve. I wish he'd take a job far far away. I wish he'd run off with a younger woman who would dump him after the novelty has worn off and he'd come crawling back for forgiveness. I wish he'd get a heart attack. A stroke would do too. Then I'd send *him* to a nursing home. I wish, I wish…

*

Steve picks me up at the body shop. I take one last look at my injured baby and get into his car.

"I'm sorry," I say.

"It's just a car. At least nobody got hurt," Steve says and hugs me.

He thinks I'm apologizing for the accident. He'll never know about my horrible wishes for him.

"I wasn't paying attention," I say, noticing a hollowness in my voice.

"I know," Steve says, copying my tone.

"It's time to pay attention."

"Yes, it's time."

The moment we get home, I go straight up to my parent's

quarters. There's a matter I need to settle with them. The TV is blasting the evening news at highest possible volume. Mami watches with interest while Baba dozes, his head thrown back and mouth open like a fly trap.

"What took you so long?!" Mami lets out her usual greeting. She doesn't know about my mishap because I've asked Steve not to alarm them.

I grab the remote and mute the TV. "I just had a car accident," I say, rushing to add, "I'm okay, but the car is at the shop."

Mami shakes Baba's arm. "Wake up. Cary had an accident. You have to help her."

She struggles to get out of her chair. "Are you hurt?"

"You have to go to the hospital," Baba joins in once he's fully awake. "You can have a whiplash or concussion. You may not feel anything yet, but when you do, it may be too late." Ignoring my protests, he feels my neck to check that nothing is broken and runs his hand through my hair to look for lumps and bumps.

"How many fingers do you see?" he says.

I'm tempted to say two, but he'll go more bananas if he thinks I'm seeing double.

"One," I say. "Hey, how come you have three eyes?"

Baba knuckles me on the head. "This is no joking matter. You should have gone straight to the hospital from the scene of the accident. Let me get the blood pressure machine. I'm going to give you a thorough checkup."

While he goes to another room to fetch his gear, I waste no time with my mother. "Mami, remember the story you used to tell me, about the little boy who cut off a piece of his flesh for his mother?"

She scrunches her brows. "Which story?"

"Once upon a time," I begin in the lilt that she once used to put me to sleep, "in a village in China, a little boy lived with his mother. They were very poor and had little to eat. Then one year famine struck across the country—"

"Oh yes, there were lots of famines in China." Mami comes to life. Evidently this is a subject dear to her heart. "Sometimes locusts ate up all the crops, other times it was a drought, or war or some other disaster. People ate anything to fill their stomachs—grass, tree bark." Mami adds with a shudder, "Even human flesh. Children were the first to be eaten. I've never seen it myself, but my nanny came from the countryside and she had lots of stories to tell. She claimed she never tried it, but she knew people who had and they told her children's flesh was sweet and had tonic effects."

"Mami, will you please let me finish my story?" I say with annoyance. "So, famine struck across the country. The mother got sick, and the boy was worried that she would die if she didn't get some nutrition—"

"The best nutrition was meat," Mami carries on for me. "Where could he find meat? The pigs and chickens were dead, even the fish were gone because the rivers had dried up. Where could he get meat from?" Her tones rise and fall for dramatic effect. I'm once again a child lying in bed as my mother lulls me to sleep with a tale of cannibalism.

"The boy went to the kitchen and picked up the big kitchen knife," Mami goes on. "Then he rolled up his pants all the way up to here." She points to the top of her thigh and raises her voice to a climax: "He took the kitchen knife and cut a slice of flesh off his thigh. Then he took the meat, put it into a pot and boiled it until it was just done. They say human flesh shouldn't be overcooked or it gets tough. Then he ladled the soup and meat into a bowl and took it to his mother. She slurped it up. Mmm, it's so good, she said. Where did you get the meat from? The boy was quiet and shaking. The mother suspected something was wrong. Come here, let me look at you, she said. The boy limped over to her bedside and sat down carefully—"

I snatch the punch line: "'What's the matter?' the mother said and put her hand on the boy's lap. He cried, 'Aya!' The mother pulled up his pants and saw the huge bloody wound."

"You remember everything!" Mami exclaims.

"How can I forget? Now, my question is, where did you get that story from?"

Mami blinks and blinks, a panicky look on her face.

"This is *not* a memory test," I say to calm her down. "Just try to think back. *Who* told you that story?"

"I don't know. My mother, I guess."

"It didn't come from Confucius?"

Mami smiles, the way she does when somebody asks her what year it is. "Confucius doesn't tell fairy tales. He's the Great Teacher. His teachings are the foundation of thousands of years of —"

"Chinese culture. I know, I know. I just want to clarify one point. So you're telling me," I enunciate clearly so there will be no misunderstanding. "He didn't say a child should shed blood for his parents?"

"No, of course not. Why would Confucius say that?"

"Are you sure of it?"

Mami's eyes blank out, as if they've rolled inward to browse the quotes archived in her head. I give her time to be thorough. After casting her eyes here and there, she lights up with a Eureka look. A mumbo jumbo of classical Chinese spews out of her. This is one Confucius Says I've never heard before.

"Let me explain," Mami says to my clueless face. "You see, every strand of our hair is precious because it comes from our parents. We should take good care of it. That's why Confucius says, 'Our body, skin, and hair are all received from our parents; we dare not injure them.'" She says it slowly this time.

Ah, I remember hearing this before. This was why both Chinese men and women wore their hair long in the old days.

"When I was a child," Mami adds, "I used to have a neighbor who refused to cut his nails because his parents gave them to him. His nails grew so long that they coiled round and round—"

"That's silly," I say. "Confucius doesn't mean it literally. What he means is we shouldn't hurt ourselves because it will hurt our parents."

"Confucius says, 'Parents worry when children get sick.' Children should stay strong and healthy—that's the first principle of filial piety."

Baba reappears, holding up a victory sign. "How many fingers do you see?" he says. I answer two.

Mami says, "Why are you asking me all these questions? Do you feel all right?" She puts a hand on my forehead to check for fever.

I let them fuss over me. It's now as clear as the fingers on Baba's hand: my parents don't want me to shed blood for them. Whoever cooked up the starving mother story should be cut into strips and stir fried!

As I sit still for Baba to take my blood pressure, I want to laugh. I feel I've stepped out of the Dark Ages into the Age of Enlightenment. The world is full of light, air and common sense. If I were to kill myself for my parents, who would take care of them? And if everyone were to do the same, how would the human race survive?

I understand now. Filial piety is taking care of my parents wisely, without hurting myself. Steve is right (for once). Placing them in a retirement home isn't abandonment. It's not like an Eskimo sending his parents to the wilderness so that a hungry polar bear will come by and put them out of their misery. Placing them in a retirement home is getting them services in addition to mine. It's also about allowing me to take breaks. *Xiao* doesn't mean I have to carry my parents on my back till I drop.

"134 over 72," Baba announces. "That's on the high side. You should see a doctor about it. When was the last time you had a physical?"

"You've been working too hard," Mami chimes in. "You need a vacation."

I do, I certainly do.

Chapter 16

Ming-Jen looks around. The grass is the young green of spring, bright and oily like well-worn jade. She loves this time of year, when the bone-biting winds that howl through the *hutongs* of Beijing calm to gentle breezes. Soon the grass will spread out and fill the bare patches of earth. The piddly plants in the flowerbed will grow and bloom through the summer. They always do—the begonias and geraniums in the courtyard that started out as a few leaves when her mother first planted them. Ming-Jen makes a note to herself to tell the gardener to give them a good soaking.

"Spring is the best time of year," she remarks to her husband. "The snow has melted and the earth is returning to life." Poetry bursts from her heart.

"What are you talking about? This is summer. We're at the tail end of August."

"August? Oh Tak, you get confused easily these days. Take a look at the plants. Can't you see they're just beginning to grow?"

"That's because the place is new. The plants were just put in. Didn't I tell you before? This is a new place, everything is new," Tak says with exasperation. "When you go inside, *do not* say anything! Let *me* do the talking!"

"You don't have to shout at me. I'm not deaf. You talk as much as you want. I never have a say in anything anyway." What's this place again? Car rides always bewilder her. One moment she's home, the next moment she's somewhere else. It's all Cary's fault. She's always bringing her to new places—new doctor, new psychologist, new acupuncturist, new lab for some test for her brain or lungs or bones. It's impossible to understand Cary sometimes. She has a habit of mumbling and running off before Ming-Jen can question her.

"Remember, we're just having a look around," Tak says. "All you need to do is smile and nod."

Ming-Jen flicks her hand as if shooing away a bothersome fly. "You don't have to nag me. I *know*," she says with brave defiance. Inside she's a little afraid, like a person groping in the haze of dusk, when everything looks familiar and strange at the same time. Has she been here before, or met this person before? It's a guessing game, a secret to be kept to herself. She hates being treated like a retarded child.

The wide glass door opens automatically. This is a doctor's office, Ming-Jen guesses. Cary greets the receptionist like an old friend. Their lips wriggle rapidly, and once in a while, one of them tosses her head back and laughs. Another woman comes out of a room. Cary waves to her, another old friend.

What's this place where Cary knows everybody? The rooms on one side have computers and desks, so they must be offices. The other side is like the lobby of a luxury hotel. The sofas look glossy and un-sat on, as if they just came out of their plastic wrap. Their flowery pattern is a perfect match for the curtains. There's also a fireplace. Though unlit, the sight of it fills the room with warmth. A collection of ceramic dolls in frocks and bonnets sits on the mantel. Ming-Jen is tempted to pick one up. Pretty things always attract her.

"This is nice, isn't it?" Cary says.

"Very nice," Ming-Jen beams.

"Hi, my name is Mercy. I'm the social worker here. I'm going to give you a tour today."

Ming-Jen looks at the woman. She's young and pretty and color-coordinated in a blue outfit against olive skin. As Ming-Jen lifts her hand for a shake, another one shoots ahead of hers. Tak grabs the woman's hand in a firm grip. Ming-Jen pays him no mind, for it's ridiculous to take offense at an old man trying to impress a girl his granddaughter's age. When they were younger, she would taste vinegar whenever Tak flirted with a woman, and there were many of them at the factory. Nowadays, she wishes he would take a concubine and leave her alone.

"Would you like to sit in a wheelchair?" Mercy says, looking from Ming-Jen to Tak.

Tak shakes his head vigorously. Ming-Jen hesitates. One part of her loves being pampered, as the elderly should be pampered, while another part hates the notion of being elderly.

"Mami, you should. It's a huge place. Look how long that hallway is."

Ming-Jen gazes in the direction of Cary's finger. The hallway is as wide as a two-lane highway. One wheelchair is traveling up and another down, and nobody is pushing them. They're running on motors!

"I don't have driver's license," Ming-Jen says.

"You don't need one," Mercy says, laughing. "You'll be in an old-fashioned wheelchair and I'll push you." In expert fashion she flips a lever, swivels aside a footrest and invites Ming-Jen into the seat.

"Let me do this," Tak positions himself behind the wheelchair and gives a muscular shove.

The first stop is the dining hall. The place sparkles with white tablecloths, shiny wine glasses, and fancy plates. Mercy leads the group to a board where the menu is posted. She explains the choices for the three-course dinner.

"I want salad, salmon, and rice pudding," Ming-Jen says.

"We're eating at home," Cary says. "I already took out a chicken to defrost."

Before Ming-Jen can express disappointment, she's wheeled to the next room. A group of women is sitting in a circle, and one is speaking animatedly.

"This is the activities room," Mercy says, turning around to face her party. "Every week we have an event called 'remembering.' And today we're remembering birthdays. Each person tells a story about a memorable birthday. We have other activities in this room also, like Bingo and exercise class."

So that's what this is, Ming-Jen thinks with relief. A senior center. Her confidence returns, for she knows all about senior centers. She knows how to navigate from one activity to another and when to line up for her box lunch. People are friendly, except for a few grouches, her husband being one of them.

She raises her hand to ask for permission to speak. "I have a story to tell," she says.

"Mami, we have to move on," Cary says. "You can tell your story another time. They have this program every week."

The wheelchair swivels around and Ming-Jen finds herself trundling down the hallway again. They stop at a place with a "nurse's station" sign, shake hands with a huge, round-faced woman, and move on again. The next hallway is lined with numbered doors. This looks like a hospital, Ming-Jen thinks. Why is she here? What tests are they going to do on her today?

A door opens and she rolls into a flood of sunshine flowing through a bay window. She wiggles to get out of the chair before they can wheel her away again. She wants to take a good look at the place. Mercy flips up the footrest and helps her up.

What a cute little apartment, Ming-Jen thinks. It's simply furnished with all the necessities for two—two sofa chairs, two chests of drawers, two closets, and a double bed. The living room is on the small side, and the kitchen is a doll house. The bedroom is almost as spacious as the one at Cary's home, and the bathroom—*Wah*, she exclaims as she steps in. It's a palace! One or even two wheelchairs can fit in it. The shower is another room of its own. One can walk in and sit down on the bench.

This beats the shower chair Cary installed over the bathtub at home. If she were to shower here, she wouldn't have to lift her feet to clear the rim of the bathtub, an athletic feat of Olympic proportions for her. Then again, why would she take a shower here? What *is* this place?

Ming-Jen feels vibration on her eardrums. Cary's voice resonates as clearly as if she's standing close by. Yet she's in the bedroom talking to Mercy. Ming-Jen's hearing aids seem to have a will of their own. When they want to, they can pick up conversations through closed doors. Ming-Jen holds her head very still, for at that angle the sound waves glide through her hearing aids with ease.

"They're staying for a week starting next Monday," Cary says.

A light turns on in Ming-Jen's brain. In her recent phone calls with Karen and Xiao, both mentioned "a week." When her children parrot each other, it means they're plotting major mischief. "It's only for a week," each one said. "Don't worry about the cost. We'll pay for it." "No harm in taking a look." So this is what she's doing now—taking a look at an old folks' home.

Ming-Jen pokes her cane up to Cary and says, "I don't want to go to an old folks' home."

"This isn't an old folks' home," Cary said. "It's called assisted living. Mercy and the other staff are here to *assist* you. And it's only for a week. Steve and I are going away to visit his uncle and aunt, remember? They're both in their nineties and always asking to see Steve."

Likely story, Ming-Jen thinks. Americans don't care about parents, let alone uncles and aunts. "Steve is sick. He can't go anywhere."

"He's recovered very well. I told you, he wants to visit his uncle and aunt in Kansas. Remember?"

"Baba and I want to stay home."

"It's *not safe* for you to be home by yourself." Cary stamps her foot with agitation. Tak clears his throat and throws her a warning glance. Cary continues in a friendlier tone, "Here, everything is taken care of. Three meals a day, house cleaning, somebody to give you your medicines. And you'll get to meet people and tell them stories."

"We'll talk about it at home," Tak says, patting Ming-Jen gently on the back. "We shouldn't waste Mercy's time. I'm sure she's very busy. She has such a big home to take care of."

You're such a gentleman in front of a pretty girl, Ming-Jen comments to herself. Well, I guess I'll have to be a lady then. The argument can wait till we get home.

"Very nice place," she says with a smile and nod to no one in particular.

*

When Tak entered the building, his mind was already set. No matter what they call it, Spring Meadows or Winter Meadows, senior living or senior dying, it's a dumping ground for unwanted parents. If his children don't want to live with him, they should rent him an apartment. He'd rather live on his own, but never, ever, will he share a home with strangers.

As he comes out of the building, his resolve is crumbling like badly cured concrete. Never did he dream that a nursing home could look like a five-star hotel. This one is brand new too, with a smell as rich as the interior of a new car. He wants to step on the gas pedal and go, just go anywhere he's never been before. Perhaps in this new world he can be twenty again. Thirty won't be bad either. As they wait for Cary to get the car, a breeze brushes his face, and his skin tingles at the zing of possibilities in the air.

Cary drives the car up to the portico. Tak helps his wife into the front seat and gets into the back. He closes his eyes and pictures himself strutting in his best suit, escorting his wife to the dining room. In Hong Kong they were known to be the best-dressed couple, he arriving in a three-piece suit and she in her red peacock cheongsam at the Garment Association's Lunar New Year banquet. At the table he pulled out a chair for his wife and smoothly slid it in after the contour of her backside. The other women ogled with envy, wishing their husbands had taken lessons in western chivalry.

Paris was where he'd learned gallantry and amour. He'd visited every year to meet his buyers and attend the celebrated fashion week. In terms of business, the trips produced dismal return; in terms of personal satisfaction, the yield was enormous. Paris brought out the man within the man. In Paris, he was no longer a struggling manufacturer but an art connoisseur, savoring the beauties who sashayed down the catwalk in splendid plumage. Walking down the Champs Elysees in spring, surrounded by glamour and glitter, he was no longer the husband of a virtuous wife but a lover whose passion was as boundless as his imagination. The whole of Paris was a fashion show. Everywhere he looked he saw beautiful women balancing deliciously on high heels and showing off their new spring clothing.

Tak chuckles softly. Ming-Jen would be furious if she found out. However, what she doesn't know can't hurt her. What could he have done? The buyer went to great expense to book a private room at the club. The women were part of the prepaid package. To turn down the hospitality would be rude, aside from jeopardizing his chances of a plum deal. Anyway, the games didn't mean anything. He saved his amour for his beloved wife, bottled safely in a vial of perfume. Ming-Jen loved the pretty bottles as much as the fragrant water inside.

"Haiiiiiiiiii," Tak heaves a nostalgic sigh. How he wants to get away again. He needs a vacation from his ninety-year-old body. For all the horny goat weed and Super T and a dozen other supplements, his engine still won't start. He's given up on doctors. Every one of them, from the internist to the psychiatrist, ophthalmologist, and orthopedist, refuses to prescribe him Viagra. They say the excitement would be too much for his weak heart. He'd quoted scientific articles about the anti-aging benefits of sexual activity, even told them that his sex-starved wife had threatened to leave him, yet none of his arguments convinced them. The porn films have failed him too. They've gone flat with time. A naked body is just a naked body.

"Haiiiiiiiiii." Another sigh gushes out of him, the despair of a man who's lost his most valuable treasure. Oh, how he wants that feeling again—to love and be loved.

Cary's eyes meet his in the rearview mirror. "It's a nice place, isn't it? Nice *people* too," she says.

"Not bad," Tak says with a little smile. Knowing how well his daughter knows him, the "nice people" she referred to can only be one. Mercy is like a gift box wrapped in tinsel paper and topped with a red ribbon. However, she's a present for somebody else, not him. It's pleasure enough to admire from a handshake's length. His present is, always has been, his beautiful and virtuous (perhaps too virtuous) wife.

Remembering Cary's recent accident, he says, "Let's talk about it when we get home."

*

As soon as we get home, I go into the kitchen and take the cleaver from the drawer. Now, this is a Chinese cleaver, with a blade as heavy as a machete. It's a multipurpose tool that can function as a chef's knife for slicing meat, a crusher for garlic, or an axe for hacking through the hardest bones. I scrape the edge on my thumb. It's as dull as the last time I used it. At the same time, it's still usable. Well then, tomorrow is another day. I rip the thawed chicken from its package and spread eagle it on the chopping board.

Baba comes in to make tea. He stays on one end of the kitchen, away from the bits of chicken flying out from under the cleaver. I glance at him with suspicion. Does he have something to say? I'm not ready for the "talk" yet. My plan is to hold off till dinner, when Steve's presence will bring a degree of civility to the table. Given his "outsider" status, Baba and Mami will give him face.

A cup in each hand, Baba leaves without a word. I'm relieved.

The senior home tour went much better than I expected. Mami behaved like a little girl clamoring to try every ride at an amusement park. She was agitated for a moment, when she thought the place was an "old folks' home." But it's just a matter of semantics. At our talk, I'll call the home a "retirement community." "Retirement" has a respectable ring. It means you've worked hard for many years and deserve to rest and enjoy your "golden years." Mami will buy that, totally.

The person I've been worried about is Baba. During the tour I paid close attention to his every twitch, to prepare myself for the kind of fight he'll put up. Indeed he twitched a lot. Whenever Mercy talked to him, whenever he stole glances at Mercy, his whiskers trembled with pleasure. He was entirely at Mercy's mercy, a turn of events I haven't foreseen. Although I should have, I chuckle.

"I don't want to go," Mami's voice comes from the living room. "I like to stay at home, sleep in my bed. An old folks' home is for old people who don't have children. I have four children. Filial piety is the first virtue..."

"You have only three children," Baba corrects her.

"I'm not going anywhere. I'd rather die than go to an old folks' home."

My cleaver pounds on the rib cage. White light flashes across my eyes. A Chinese boy's face appears—long, yellow, and tragically handsome. I recognize my nemesis immediately.

"You're still around," I say. "I told you I don't believe in you anymore. You're just a lie somebody made up to brainwash children. Mami says so herself. She doesn't want me to shed blood for her."

The boy smirks at me, as if he knows something I don't.

My heart drubs a double beat. What if Mami isn't aware of what she's doing to me? Her mind isn't quite all there. She doesn't know the stress of caregiving is tearing my marriage apart. She doesn't know she was the cause of my car accident. She doesn't know I stay up nights racking my brain over what to do with her and Baba. She doesn't know she's the source of at least half my gray hairs.

She doesn't know! That's why! I've given her several slices of my meat already, but she doesn't know it. I'll die if I give her anymore. Somebody has to tell her. I grip the cleaver and run out to the living room.

"You want another piece of my flesh? Is that what you want?" I shout at them. I press the blade on the tender side of my forearm. Thank goodness the edge is blunt.

Baba gapes at me as if I'm speaking Greek. Mami squints with the disapproving look that usually accompanies, "You can't go out dressed like that!"

"Are you going to the old folks' home or not?" I shriek.

"Heh heh heh," escapes from Baba's jagged mouth.

How can he laugh at a time like this? Don't tell me I have to carry out my bluff. I appeal to my mother, who answers with a flurry of blinking. The cleaver is getting heavier and heavier. I can't keep it suspended much longer.

"Heh heh heh," Baba cackles again. A tear rolls down his cheek and soaks his mustache.

"Are you going or not?" I squawk.

Mami is blinking an urgent Morse code.

I hear footsteps on the staircase. Hallelujah, my savior is

here. Steve is coming to rescue me from myself. But why is he so slow? No, Steve doesn't have long claws that click on the floor. Besides, I remember now, he has a late afternoon meeting with a client.

Laozi saunters up to Mami and slurps her in the face.

"Go, go," she blurts.

"G-g-go." Baba stammers.

"Go, go," Mami blabs again.

I stagger back to the kitchen. The Chinese boy who fed his flesh to his mother is gone. "Good riddance," I say out loud.

Chapter 17

I sling the clean plastic-bagged clothes over my shoulders. Now that my parents gussy up for every meal, I'm constantly ferrying their dressy clothes to and from the dry cleaners. They've been at Spring Meadows four months now. Fallen leaves have given way to snow, and the home's response to both seasons has been most satisfactory. The driveway is clear and the walkways salted. There aren't going to be any fractured bones in this place.

Past the lot, a doe and her twins graze on a green patch. Many aspects of the home impress me, none more than its truth in advertising. Unlike the Oak Streets, Pine, Maple, or Chestnut Streets named posthumously after the trees that have been chopped down, Spring Meadows really does have a meadow. In spite of its location at the intersection of two main thoroughfares, the bucolic surroundings give it the feel of a country retreat.

Mercy looks up and beams as I walk into her office. "We did it," she crows. "They were both there yesterday."

I know immediately what she's talking about. That's all we talk about when we meet.

"My parents went to exercise class?" I ask just to make sure.

"Yup. They were there yesterday, your mom and your dad." Her sharp cheek bones glow with triumph. I think of her as Spanish mixed with Inca.

"Congratulations. How did you do it?"

"When the aide went to get your mom this morning, your dad blocked the door to the bedroom. He said your mother was still sleeping, and he wouldn't let anyone wake her. So I decided to go talk to your dad personally. You know, we can't force our residents to do anything they don't want."

I nod to show I understand this is a home, not a prison.

"I knocked on his door," Mercy says. She proceeds to stand up to reenact the scene, displaying the length of her shapely torso.

"He invited me in and offered me tea and cookies," Mercy chuckles. "I told him what I came for. He bowed to me—your dad is *such* a gentleman—and said fine, no problem. He let the aides go in to dress your mom. Later on I passed by the exercise class and saw both of them there. He was wearing his track suit and pumping weights like a champ. I think your dad is just *wonderful*."

I struggle to tweak my sneer into something more benign. "Oh Mercy, what will we do without you? Thank you, thank you so much."

I go on down the wide two-wheelchair corridor, greeting everyone I pass. The staff wear name tags pinned to their chest, thank goodness, or I'll never remember names such as Afsaneh, Haweeyo, Tsering, and Saccandrika. I've also learned the differences between a nurse, med tech, and nursing aide, so I can go to the right person for assistance.

I'll forever bless the man who told me about this place. He was the social worker at the eighth home I checked out. I'd been quite ready to drive my parents to a faraway outlet mall and dump them there.

Who knew the search for a home could be as frustrating as panning for gold? Even when the price seemed right, it would turn out wrong after the "care packages" were tacked on. "Who can afford eight thousand dollars a month per person?" I exclaimed at my first home. The social worker replied, "Don't your parents have a house to sell?" My answer was a sigh and a no.

I also had no idea of the complexities of elder care. I always thought old age was the only qualification for entering an old folks' home, until I learned about the many grades of old. The ADL test for the elderly is the equivalent of the SAT for college applicants. ADL stands for Activities of Daily Living, such as dressing, toileting, and eating. The number of ADLs you're capable of determines your score, which in turn determines which of these institutions you can gain admission to: continuous care (people who don't have a wad of cash to put down need not apply), independent living (Mami and Baba are past that stage), assisted living (just right for them), and nursing care (not yet and hopefully never). Although "nursing home" is often used as a generic label, it's actually as exclusive as an Ivy League school. Only those with the highest needs can enter.

The first time I walked into Spring Meadows, my thought was: luxurious home, luxurious cost. I went through my list of questions anyway, just to make sure no stones were left unturned. And what a stone I found! I'd been panning for gold, but the nugget shining at the bottom of the basket was diamond! Spring Meadows is privately run and publicly financed. Thanks to the taxpayers in the county, the charge is only three thousand a month for a couple, a fraction of the other homes I looked at. Since then, every time I walk through my neighborhood, I quietly thank all my neighbors for subsidizing my parents.

*

I stop by the nurse's office. The round black face cracks into a grin, then a laugh. The nurse is a roly-poly Ghanaian, as wide as she's tall.

"No 'heart attack' this afternoon," the nurse says, quotations implied. "I think he misses you too much. His heart is fine the moment he sees you."

"I am flattered," I say tongue in cheek. "Thanks for

checking on him. When he called me at seven this morning, I almost jumped out of bed to run over to see him. Then I thought if he were having a *real* heart attack, it would be too late by the time I got there. That was when I thought of calling you."

"That's what I'm here for. Tell him next time he has a heart attack, there's no need to call you. He should pull the red cord in his room. Somebody will go to him immediately."

"Do you know how many times I've told him that?"

"He just wants to see you." The nurse chortles. "You should see his face when I went to check on him. He looked so surprised. *Why are you here? No, I'm not having chest pains. No, I didn't call my daughter.*"

I can just see it: Baba rounding his eyes with angelic innocence while lying like the devil.

"I checked his vitals and everything was fine," the nurse says.

"By the way, has my mom's new medication come in?" I ask.

The nurse gets up and pulls a file from the shelf. The information is right on the first page. "The Procardia? Yes, it was delivered yesterday and she had her first dose this morning."

"Can you please keep an eye on her blood pressure? It tends to go up and down after the doctor adjusts her medication." At the risk of nagging, I add, "You've stopped the Norvasc, right?"

The nurse turns a few pages and puts her finger on it. "Yes, I've crossed out Norvasc."

I leave the office, once more convinced that my parents are getting better care here than at my home. It doesn't mean I've passed the responsibility to others, only that I've been promoted to supervisor. No more do I have to run to the pharmacy and wait around for the prescription to be filled. Others do that job now, and my role is to make sure they do it in a timely fashion. Because this is "assisted living," there's one nurse for sixty residents and one nursing aide to eight residents. I consider them my helpers, and the one I hold accountable is myself.

The sound from my parents' TV broadcasts into the hallway. I knock until my knuckles hurt. Baba finally opens the door. "You come at the right time," he greets. "I have many things to tell you."

The room looks homey, cluttered with knickknacks and family pictures as a home should be. Baba and Mami have been sitting on their respective personal chairs, both brought from my home, and watching TV hooked up to the same cable channels as before. Two cups of tea and a plate of assorted cookies lie on the coffee table. A portrait of domestic bliss.

I pull up a folding chair and turn down the TV. Mami smiles fondly at the daughter whom she doesn't get to see daily, hourly, and minutely.

"How are you doing?" I say, stroking her gnarled hand. Once again my mother is the most beautiful woman in the world, not the wicked old witch who's cast a miserable spell on my life.

"My pain here is bad," Mami says, kneading her lower back. "It's like somebody is cutting it with a rusty saw. From side to side, back and forth, it never stops."

My mother's descriptions of pain are her exercises in creative writing. "You have to tell the nurse when you're in pain. She'll give you an extra dose of medicine," I say.

"I don't want to bother her," Mami says.

"It's her job to be bothered." I almost add, "You never minded bothering me."

"I have many things to tell you," Baba says as he sits down

with a piece of paper in his hand. "Number one," he reads from his list (guess where I got my habit from?), "the workers in the home discriminate against me. They're good to white people, but they don't like Chinese. They look down on us Chinese."

I take a long deep yoga breath. Baba's honeymoon is over. The relationship started to sour a few weeks ago and is fast deteriorating into divorce. I glance at the clock on the DVD player. In fifteen minutes they should be walking out to the dining hall. In fifteen minutes I'll be saved.

"Let me give you some examples." Baba moves his finger down the list. "They refuse to accept tips from me. They think my money is no good—"

"This isn't a hotel," I interrupt. "You can't tip the workers here. They're supposed to treat every resident the same. They can get into deep trouble if they take your money."

"Why won't anyone accept money? There's no such thing. Everyone wants money."

I look at the clock again. Only two minutes have passed. Then I remember Mami needs to get dressed, and that requires a number of minutes.

Baba's finger moves down the list again. "Here's another example. Your mother and I are always the last to be served. We often have to sit for half an hour before we get our food."

"That's because you chose a table farthest away from the kitchen. When you first moved in, the dining room was half empty. You could have picked any table, but you wanted the last one, the one at the very edge of the hall."

"No, I didn't pick it. They assigned it to me."

I draw another deep breath. "Okay, okay. I'll talk to Mercy about it. I'll ask her to put you at a table closer to the kitchen."

"You want me to die?" Baba shouts, a rope of muscle tugging at his jaws. "If you tell them, they'll poison my food."

"You think Mercy will poison you?"

"Not Mercy, but the others will. Once she knows, everybody will know. I will surely die here."

"So what do you want me to do about it?"

"Don't talk to anyone about it!"

The gulps of breath are making me dizzy. "It's time to get ready for dinner," I say. "Hey Mami, your silk blouse is back from the cleaners. You know, the one with the little peach blossoms. It will go very well with your beige pants."

Mami is delighted.

Baba shouts after me, "I'm not finished yet."

I bury my head into the closet and make a mental note to call the psychiatrist. It's been a while since Baba's last appointment. Perhaps a higher dose of Prozac is in order.

*

The residents migrate toward the dining room in different modes of transport—some on foot with the help of canes and walkers, and others on wheels either motorized or manual. I push Mami out in her wheelchair and merge into the procession. Baba walks next to us, jauntily dressed in an open-collar shirt and sports coat. He's wearing his public face, a benevolent Buddha smile lifting the corners of his lips, eyes as serene as Lake Placid. Mami waves to everyone she passes, like a queen to her royal subjects.

A few units down, a woman exits her room on a scooter. From her perch she leans forward to close the door with a hook fashioned from a hanger. She's obviously having difficulty reaching the handle. Baba springs into action. He runs ahead to close the door for her. Noticing that her oxygen tube has tangled around the scooter bar, he carefully picks up the plastic coil and straightens it out.

"Thank you! You're such a gentleman," the woman, a dyed red-head, says as she adjusts the prongs in her nostrils. *Psst...*

psst, the oxygen agrees. "Oh hello, I see your daughter is here."

"Her name is Cary," Mami says proudly. "I have three daughters and she's my oldest."

I look at her with astonishment. Is she joking or is she really that demented? And yet she can recite long tracts of "Confucius says" word for word.

"Your parents are wonderful," the woman says to me. "You're very lucky."

This time I reply with ringing endorsement, "Yes, I'm very lucky." Yes, my parents are wonderful. The only time they're *not* wonderful is when they're alone with their daughter, who brings out the worst in them. There should be a law to protect the elderly from such harmful contact.

As I follow the procession into the dining hall, my heart bursts with gratitude to all the residents. They're miracle workers, each one of them. They heal my parents in ways doctors can't. They can transform an antisocial psychopath into a Good Samaritan and a miserable invalid into the Empress of China. They're better than all the anti-depressants, steroids, and narcotics put together. Best of all, they come with no side effect.

It's no wonder I've felt overwhelmed. I was doing the work of thousands—the residents and staff at the home, the county Board of Supervisors, voters, and taxpayers. If it takes a village to raise a child, it takes a county to care for the elderly.

Chapter 18

Ming-Jen takes a chair in the circle. A dozen other women plus one man are already seated, and more are coming. She's sneaked out of her room while Tak was snoring. Otherwise, he would have kept her from coming, or even worse, come with her. He would fidget and bug her to leave before it's over. Today, she can't afford to be distracted. Today is her big day.

At the stroke of three "cuckoos," Mercy opens the meeting. "Welcome to Stories, everyone. We have an *exciting* hour ahead. First, Ming-Jen is going to tell us stories from China. Then Mabel will talk about growing up in Tennessee. Last but *not least*, Kate will tell us the Irish stories handed down from her grandparents."

Mercy gives the floor to Ming-Jen. For the occasion Ming-Jen has put on her Chinese jacket with dragons swimming in clouds.

"Ahem," she begins. "Confucius say filial piety is most important virtue. We Chinese people love our parents very much. We even compete who love parents more. You do something good for your parents, I do *more better* for my parents." Ming-Jen thumps her chest.

"We Chinese don't have Superman. Our heroes are filial sons and daughters. There are twenty-four stories about these *awesome* people, and today I will tell you three." Ming-Jen is glad to see her Americanisms resonate with her audience.

"Once upon a time, there is a young man called Chung. His father die already and Mother is sick. In winter it's very cold. She wants to eat hot soup with bamboo shoots. Chung is too poor to buy bamboo shoots, so he goes to bamboo forest. But there is no new shoots. They come only in spring. He kneels down and cries and cries. Heaven look down and is move by his filial piety. The earth open and many many bamboo shoots come out. He bring them home to make soup for Mother. She eat soup and get well."

"What a *beautiful* story," Mercy remarks.

"I wish *my* son would make me soup," says the woman with a bandage on her nose. "He doesn't even come to see me, and he lives only a few miles away."

A number of gray heads nod in sympathy.

"Have you been to the Chinese restaurant down the street?" the woman sporting a giant pink hair bow asks Ming-Jen. "Is it any good?"

"I had a dish called *moo shu* pork," someone answers on Ming-Jen's behalf. "I think it's got strips of bamboo shoots, and it was yummy!"

"Let's get back to the stories," Mercy intervenes. "Ming-Jen has two more to tell."

Once upon a time, there was a little boy named Meng. He was eight years old and very good to his parents. The family was poor and couldn't afford to buy a mosquito net to put over the bed. In the summer, mosquitoes swarmed over them and sucked their blood. While others tried to shoo the mosquitos away, Meng let them feast on him, so they wouldn't bite his parents.

"I hate mosquito bites," cries the Pink Bow, scratching her arm.

"That's not the point!" somebody contradicts.

Ming-Jen looks around and is pleased to see that everybody else gets the point. Eyes pop open, heads shake with wonder, and one exclaims "Wow!" They can see the superiority of Chinese culture. Well, if they're impressed with this story, wait till they hear the next one. She's saved the best for last.

Once upon a time, there was a man named Ju. He had

a three-year-old son and a mother. Because he was poor, he couldn't provide enough food for both. He felt ashamed he couldn't feed his mother properly. One day, he had an idea. If he buried his son, there would be more food for his mother. He started to dig a hole in the ground, and suddenly he struck something hard. It was a pot of gold, and it had his name written on it. The heavens were rewarding him for his filial piety.

The audience is speechless. Even the loud-mouthed Pink Bow has lost her tongue. Slowly Mabel raises her hand. She and Ming-Jen are table mates in the dining hall. Ming-Jen has great respect for this retired school teacher.

"I'm really impressed with your stories, Ming-Jen," Mabel says once permission to speak has been granted. "They're like parables, meant to teach people moral lessons. But sometimes these stories exaggerate, which means you can't take them too literally. What I'd like to know is, how do ordinary folks serve their parents. For instance, what did you have to do for them?"

Ming-Jen sighs. "My father die in labor camp. Communists take him away because he is *intellectual.*" The word feels luscious on her tongue. "He's only fifty-five years old. In labor camp, there's no food, no doctor, and he has to work very hard. When he die, no family is with him. Very sad." She bows her head with gravity.

"I hate communists," Pink Bow cries. "I used to know a communist. He was my neighbor. Never mowed his lawn or raked his leaves. He just let them blow over to my side."

Mabel raises her hand again. Mercy nods.

"What about your mother? Did you get a chance to take care of her?" Mabel says.

Ming-Jen feels a punch in the guts, but she's determined not to show it. "My mother die in Beijing. I already in America. Too far away to go back."

"How far is that?" somebody says. "About five hours by plane?"

"It's more like six or seven," somebody else says.

Mercy moderates, "Thank you very much, Ming-Jen, for your wonderful stories. Come on, everyone, let's give her a hand."

Ming-Jen tips her head to the applause. She'd like to go to her room now, but she can't be so rude as to get up and leave before the other speakers have their say. She sits there, weeping silently.

After Father had died, her mother wrote her. The elegant calligraphy is forever engraved in her mind. "No one can blame you for not serving your father when he was sick," her mother wrote. "But this you must do to fulfill your filial duty: return to Beijing and mourn for your father at his funeral."

Tak vetoed the trip. "What if the communists detained you? What's going to happen to the children?"

"My brother promised the communists will leave me alone. He's quite high up in the Communist Party."

"If he's so powerful, why can't he protect his own father?"

She begged and cried. Karen, a toddler then, clung to her leg and bawled with her. Tak tried to comfort her, but she'd have been better off without his kind of consolation.

"Your father is dead already. His troubles are over. It's not your fault he died alone, without any family member at his side. The communists did it to him. They probably tortured him too. You know what the worst torture is? It's poking a needle under your fingernail. They say the nerves in your fingertips go straight to the heart."

Married to a man like that, it's no wonder her tears have run dry. She has to use artificial tears these days to lubricate her eyes.

Many years later, her brother pleaded to Ming-Jen to return

to Beijing. Their mother was fading fast. The old woman couldn't recognize anyone anymore, but her eldest daughter's name was constantly on her lips. This time Ming-Jen didn't consult Tak. Her bank account balance plus the two pending college tuitions made the decision for her. A plane ticket from San Francisco to China meant that one of her children would have to drop out for a semester. She could have buried either Karen or Xiao, but she couldn't do it. Her devotion to filial piety wasn't strong enough.

Before the month was out, she received a call from her brother. Their mother had passed away.

Confucius says, "Filial piety is the foundation of virtue, the root of civilization." Ming-Jen has been mouthing this ever since she could babble. But when the time came for her to practice it, she was too weak to carry her parents on her back. She couldn't even fulfill her mother's dying wish.

As the last storyteller takes the stage, Ming-Jen feels a headache coming, and it isn't the stabbing-with-knife or pounding-with-hammer kind. She can get rid of those with a couple of pills. This headache is the tightening-with-vise kind, which no medicine can help. The vise is pressing at her temples now, and it will get tighter and tighter until her eyeballs want to pop out. There's nothing to do except close her eyes, lie as still as a cadaver, and ride it out for a day or two, sometimes three.

Ming-Jen anchors her eyes on one carpet square, waiting patiently for the stories to finish and Pink Bow to shut up. Finally, applause flutters in her ears. Ming-Jen taps her fingers together politely. With all the strength she can muster, she leans on her quad cane and hoists her body up. When Cary presented her with the new cane, she'd balked at the ugly claws at the base. But she also knew if she didn't obey, Cary would fly at her. Some days, however, such as today, she's thankful for the extra stability.

Clump, clump, clump, the unsightly quad leads the way.

Passing the paintings in the corridor, she turns her head to admire them as always. The rosy-cheeked women with narrow waists and flouncy floor-length skirts come from a past era, and the past is always better than the present.

Oh, look at the woman in the pink gown—she's walking out of the painting! Ming-Jen blinks to clear her vision. A thud jolts her. What happened? One leg sprawls in front of her. Where's the other? Ah, here it is. She finds it bent backward to one side. The floor shakes. She looks up and sees people running toward her.

*

Ming-Jen opens her eyes. "Cary, there you are," she says with relief. Whatever happened, Cary will take care of it.

"Mami, you broke your hip. You have to go through surgery," Cary says.

"Surgery? No, no, I want to go home." Ming-Jen bounces up and swings her legs off the bed. She feels no pain. How can she have broken anything?

Cary grips her shoulders. "The doctor says, if you're not operated on, you can get a blood clot and die. You don't want that, do you? Be a good girl now. Let's lie back down. Come on."

"My parents are waiting for me. I have to go home and make soup for them," Ming-Jen whimpers.

"Tell you what. You stay here and have a good rest. When I get home, I'll make a *big* pot of soup. Tell me what you want in it."

"Lots of bamboo shoots."

Chapter 19

Tak bends down to embrace his wife. "You're going to be all right," he says, brushing her lips with his mustache.

"The doctor says the surgery went very well," Cary says. "You can go home in three days."

Ming-Jen thrashes around to get up. "My baby, where have they taken my baby?" she cries frantically.

Tak and Cary look at each other in puzzlement.

"Hoo hoo hoo!" Ming-Jen wails. "My baby is dead. Where did they take my baby? I want to look at him." She searches under the sheets.

"I'm your baby," Cary says, placing her face squarely in front of her mother's. "And I'm right here. Mami, you're in the hospital because you broke your hip. The doctor fixed you up. You're going to get well soon."

"Hoo hoo hoo," Ming-Jen can't stop crying.

"Look at me. I'm Tak, I'm right here with you."

Ming-Jen glowers at him as she would a stranger who's pinched her in an indecent spot on a crowded bus. "My Tak is young and handsome. You're an old man. Hoo hoo hoo. My whole family is dead. My husband, my children…my baby."

Tak feels a stab in his heart. He's always blamed himself for Ming-Jen's miscarriage. If he'd been home instead of gallivanting with fashion models in Paris, Ming-Jen might not have slipped and fallen. The fetus was five months old with features that reportedly favored Tak. And it was a boy. They could have had two sons.

Cary pulls him aside and says, "She hasn't quite wakened up from the anesthesia. The doctor says at her age, it will take some time for her head to clear."

"It's a bad baby," Ming-Jen says, her mood swinging from sadness to anger. "Let them take it away. I don't want it."

Tak strokes his wife's disheveled hair and makes a silent oath. Oh Ming-Jen, I'll make it up to you. I'll do everything in my power to take care of you. I'll never leave your bedside. I'll watch over you whether you're awake or asleep. I'll carry you wherever you need to go. I won't allow anyone to hurt one strand of your hair. I'll get strong, you'll see. As long as I'm alive, you will be too.

Two nurses enter the room. Tak steps aside to let Cary take over. He's tired of people snapping at him with "Say again?" His accent is pure Queen's English, which he'd acquired straight from the mouths of the British educators at the Anglican school he'd gone to. Americans don't understand him because he doesn't slur his words like they do.

The tall nurse says something to Cary. They go back and forth and finally Cary gestures "go ahead."

"Ayo yo," Ming-Jen hollers as the tall nurse pulls her to a sitting position and the short one scoots her legs off the bed.

"Don't touch her! She just had surgery," Tak wants to yell at them. Yet only hot air comes out of his open mouth. He turns to Cary with a do-something plea in his eyes. Cary looks distressed, her fists clenched as if they're about to strike. He signals to her to go ahead. Punch them out. Atta girl.

A string of sounds comes out of Cary's mouth. He can see them floating in the air. *Kwang, kwang, kwang.* He imagines reaching out and grabbing at one, only to see it pop like a soap bubble. The nurse opens her mouth and the same *kwangs* stream out. Tak swings his head from side to side like a tennis spectator. He dials up his hearing aid, but all he gets is louder *kwangs*. The doctor has told him he has "nervous ears." The more he tries to understand the less he does.

Cary taps him on the shoulder. She faces him, her lips moving slowly now, giving him time to latch on to the sounds. After asking Cary to repeat several times, Tak comes to understand that the pain and torture the nurses are giving Ming-Jen is called "Physical Therapy." It's supposed to be good for her.

He stands by as the nurses manhandle his poor wife to her feet. When they catch her leaning on her good leg, they straighten her so that the broken leg gets its full share of torment. "Ayo yo," Ming-Jen cries. Tak wants to whisk his wife away from the horrible place. He commands his legs to get going, yet they remain rooted to the ground like tree stumps. He can only watch helplessly as the nurses force Ming-Jen to take a step. Her face is bloodless as a corpse's. She's quiet, trembling like a condemned person walking to the guillotine.

*

Tak locks the door to his suite at Spring Meadows. He changes out of his dress clothes into gym gear—sweat pants, a crew neck tee, and white Adidas running shoes—and drags out all the weights from his closet. He lines them on the floor, the dumbbells and barbells, wrist weights and ankle weights, in the ascending order of their heaviness. His muscles have atrophied from disuse, but they'll bulk up quickly once he embarks on his tried and true program. It's worked for him at the age of twenty, forty, and sixty. Why shouldn't it produce the same results at ninety? By next week, he'll have regained the strength to carry Ming-Jen around. She'll never fall again because she'll never have to walk another step.

He picks up a three-pounder and flexes his biceps several times. "One two three four," he counts silently. At "three two three four" blood begins to hum in his veins, and it feels good. How he misses those days. At the peak of his martial arts training, two-hour workouts four times a week were routine. His coach was a tall, broad-chested old man originally from Shandong province, where men were famous for fighting tigers bare-handed. Although he was just a coach in Hong

Kong, the gym owner kowtowed to him. (Rumor had it he was once a mafia hit man in Shanghai.) His pep talks were famous throughout the colony. "Push harder, harder, harder! Show her everything you've got! You're not impotent!" followed by expletives that burned the face of the hardest core. This training technique never failed as no man wanted to fall behind on this front.

On the first day of training, however, the old man's advice was always discretion. "Think of it as a first date with a pretty girl. If you rush into it, she'll slap you in the face. If you take your time and warm her up, the fun can last a long, long time."

Tak pauses after ten rounds. The humming in his veins has swelled to a full-throated operatic warble. Remembering the coach's warning, he reaches for a lighter weight, the one-pound baby. His fingers caress her cool, smooth skin. The grip, however, feels as arousing as holding hands with a chicken. He puts it down and wraps his hand around a five-pounder. The heft is just right. His lips warp into a devilish smile. Coach was both right and wrong. Some women need warming up. Others don't. Before Ming-Jen came along, the women he'd gone out with had arrived at the door already steamy.

One, two, three, four, Tak starts with his right arm. Inhaling, exhaling, his body slides easily into the groove. His eyes stare ahead, filled with vision of one woman. He must get back into shape so he can protect her from all harm. The image of Ming-Jen's agony is fresh on his mind, her cries still ringing in his ears.

Seven-haah-two-haah-three-haah-four-haah. What's the matter with him? Fifteen minutes of working out and he's choo-chooing like a train already. Pumping light weights used to be no more than a stroll in the park. Just because he's ninety doesn't mean he can't do what he used to. He's still the same man, isn't he?

He can't fail this time. Ming-Jen is more precious than life itself. Although she's the prize he doesn't deserve, to lose her now will be too, too cruel. He's gladly accepted all his other losses—his businesses, money, reputation—for they were only retribution for sending his friend to his death. Whatever revenge Mushroom has taken on him is fair, as long as the victim is him and him alone. The matter concerns no one else.

Take that and that, he punches at the ghost. The mushroom head wobbles on a narrow stem of neck, and yet the silly grin refuses to go away. You're not going to get me this time, Mushroom. No matter what you do, I'm not going to fail. Even if you trip me, I'm going to get up and keep going. You wait and see.

Tak freezes, his arm suspended in mid-punch. What's that he feels in his back?

Chapter 20

Mami and I sit in the rehab center courtyard, soaking in the recommended daily dose of vitamin D. While the UVA rays of the July sun bombard our bare arms, the shade of a giant oak protects our faces. Mami slumps in the wheelchair despite a heap of cushions to prop her up. She's well groomed, her hair curly from a visit to the in-house beauty shop, and her fingernails freshly painted and manicured by an aide. Her flowery print blouse, however, has withered from too much washing. Because of the frequent mix ups in the laundry room—somebody else's clothes are sometimes hanging in Mami's closet, and her clothes are sometimes seen hanging on somebody else's body—I've brought the lowest end of Mami's wardrobe to the rehab center. The Mami of yesteryear would rather have died than appear shabby in public, but these days her esthetics have grown dull. Even the stain on the front of my T shirt doesn't offend her.

"What did you do this morning?" I ask.

Her eyes glint with outrage. "You know, Madame is in town. She's bossy as always. This isn't right, that isn't right. You have to do it again. Fifty times she told me to do it over. But what choice do I have? She's the customer, our rice bowl. Without her we'll be out of business."

I think she's mixing up two people—Madame, the French buyer of the garments produced in Baba's shop, and Linda, the physical therapist. I've seen Linda yell at Mami for falling short by one arm cycle. She means fifty when she says fifty. But it's a good-natured kind of bawling, and well-intentioned, so I don't complain.

"How are the workers treating you?" I ask my mother to make sure there's been no abuse.

"The workers?" Mami wags her head slowly. "Just because you're the boss doesn't mean you can treat them however you like. You'll be in trouble if they walk out on you. You have to smile at them, tell them what a good job they're doing, and pass out candies and cakes."

"You're right," I say, glad that she tries to endear herself to the staff, because once I leave, she's entirely at their mercy. "It's best to get along. Confucius says, 'If there's harmony in your heart, there's harmony everywhere.'" I'm not sure he actually said that, but it's close.

"Harmony," Mami repeats several times, like a child learning a new word.

I want to cry. My mother has gone through extreme physical pain and mental anguish in the past month, yet she keeps finding new ways to cope. The doctor says the anesthesia has aggravated her dementia, as it sometimes does to the elderly. But I'd rather call her condition ingenuity. If she can't change her circumstances, she can change her attitude. She's now the owner of the establishment, and everyone working here is her employee.

I put my hand over hers. My fingers seek out the big fat vein on the back of her hand and roll it around. Squishing her veins gives me a peculiar pleasure, like playing with earthworms. Since her fall, it's been my pastime when we sit together wordlessly for long periods.

"Why isn't Baba here?" Mami says suddenly. "This is the busiest season. We've been up all night finishing the order."

"He's resting today. He hurt his back and can't get up. He'll come see you when he feels better," I add hopefully, "in a few days."

The Spring Meadows nurse called me yesterday and told me Baba couldn't get out of bed. I found him lying flat as a pancake, unable to move a finger or toe. "I don't know what happened," he moaned. "My back gave out for no reason."

Sure, and the dumbbells crawled out of the closet on their own. I almost tripped on one.

"He must have gone to Paris again," Mami says. "He goes there all the time to see his girlfriend."

"No, no. He loves you and only you."

"He must have moved in with her. Go ahead, I don't care."

There's something I haven't told her yet. From now on, she'll live separately from her husband of sixty-two years. Spring Meadows has refused to take her back because she's graduated to the next level. She now needs 24/7 care, which the assisted living doesn't provide and the county can't afford. When her rehab program ends next week, she'll move to the nursing home next door. The state and federal governments will step in to cover those expenses under Medicaid. The country, not just the county, will help me take care of my mother, just as my taxes help others take care of theirs. I have a feeling Confucius would approve if he were around today—kind of a communal filial piety.

Karen, George, and I have conference-called to discuss what to do with Baba. Although the nursing home is willing to admit Baba for compassion reasons, we believe they're better off in their separate homes. Baba needs privacy, while Mami needs attention. A nursing home is like a hospital—two to a room and nurses walk in every two hours to check on the patient. Since there are no locks on the doors, Baba will push every piece of furniture against the door to barricade himself in. We feel like monsters tearing the lovers apart. However, the distance is only a fifteen-minute taxi ride, and we make it up by financing Baba's cab fares.

No, this isn't a good time to break the news to Mami. I have a more interesting subject to bring up.

"Look what I brought you!" I haul a hardbound volume from my tote bag. "It's your book of Confucius sayings."

Mami beams and reaches out like a child for a lollipop. I place the heavy tome carefully on her lap. The pages are yellowed, some of them barely hanging onto the binding. Each page is split into two columns, Chinese on the left, English on the right.

"You want to read it aloud?" I say.

A knobby finger homes in on the Chinese column. Mami pokes at the characters she recognizes and skips those she can't. Giving up, she closes her eyes and recites the passage, head swaying with the rhythm.

"Wow, that's very good," I exclaim. How can anyone say my mother has dementia? She can remember a whole paragraph from *The Analects*.

I tilt the book so the English translation column is visible. I read softly to myself, "The Master said, 'At fifteen, I set my mind and heart on learning. At thirty I stood on my own. At forty, I had no doubts. At fifty, I knew heaven's decree. At sixty, my ears were in accord. At seventy, I followed the desires of my mind-and-heart."

Too bad Confucius didn't comment past his seventies. I recall learning he died around seventy, probably of a disease that's entirely curable today. If modern medicine had prolonged his life, what example would he have set for people in their eighties and nineties? And if he had dementia, what kind of adages would he be spouting?

Mami flips through the pages.

"What else do you want to read?" I ask.

"*Xiao*," the reply shoots out as fast as a rock from a slingshot.

I should have known better than to ask. Begrudgingly I take over the volume and flip to the index at the back. "The Book of Filial Piety" shows up. Of course, there has to be a whole book dedicated to the subject.

Mami is already reciting from memory: "Filial piety is the foundation of virtue and the root of civilization..."

As Mami intones, I follow the English translation. My Chinese language ability is limited to everyday conversations. Of all the characters in the text, the only one I recognize is 父 for father, the picture of a man wearing a mustache.

The English column reads: "A disciple asked Confucius what filial piety was, and he replied, 'Our body, skin, and hair are all received from our parents; we dare not injure them. This is the first priority in filial duty.'"

Oho, listen to this—"first priority!" Not just one of the filial duties, but the first! I grab the book from Mami's lap and demand my turn. I recite in English: "To establish oneself in the world and practice the Way; to perpetuate one's name for posterity and give glory to one's father and mother—this is the completion of filial duty."

This is a lot to swallow in one gulp. "To establish oneself in the world and practice the Way. Now, how do we do that?" I ask Mami for guidance.

Mami replies without hesitation, "It means work hard, save money, be a good person—"

"I know, I know. But I didn't know these things were part of filial piety. I thought filial piety is to hover over your parents, wait on them hand and foot, give them whatever they want, bow to them, and call them 'honorable parents.'" I clasp my hands and lower my head in mock reverence.

Mami eyes me suspiciously, unsure what to make of my flippant remarks.

I carry on: "Let's see, what else does it say here... 'Perpetuate one's name for posterity and to give glory to our parents.'"

"Well, of course, if you made a name for yourself, your parents would be so proud. I know that's all I ever want from Fred and Maggie. Nothing pleases me more than to see them pursue their dreams and succeed in whatever they do." An Oscar footage plays in my mind: the winner goes up the podium to receive his award and intones in a British accent, "I want to thank my mum and dad...."

I can't believe what I've read so far: There are many ways to practice filial piety, and one of them is through personal achievements.

I read on, "'Thus filiality begins with service to parents, continues in service to the ruler, and ends with establishing oneself in the world.' Well, we don't call them 'rulers' nowadays, at least not here in the U.S."

I look to Mami for enlightenment, but she's engrossed with watching a sparrow pecking at a crumb. Well then, let me venture my own interpretation: "We have no rulers to serve nowadays, but we do have to kowtow to an authority, which we call the law. Serving our ruler today is being a law-abiding citizen...a useful member of society."

"I really like those two trees," Mami says. "One is big, one is small, and their shapes are exactly the same. Like mother and child." She cups two hands together into the shape of a cypress.

"Yes, they're beautiful," I say without looking up. Mami has made the observation as many times as we've sat in the courtyard.

"So filial piety is a three-step process," I say, wrapping up the discussion before Mami's mind wanders farther. "First you serve your parents. Fine—'Charity begins at home.'" If it were up to me, I'd add a footnote: Sometimes family are the hardest people to be nice to.

"Second, you extend this service to society at large." I pause to ponder what this means for me. "For me, it's teaching and performing, bringing the joy of music to others, helping others less fortunate, scooping up Laozi's poop...."

I look down at the page to remind myself of the third step. "And ends with establishing oneself in the world."

I sit up with astonishment. "Does this mean that the end of filial piety is to establish oneself?"

"Let's go inside. Madame must be looking for me," Mami says.

"Wait," I say. "Am I reading this right? The goal of filial piety is to establish oneself. Is this why I'm taking care of you? Is this all for my benefit?" I sweep my hand across the landscape of wheelchairs, hearing aids, adult diapers, and pills, pills, and more pills. In spite of all my efforts, my parents are sliding inexorably to the brink. Even if I were to feed them more fillets of my flesh, my parents would still suffer and die. No amount of filial piety can save the elderly. Perhaps it's meant to save the young?

"We better go see what the workers are up to," Mami says, tossing me a you-know-how-they-are look.

I close the book and place it respectfully in the tote bag. This is going to be my bedtime reading in the near future. All these years I've been getting bits and pieces of "Confucius says" from Mami. They sound as ridiculous as the strips of paper in fortune cookies. It's time to get the unabridged version from the horse's mouth.

BOOK THREE

Confucius says, "When parents are alive, to serve them with love and reverence; when deceased, to cherish their memory with deep grief—this is the sum total of man's fundamental duty, the fulfillment of the mutual relations between the living and the dead, the accomplishment of the filial son's service of his parents."

Chapter 21

What would Confucius do? I ask. For Christians, the question is "What would Jesus do?" and for Muslims "What would Mohammed do?" Since my mother's faith is Confucianism, what Confucius says is the closest proxy of what Mami wants. If Confucius were in my shoes (a pair of washed out made-in-China sneakers), what medical decisions would he make for Mami?

I browse through *The Analects* to see what Confucius has to say about death. To my disappointment, this is all I find: When a disciple asked Confucius about death, he said, "While you do not know life, how can you know about death?"

Thanks a lot, Mr. Confucius. This sounds to me like fudging of the highest order. You could have simply said, "I don't know." It's okay to admit it even if you're Confucius.

To be fair though, how could Confucius have an opinion about a postmodern phenomenon we crudely call "pulling the plug?" He couldn't have imagined such a dilemma. In his day, a person with an infection either got over it on his own or died. A patient had no choice in this matter until the invention of penicillin in the 1940s. Nowadays the array of antibiotics is as plentiful as cereal brands in a grocery store. If one class of drugs fails to work, there's always another. Sometimes a person can't die unless he's so worn out that he or his family chooses to stop the drugs. In this sense, dying has become increasingly optional.

Not right now, but soon, in the not too distant future, I'll have to decide for Mami. I've attempted to have this chat when she's lucid, but the conversation never gets very far. ("You want to kill me?" she said.) It's too late now. She's been diagnosed with dementia—not the Alzheimer's that she always dreaded, but the result of a series of mini strokes. Unbeknownst to us, her headaches and dizzy spells are the death throes of her brain cells.

The ethical issues over "pulling the plug" have stirred heated debates. Some call it a crime because they believe life is sacred, an absolute good. Others call it "allowing death to happen," or "letting nature take its course." This school believes that when the body and spirit are ready to move on, holding it back by extraordinary means is cruel as it only prolongs suffering. Just talking about the subject is controversial. The pro-choice camp calls the discussion "end of life conversation," while the pro-life camp calls it "death panel" deliberation.

*

On a blistering July day that Washington DC is famous for, Karen, George, and I sit down for a whatever-you-call-it discussion at the nursing home. We take our seats on one side of the conference table, I in the middle and my siblings on each side. People's remarks on our resemblance to each other always take me aback. In my eyes we have nothing in common. One sister is a replica of one parent, the other the other, and the brother, now that he's gained another twenty pounds, is a breed unto his own. Nonetheless I've read that the genetic makeup of siblings is closer than that of any relation. Even if I can't see it myself, the shared DNA strands must spring out at observers. I'm so glad to have my two gene-mates by my side today.

The hospice nurse and social worker introduce themselves, although their appearances are introduction enough. Diana, the nurse, is robustly built, square-jawed, with the fearless eyes of someone who stares down Death as a daily routine. Joanne, the social worker, has a slender frame and a sweet and soft marshmallow face that seems capable of absorbing all the sadness in the world.

Joanne starts, the skin around her eyes crinkling with

kindness, "First of all, I want to say that I really enjoy working with your mom, and your dad too. I've been talking a lot to him, and he's just wonderful."

I smile gracefully, noticing my siblings doing the same. A day after the Californians' arrival, our "wonderful" Baba has already threatened to disown them thrice: "You're not my son (or daughter) if you don't move me into your home."

"I'd like you to know that hospice isn't just for the patient," Joanne goes on in a menthol voice. "It's also for the family. We're here to help you go through a very difficult period. If you have any questions and concerns, please feel free to let us know."

My siblings and I glance at each other, uncertain who should speak first. Normally the pecking order in a family is as unalterable as birth certificates, but in this family the roles have been shuffled around. Our eyes dart around in confusion. Finally one pair steadies. George leans forward.

"As far as I understand," George says with the authority of the CEO that he is, "hospice is for terminally ill patients with a prognosis of six months of life. Does this mean my mother has only six months left?"

I flinch at my brother's query. I explained the hospice business to him months ago and got his agreement. Is he double-checking on me?

"Let me give you some basics about hospice care," Diana replies, gathering her massive shoulders. "It started out as a movement to provide palliative care for terminally ill patients. Its focus was to give comfort, peace, and dignity to the dying. Since then hospice has broadened its services to other categories of patients. Your mother entered the program under the category of 'adult failure to thrive.' And the reason is...." She flips the chart to the right page. "She lost twenty pounds in two weeks. She was also in pain, and pain management is one of our key functions. So she met two criteria for hospice care."

"How much does she weigh now?" Karen said.

Diana flips the chart back to the front page. "She's now ninety pounds…from one hundred and twenty-six when she first came to the nursing home a year ago."

"Yes, I was quite shocked to see her," George says. "Can't you give her more of that liquid supplement?"

"The aides make their rounds regularly. Their reports say your mother can finish a quarter can at a time," Diana reads from the chart. "They've tried every flavor on her, strawberry, chocolate, and vanilla, but she doesn't care for any of them."

"Can't you force her?" George says.

"We can't force anyone to do anything he doesn't want," Joanne interjects. "We can only encourage."

"Look, your mother is shutting down," Diana says. "She's not eating or drinking. That's why she's been getting one UTI after another."

"UTI is urinary tract infection," I explain to George.

The nurse continues, "It often occurs when the immune system is weak and also when the person is dehydrated."

"I know it must be hard for you to accept," Joanne says, three worry lines drawn across her forehead. "Your mother is in the last stage of her life."

Karen and I nudge each other in the elbow. Mami's nourishment has been the subject of our phone conversations many a midnight. With dedication and deception, I can get Mami to finish a can of supplement. One "last gulp" leads to another, and there are precisely twelve last gulps in each can. It can be done, even if it takes hours. However, what's the point? Karen and I have discussed the pros and cons of stretching out the already thin thread of life. Mami's rejection of sustenance means she's ready to go. Is it a favor to her to hold her back? Or is it a favor to our own consciences? Our calls always end with Karen's parting advice, "Just play it by ear." The problem is I've never been good at it. I prefer the written note that leaves no doubt as to what the composer wants me to do.

"How often does she get the UTIs?" Karen says. The question is really for George's benefit as she already knows the answer.

Diana flips through the pages. "She had two last month."

"What can be done to prevent it?" George says.

"Drink plenty of water," Diana states simply.

My siblings and I look at each other helplessly. The solution is simple, the implementation impossible. We've witnessed how much water our mother drinks. When forced to, she takes a little sip through a straw. Sometimes she pretends to sip. Only a person holding the straw will notice there's no water coming up.

"Can't you feed her water through an IV?" George suggests in desperation. His mouth turns down as if he's about to cry.

"George, I thought we've agreed not to put her through any invasive procedure," Karen says, craning her neck to address her brother. I sit back so as not to block the full glare of Big Sister's ire.

"Right, right," Little Brother says, retreating.

"Hospice doesn't provide this kind of care," Diana says. "The nursing home doesn't have the equipment either. Your mother will have to go to a hospital for an IV. In which case, she'll be taken out of the hospice program. Of course, you can re-enroll her later."

"No, we're not going to hydrate her with an IV," Karen states flatly. "Cary tells me that our mother is on antibiotics all the time. She gets an infection, takes a course of antibiotics, and a week after the course is done, she gets another infection. This is really a chemical lifeline to keep her going, isn't it?"

I'm relieved it's Karen raising the subject. As caregiver in chief, any hint of letting go can lead to suspicions that I'm tired of taking care of my mother. If the suspicions were entirely groundless, I could shrug them off. But they're not.

"Yes, it's a chemical lifeline," Diana says. "Withholding antibiotics is an option for families to consider. I've even seen patients picking this option for themselves. Unfortunately, your mother is in no condition to make decisions. It's up to you and your father—"

"My father is totally irrational about this. No, we don't want to involve him," Karen says. George and I nod vigorously.

"It all depends on her quality of life," George weighs in. "If there's no quality left, then there's no reason to go on. At this point, she still enjoys some things. Yesterday we took her out for dim sum, and she ate everything we put on her plate."

"I had to give her two tablespoons of Imodium for dessert," I remind my brother. "Or she would have an accident in the car."

"She still knows us," George goes on. "When I walked into the room, she smiled and waved to me."

"She called you her brother, and when you corrected her, she didn't believe you. She said you looked too old to be her son," Karen says, suppressing her smirk. I find myself covering my mouth with my hand. George touches the gray hair on his temple, a subconscious act, I suppose.

I regret not having given my brother a blow-by-blow account of Mami's battles with infection, as I have with Karen. Whenever a UTI hits, Mami lies in bed for days, seemingly comatose though still conscious enough to scrunch her eyebrows together to show discomfort. I'm shocked when I hold her hand. In spite of fevers of a hundred and two or three degrees, Mami's hand is icy cold. I've figured out why—Death has a firm grip on her hand, and just as He begins to lead her away, a miracle drug yanks her back. Lately, one miracle drug hasn't been enough to make her stay. She's been needing two or three, and no sooner has she recovered enough to resume eating than Death drops in for another game. It's a tug of war between Nature and man's cunning, and Mami is the prize in the middle, a very tired prize by now.

"Let me lay out an option that you may want to keep in the back of your mind," Diana says. "If you think your mother is suffering too much from the infections, and the antibiotics are merely prolonging her suffering, you have the choice of withholding the chemical lifeline. If this is what the family decides, you can be assured that your mother will be kept comfortable. We'll give her medicines to lower her fever, oxygen to ease her breathing, and morphine to keep her comfortable."

"I know this is very hard for all of you," Joanne says, her face crumpled into a ball of empathetic pain.

"My gut feeling is that as long as my mother has something to enjoy, even if it's only one thing—" George waves a thick forefinger—"let her enjoy it."

"I believe that life is divided into many phases," Karen says, "and each phase has its own focus. My mother has lived a full life. She's gone through all the phases. This is the last one, and she's reached the end of the end. Her focus now is on transitioning to the next...." She gestures the obvious with her hand. "The focus of the family should be to help her attain a peaceful and painless passage."

I suck in my breath. My sister has flung the taboo against the wall and shattered it into a million pieces. Although Karen never once mentioned the word "death," the unspoken word is as noticeable as a stripper dancing on the conference table. I look around and see that all eyes are on me. My siblings have spoken, and they're now waiting for me. I wish I could tell them the truth: I'm emotionally drained, beat up, wrung dry. I can't go on much longer. Every time I leave, Mami clings to me and whimpers like a child, shredding my heart with a scalpel. Her arms have grown strong with all the therapy. The only way I can get away is to lie: "The doctor is making his rounds. He's just a few doors down. Be a good girl now and lie down."

I want this agony to end. No, I can't tell my siblings that.

"I wish we didn't have to decide for her," I hedge. "I wish she would tell us when she's had enough."

"That's why we have advance directives," Diana says.

"My mom has had several advance directives," I point out. "In the latest one she could only put an X on the dotted line. I tried to explain to her there will be no resuscitation, no invasive procedure, but I'm not sure she understood. Besides, she's always changing her mind. One day she says she's so miserable she wants to die, and the next day she begs me not to let her die. What am I supposed to go by?"

"Your mother has dementia," Diana says. "She may not fully understand what she's saying."

"She's not completely gone," I retort. "Sure, sometimes she doesn't even know me, but then there are times when she's totally lucid. She knows who she is, where she is, and the U.S. President's name. Sometimes she can go on and on reciting Confucian sayings."

"I know it's very confusing," Joanne coos. "That's how dementia is. She has good days and bad days, which makes it very hard for the family to accept that she has dementia. That's why we're here, to offer guidance and consolation to the family."

"It's only going to get worse, not better," Diana adds, matter-of-fact.

My brother cackles, his bulk shaking with laughter. I look to my right to see what can be so funny. No, he's not laughing. He's crying! He hoods his eyes with a hand, but his lips are trembling visibly. Karen gets up, and we both hug him. Joanne slides a box of Kleenex across the table.

"I can't believe we're talking about this," George sobs, "on her birthday."

"I thought since you're both here, we might as well—" I swallow back, "kill two birds with one stone." The metaphor doesn't sound right.

"We don't have to make a decision today," Joanne says. "This is just a discussion about where your mother is and what the options are when her condition changes."

George blows his nose and wipes his eyes. "I'm going to sell my bank and stay home to take care of her. I'll spoon feed her myself. I'll...I'll get water into her somehow. She won't have any UTIs at my place."

"You can discuss it with your wife later," Karen says, puncturing his hot air balloon with one prick. Our brother has the best of intentions, but his heart often speaks faster than his head.

"As Joanne said, we don't have to decide right now," Diana says. "We'll keep her on the same meds and continue to monitor her. When she gets sick, we can decide on the treatment on a case-by-case basis. Cary is here, and she has the power of attorney. We'll work with her as the occasion arises." Addressing Karen and George, she adds, "If either of you have any questions, please don't hesitate to call me." She hands out her card.

"The power of attorney doesn't mean anything," I say to my siblings. "I'm not going to do anything without consensus from you two."

"Consult with us if you can," Karen says. "But if you have to decide on the spot, or if one of us can't be reached, do what you think is best. We trust you completely. Right, George?"

How else can my poor brother respond than by mumbling, "Right?"

My eyes appeal to the professionals across the table. How will I know what's "best"?

"Don't worry, you'll know when the time comes," Diana

says, reading my mind.

"We'll be here to help you," Joanne adds.

*

As my siblings and I enter the room, Mama greets us with, "Where have you all been? We're going to be late for the party." She's all abuzz in her wheelchair, ready to roll.

"What took you so long?" Baba says. He's decked up in suit and tie and smells of aftershave. Yet no amount of grooming can hide the fact that he's aged ten years in the one year since Mami's fall. The tailored jacket hangs like a sack on his sunken shoulders and the legs of the trousers pool around his ankles. The swagger in his gait is gone, and so is the fire in his eyes, the mischief in his grin. He's a dwindled version of himself in every way.

"What did the nurse have to say?" Baba presses. Even his voice has grown thin.

"We better hurry up and get Mami ready," Karen says, dodging the questions.

"Mami, we're going to celebrate your ninetieth birthday!" George shouts with ebullience to hide his hoarseness from crying.

"I had my ninetieth birthday already. My sister brought me a very nice cake with lots of strawberries. I must be ninety-one today."

I laugh and explain to my puzzled siblings, "The home had a cake for her on Tuesday, the day of her birthday. She was ninety then, so she must be ninety-one now. I told you, she can be very lucid sometimes."

Turning to my mother, I say, "Now we're going to dress you up in beautiful clothes! Look what I brought." I pull out of the closet the suit Mami reserves for weddings, birthdays, and new years. It's a loud, boisterous red, the Chinese color for uncontainable joy and new beginnings.

After the men are shooed away to wait in the lobby, I pull the sweatshirt over Mami's head carefully so as not to mess up her fresh curls and thread her arms through the sleeves of a pink blouse. Mami raises her chin as Karen paints her lips. Rubbing her lips together to even out the rouge, Mami looks dreamily from one daughter to another. I click a mental snapshot of this moment and store it in my heart. In case my brain fails one day, this precious picture will still be accessible.

"Mami, you have to stand up now. I need to pull up the skirt," I say. Karen holds her up. As expected, her waistline has shrunk. I've come prepared with a box of safety pins to do last-minute alterations.

"Ouch," Mami cries.

"What? Did I poke you?" I say, recoiling.

"It hurts." Mami points at her stomach area.

Oh no, I think. A stomachache already before the banquet? I'll have to sneak her a tablespoon of Pepto Bismol before we leave. The home forbids anyone except its nurses to dispense medications. Even for over-the-counter drugs, the procedure is for the family to make a request to the nurse, who then calls the doctor for authorization. From the time of request to the resident receiving the drug, a day is considered lightning speed. I've learned to bypass this frustrating rule, as well as a few others.

"Don't worry, I'll give you medicine before you go," I say. I tighten the waistband a little, and Mami cries out again.

Karen pulls up the blouse. A brownish growth foams on the pale skin. We bump heads as we bend down for a closer look. What can it be? We've never seen anything like it before.

"It hurts just a little bit, right? Not a lot?" The answer I'm hoping for is obvious.

"A little bit," Mami echoes.

I raise my eyebrows at Karen. "We can tell the nurse *after* the party. I'll pull the skirt down so it's not touching that thing."

"She doesn't seem too uncomfortable," Karen says, agreeing.

Two heads pop into the doorway, one above the other. "Happy birthday, Popo!" two voices ring out. Fred and Maggie parade in amid bouquets of flowers and balloons.

Chapter 22

Ming-Jen feels a familiar weight dent her mattress. Whenever she oversleeps, her mother sits down on her bed and strokes her cheek until she wakes up. Slowly she opens her eyes. Her mother is smiling at her, and oh, Father's here too. He's looking at her fondly, his handsome face glowing in the pale light. Mother leans over and kisses her on the cheek. Father kisses her on the other cheek. Without a word, the couple turns around and leaves.

"Wait, come back," Ming-Jen calls after her parents. She touches her right cheek to feel the wetness of her mother's lips, then her left. Why are they in such a hurry? How can they leave without having a cup of tea?

Ming-Jen wakes up feeling refreshed. She hasn't slept so well in a long time. In fact this is her first pain-free day in what seems like a lifetime of pain. The ring of fire around her waist is gone. So is the knitting needle whipping in her knee, the crown of nails burrowing into her brain, and the knife sawing in her lower back.

Lying in bed, enjoying the quiet before the day's bustle begins, she relives her parents' visit. Mother was dressed in the casual *samfu* she always wore at home. Her hair was tied back in a bun, and the skin on her face showed only the least hint of a wrinkle. She looked exactly the same as the day she sent Ming-Jen and her siblings on a train to Hong Kong. Her last words to Ming-Jen were, "Silly girl, there's nothing to cry about. I'm sure things will settle down in a few months. You'll be home before the Moon Festival." Her smile was kind and comforting, but when the train pulled away, Ming-Jen saw her dab her eyes with a handkerchief.

Ming-Jen turns her thoughts to her father. He wore a navy

blue robe, his back straight and strong, and his face square and just. One look at him and you could tell he's every bit the "superior man" Confucius talks about. During his brief visit, his face lit up the way it did whenever he inspected her brush calligraphy. "Of all my children, you have the most strength in your stroke," he's said many times.

"Guess who came to visit me this morning?" she opens her mouth to say to Tak the moment he walks in. To her dismay, her tongue feels numb as if the dentist has given her a Novocain shot. All that comes out is, "Ah ah ah ah."

"Speak louder, I can't hear you," Tak shouts, cupping a hand around his ear to enlarge the reception dish.

"Ah, ah, ah."

"You see, you always say I'm deaf. How am I supposed to hear when you mumble like that?"

Ming-Jen turns her face away.

"You don't want to talk to me, or you can't talk?"

How can I tell you I can't talk when I can't talk?

*

Tak glances over at Ming-Jen's sleeping roommate. He pulls the curtain all the way around Ming-Jen's bed, enclosing her in a fabric cocoon. Good. Now they're hidden from the prying eyes of the nurses and aides. He pulls a chair right up against the bed, as close as possible to his wife's face, and sits down. She drops her eyes to her nose.

"Whether you look at me or not, I'm going to take care of you," Tak vows to himself. "You haven't touched your breakfast," he says, grunting at the thought of the good-for-nothing aides. Almost nine in the morning, and they still haven't come to feed her. Cary always comes to their defense. They're busy with other patients, she says. You have to wait your turn. Press the call button if you need anything. Somebody will come to help you.

Yeah, sure. His bones will have turned to ashes by the time somebody arrives. He scoops up a forkful of scrambled eggs and brings it to Ming-Jen's lips.

"Open up, come on," he barks.

She clamps her lips together and sucks them in.

"You have to eat," he goes on barking. "How can you get better if you don't eat?"

She closes her eyes to shut him off more completely.

"Have some juice then," he says, softening since the harsh method doesn't work.

He drills a straw into her lipless mouth, but she refuses to sip.

He gives up, for the moment at least. When she isn't looking, he'll shove a piece of sausage into her mouth.

"You want to go to the bathroom?"

Her eyes flicker. He takes it to mean yes. Tak gets up, pushes the chair aside and positions the wheelchair at just the right spot. His body-building program came to a full stop after he hurt his back and Cary confiscated every barbell. It doesn't matter though. Now that Ming-Jen has lost weight, he can pick her up with one arm. Well, maybe two.

He clasps his wife's hands. Her limpness gives him pause. Normally she returns the grip and works with him to get to the edge of the bed. Today, her hands feel like cotton. There's nothing to hold on to. Tak braces his legs and gives a mighty tug. There, Ming-Jen is sitting up. Ignoring the twinge in his back and the thumping in his ears, he drags her feet off the bed.

The next maneuver has to be carefully planned as there's no margin for error. Tak rehearses it in his head. He'll insert both arms under her armpits, forklift her just a little, and swivel her into the wheelchair.

The first step is easy, the second is hard though not too

hard since he's doing it. The third has to be fast, decisive…like this. Ooof! Tak finds himself sitting in the wheelchair. He tries to get up but a heavy pile pins him down. He looks and sees that the pile is his wife!

"Ming-Jen, are you all right?"

"Ah, ah, ah."

Good thing he caught her. No harm done, he assures himself. Nobody needs to know about this. All he has to do is lift her up and put her back on the bed….

*

I march straight to the nurses' station. "Francis, how are my parents?" I ask the head nurse.

The nursing home had called me an hour ago to report my parents' mishap, but since no harm was done, I waited till a gap between lessons to come. My nose is a bit out of joint because this isn't my day to visit.

"They're okay," Francis says, his broad Sri Lankan face dimpling with sympathy. "Coco went in to check on your mother and found your parents tangled up in the wheelchair. I've examined them. They're both fine."

"I don't know how many times I've told my dad not to help her get up," I say with irritation. "He should've pressed the call button."

"Your father likes to do things himself," Francis says. "Your mother is a little weak today. She usually talks to me in her own language when I give her medicine. Today she didn't smile or say anything."

"She must be having a bad hair day," I joke, reminding myself to always put up a friendly face to the staff.

"We call it waxing and waning," Francis says, drawing on the lunar phases to describe his ward's condition.

"It's a pity she's forgotten her English. You must have a hard time understanding what she wants."

"We find ways to communicate." Francis bobs his head wisely.

"Thanks, you're doing a *wonderful* job," I sing.

After banging my head against the nursing home walls a few times, I've learned to be lavish with my praises and frugal with my complaints. Positive feedback seems to produce better results and avoids the danger of retaliation against the helpless patient.

I debate whether to peek in on Mami. The moment I show my face, my parents will swamp me with demands, and the intended five minutes will stretch into an hour. On the other hand, I check my watch, my next lesson starts in forty minutes. I have a bit of time, and when I have to leave I'll have a good excuse.

Baba is startled to see me.

"I heard Mami fell this morning," I say.

"Oh, let me tell you about it," Baba buzzes like an excited bee. "I came out of the bathroom and saw her standing on her own. I immediately ran up to support her. Right at that moment, she fell. I caught her and tumbled into the wheelchair with her on top of me. Fortunately, my kung fu training has taught me how to fall without getting hurt." To demonstrate, he tucks his head and arms in like a turtle.

I throw him a "likely story" look and turn my attention to Mami, who's reclining at an odd angle on the bed. One side of her face droops a little, but it's hard to say if the asymmetry is from a past stroke or a current one. Oh heck, what does it matter? The damage has been done and another corner of my mother's mind chipped away. Mami is like an old leaky boat. The moment you plug one hole, another springs open.

Pinching a corner of her blouse, I peek under, careful not to touch the skin. The brown growth is a viral infection called shingles. Good, the spongy substance has dried to a scab. This "case by case" decision has been straightforward. I didn't have to think twice about authorizing the antiviral because shingles is awfully painful, I've been told.

"How are you feeling?" I ask my mother.

A dull film shades the half closed eyes. I shove my face closer. "Mami, look at me. Who am I?"

"Ah ah."

"Who *am* I?"

"Ah ah ah ah."

The ahs rise and fall in the four pitches of Mandarin. I hear tones that sound like "Stop asking me that." This is one advantage of a tonal language that I've never thought of.

"Okay, okay," I say. "You're tired today. I'll let you rest."

A nursing aide appears. It's Coco, a squat Hispanic with a bawdy sense of humor such as pretending to suckle her male stroke patients. She's also notorious for pouring supplements down people's throats.

"I check your mama's diaper," she says.

"Oh Coco, don't you know her by now?" I say. "She'd rather die than soil her diaper. Anyway, since you're here, you can help me take her to the bathroom."

"Your mama no good today. I check."

I step aside. The tear of Velcro scrapes the air.

"Oh Mama," Coco cries. "You did big boo boo!" Stubby arms akimbo, she adds, "Wait. I go get help. Don't go away." She shakes a finger at the patient.

By reflex I switch to oral breathing. My eyes travel up to Mami's face and see that she's looking at her mess. Her shock gives way to shame. Mami closes her eyes, her lips trembling. If her glands were functioning normally, tears would be streaming down her face. She's weeping.

"Baba, go to the lobby and get some tea. There are too

many people here. I'll stay, you go." I tug at his elbow and am pleasantly surprised by the lack of resistance.

Coco returns with reinforcement. I stand aside to let the pair of aides put their training to use. Their movements are as exquisite as a tai chi duet borrowing energy from one another. When one pushes the other pulls, one rocks the other rolls. Without forcing, jerking or lifting, they clean their patient, change her clothes and diaper, replace the pad under her, and wrap her like a newborn infant in fresh sheets.

From the foot of the bed I look down at my mother's entire length. There's something very unusual about Mami, something I can't quite put my finger on. Her silence is no cause for alarm. She's gone into hibernation several times before, curling up in her nest for days in a row, refusing to perform any activities of daily living except breathe. Once, when everyone was about to give up, she woke up one morning and said to me, "I haven't seen you in a while. Where have you been?"

No, it isn't her silence that's odd. Perhaps it's the way she moves, or doesn't move?

I reach under the sheet to perform a test I've seen the nurses do. Hooking a finger, I draw a straight line down the center of Mami's sole. No reaction. I pull off the pink nursing home sock and scrape hard on her flesh with my nails. Still nothing. Mami watches the proceeding as though the foot belongs to somebody else. I realize *that's* the very unusual thing about my mother today.

I sit down on the bed and caress the doughy face. This is my chance before Baba returns. I've been meaning to have this conversation for a long time.

"Mami, you've had a wonderful life. You've also been a wonderful mother. Karen, Xiao, and I love you very much."

Mami's eyes flicker like a candle flame.

"They've been here to see you recently. Remember your

ninetieth birthday? We had a nice banquet, didn't we?"

The flame shoots up, singing and dancing.

"Mami, I have something to say to you. You know the Chinese saying—there's no banquet that doesn't end. If you need to go, rest assured that we'll take good care of Baba. Karen, Xiao, and I are all doing well. Our children are all right too. You can go in peace."

The candle goes out. My mother's face plunges into darkness.

"I don't mean I want you to go," I rush to explain. "Only if *you* want to. If you feel living is too hard, you don't have to hang on for our sake."

Her reproachful eyes pierce my heart. Is Mami mad at me for saying it's okay to die? I'm merely following the advice of the hospice handbook. It says that sometimes a person can't move on until the family gives him permission.

"I hope you feel better soon." I squeeze the slack hand. "I have to go to my lesson now. The doctor will check on you, and Baba will be here all day. I'll see you tomorrow."

"Ah-ah ah," Mami says. The tones are the same as Mandarin for "Don't go."

I plant a kiss on each cheek and tear myself away.

Chapter 23

The day is Friday, the date July 29, the year 2011. Her name is Ming-Jen, she turned ninety a few weeks ago, and the president of the United States is Obama. If the doctor were to quiz her on where she is, she'd tell him she's standing on top of the highest mountain in the world, so high that she can reach up and pluck a star from the sky.

A panoramic view lies at her feet. Looking down one side of the mountain the landscape of her life rolls out as far as her eyes can see. There are the green pastures where her children played, the courtyard house she grew up in, and the moon-lit park where Tak declared his love. There are also the desert, the raging river, and the burning houses and streets. She gazes at them all with fondness, the beautiful and the ugly, that make her tapestry rich and remarkable. She is where she is because of the terrain she's traveled through, and there's no better spot than to be ninety and cherished.

Looking down the other side of the mountain, she sees the faces of people she loves and who have loved her: her father, mother, brothers and sisters. They're smiling and beckoning to her. She casts her eyes further. *Who else is over there? That French vixen who tried to steal my rooster? Well, so what if she is? The rooster is mine and always will be.*

She feels Tak's palm on her forehead, then her cheek. "I think she has a fever," he says. "Where's the doctor? Why isn't he here yet?"

"He was here earlier this morning," Cary says. "The nurse just checked Mami's temperature. She said it was normal."

"Why is she sleeping so much?"

"She's probably tired."

"You should find her a better doctor," he says, his voice shrill with anxiety. "There's got to be a medicine for her illness."

"Baba, I think we should be prepared. She may not get out of this. Look, she hasn't talked for five days. She's never done this before. And now, she…"

Shshsh, don't tell him too much. If he knows I have pneumonia he'll send me to the hospital. Please, no needles for me ever again.

"She should rest," Cary finishes her sentence.

"Wake up, it's almost noon," Tak shouts. Ming-Jen feels an angry shove against her shoulder.

"Leave her alone," Cary hisses.

Tak sits down by her side. He's quiet except for the old man noises he makes unconsciously—the belabored breathing, the profound sighs, and the "umph" that escapes from time to time.

A cheerful tune rings. Ming-Jen recognizes Cary's cell phone. "Hello…yeah, hi," Cary says while walking away from the bed. "She's gone into a coma," she murmurs.

What do you mean I'm in a coma? I can hear everything that's going on!

Actually Ming-Jen is quite amazed at the sharpness of her hearing, and she isn't even wearing hearing aids. She wants to tell her children there's no need to hide anything from her. The greatest secret of life is unfolding with sparkling clarity. Since she made up her mind, Ming-Jen's heart has become as clear as the water of a deep well. The layers of earth have filtered out all the impurities that cloud her life. At this point she wants only to laugh.

"She looks comfortable," Cary continues in a muffled voice. "The hospice doctor is giving her everything to make sure of that. They've also moved her to a vacant room, which is great, because Baba can sleep in the other bed. We spent the night here—Hey, Baba, what are you doing?"

Help, help! Get him out of my bed!

"Baba, please don't be like this. You're just making it harder for her. Come on, please, get off the bed....Or I'll have to call the nurse."

The sack of old heavy bones slides off Ming-Jen. She can breathe again.

"He climbed on Mami's bed and was about to lie on top of her," Cary says to her caller. "I better ask the doctor for some sedatives for him. Right, yeah…"

Ming-Jen's hearing is good, but not that good. She can't hear what the other party is saying, although she has a strong hunch who it is.

"Sure. You want to talk to her? You can try. They say the hearing is the last to go. Okay, I'm going to put the phone on her ear."

"Mami, it's me, Karen. Can you hear me?"

Please don't shout. You're making me deaf!

"I think she heard you," Cary says. "Her eyebrows twitched."

"Mami, I'm sorry I can't be there with you, but I'm with you in spirit," Karen says. "You've led a fantastic life. It's all right to let go. Your children and grandchildren are all doing well and we'll take care of Baba. Just think of yourself as a ship and your life on earth is a stop in your voyage. You've anchored at this port many years and seen all the wonders of this place. It's now time to set sail again. As your boat goes over the horizon, the people on shore will lose sight of you. But soon you will enter another harbor. There will be other people on the other shore, waving to you, welcoming you."

Karen, you're my eldest and favorite child. You've always been wise beyond your years. How did you know I was going on a trip? You're wrong on one point. I'm not sailing—it's too slow. I'm going to fly!

"You've been a wonderful mother. You gave us everything

we have today. I love you, and I—" the voice cracks—"wish you smooth sail."

Don't cry, my dearest. We will meet up again. When your plane appears on the horizon, I'll be waiting for you on the tarmac and shouting "Here she comes!"

Hardly has the phone been taken off her ear than the cheerful tune rings again. Ah, it's going to be a busy day.

"Mami—" he's choking already—"I've been a terrible son. Can you forgive me?"

Xiao, you're my only son and favorite child. You've done your best for me. How can I ask for more? I don't want you to go through life begging for my forgiveness. A mother only wants happiness for her child. All you have to do is look into your heart as a parent and you'll know what I mean. Confucius says, Serve your father as you would require your son to serve you. And no more."

"Oh Mami, please don't leave us. Hoo hoo hoo…"

Stop crying. I've always told people, my girls never cry when they get their vaccinations. But my son bawls just at the sight of the needle. All right, all right, I'll come visit you as soon as I can get away.

Xiao is too choked up to go on. Cary takes the phone back.

"I'm going to the bathroom now," Cary says to Tak. "You promise not to bother her?"

A sullen silence is the reply. As soon as the bathroom door clicks shut, Ming-Jen feels a poke on her arm.

"Open your eyes," Tak says.

You can't tell me what to do anymore. I'm going on a trip and there's nothing you can do to stop me. Ha ha. My tickets and passport are ready. First I'm going to fly to Beijing to see my parents, with a stopover in California to make sure Xiao is okay. Then I'm traveling on to Paris to visit the sights you promised to show me and never did.

Something tickles her palm. "Squeeze my finger," he says.

Stop ordering me around.

"You're useless! You can't do anything!"

Forget it, Tak. I'm not going to fight with you anymore. My eyes may be closed but I can see right through your thick bones into your heart. You get nasty when you're afraid. And you've never been so afraid before in your life.

The bathroom door creaks on its hinges. Cary's sneakers patter softly to the foot of the bed. Next comes the scrape of a chair and the flipping of pages. Cary's face must be buried in her book. Ming-Jen feels another jab.

All right, Tak, let's have it out. I have a confession to make. From the first day of our marriage, I've wanted you to be somebody else—a high-level civil servant, a literature professor, or an engineer designing the tallest building in the world. Let's face the truth. You don't have the brains, the diligence, or perseverance. You're not and will never be one of them.

And I'm glad, because otherwise you won't be Tak, and nobody can love me as much as Tak does. Even in my wasted state, you want to climb into bed with me. Only you, Tak, can look at me with desire now.

All my life, I've pined for things I don't have instead of appreciating what I do have. Right now, my possessions are reduced to one, and it's blooming like a red red rose in my heart. This is my family's love for me and mine for them. The filial piety I've been nagging my children about is just that. Filial piety is appreciation for what your parents have done for you and doing what you can for them. Of all the people in the world, I should be the first to understand that every person has his constraints. My children have to balance their obligations to me with those to others. That's what Confucius calls Doctrine of the Mean. *I don't know how I could have been so blind before. The treasure I've been searching for has been right under my nose.*

*

Kung pao chicken. That has to be it. Ming-Jen sniffs out the earthy smell of peanuts, the musty scent of sesame oil, and the nose-tickling spice of stir-fried chilies.

"I brought lunch," Steve says. "How's she doing?"

"The hospice nurse said she might not last the day," Cary whispers.

Ming-Jen senses the warmth of the bamboo pole body at her bedside. *Steve, thank you for everything you've done for me. Now you know what it means to marry into a Chinese family. It's a lot of trouble, but it has its blessings as well. You can be sure you'll be taken care of in your old age.*

"Why is her mouth open?" Maggie says.

Ah, my beautiful granddaughter, you're home on vacation.

"She's very relaxed, I guess," Cary says. "We're supposed to swab her lips with water every now and then. Here, you want to do it?"

The cool water soothes Ming-Jen's parched lips. *Thank you, Maggie. You're my favorite grandchild. In spite of your mother, you love beautiful things as much as I do. I wish I could have done more with my talent, but it's all right. A person can't do everything in one lifetime. You'll carry on my love for art and enjoy it more than I have.*

All afternoon, people come and go. Every so often, the nurse drips the bittersweet morphine under her tongue, and the aides wipe her down and change her diaper although it needs no changing. There are other visitors too—her friends at the senior center, Cary's friends, and the nursing home residents and workers who have become as close as family. She recognizes every voice and silently acknowledges each by name. Her memory is as sharp as when she was twelve, when she could recite a whole book of Tang poems.

Maggie strums her guitar and sings the English songs that Tak crooned to her in the early years of their marriage. Her favorite is *One Day When We Were Young* from the movie *The Great Waltz*. The scene moved her to tears when the beautiful actress stands on the deck of the boat, waving to her lover on shore. As the boat pulls away slowly, she sings the song while her lover strains to catch one last glimpse of her. Ming-Jen has taught this song to her children, and they've passed it on to their children. Maggie sings with a strong voice. She'll live a long happy life.

Dinner is pizza, and the delivery boy is Steve again. He also does something naughty—sneaking in a bottle of wine. Ming-Jen hears the cork pop and whiffs the fermented fumes. She drinks only on special days, such as the Lunar New Year or the Moon Festival. Today counts as one of those special days.

After dinner, the music resumes. Cary even digs up the Chinese lullabies that Ming-Jen sang to her once upon a time. Ming-Jen hums along, reliving the joys of motherhood. Her favorite part is sniffing the baby's head. The smell of sour milk is an addiction that she can never get enough of.

By and by, the voices begin to wane. The air in the room has grown stale. Ming-Jen senses the fatigue. Too much partying can make a person sick, and Ming-Jen doesn't want anyone to get sick on her account. She hears Maggie pack up her guitar and talk about her flight back to Seattle the next morning. Somebody is going around the room putting things into a trash bag. It must be Steve, the one who takes the garbage can to the curb every week.

Tak is still holding her hand. She wishes he would go to bed. *Say something, Cary. He'll listen to you.*

"Baba, it's time for bed. Come on, she'll be fine. The nurse will check on her every two hours."

Ming-Jen feels his stubbles on her cheek, then a long silence. She imagines him looking at her with his soft brown eyes. They can be hard as rock too, but when they're soft, they're like lambskin.

All right, that's enough now. Go to bed. She doesn't want him to see her leave. Tak is capable of creating the most embarrassing ruckus. At his mother's funeral, he banged his head against the coffin until he knocked himself senseless.

Finally he lets go of her hand. Ming-Jen listens to his every move: the shuffle into the bathroom, followed by the *chig chug chig chug* of his toothbrush, the *ting-a-ling* in the toilet bowl, then more shuffling, and the bed going *eeek aaak* several times. Then all is still.

Cary, my baby and favorite child, you know much more about filial piety than I do. Thank you for the extra years on earth. Without your care, I would have gone much earlier. From now on, live your life in peace and joy, for my blessings will always be with you.

All her channels are fully dilated. Her soul is struggling to be born. Ming-Jen feels the urge to push, coming in waves as irresistible as late-stage labor contractions. Nothing can hold her back now. *Cary, I'm going.* She pushes once, twice, thrice, and with a gentle sigh of astonishment and ecstasy, her soul bursts out of the confines of skin and bone. She lingers at the ceiling, watching Cary and Maggie huddled around her bed and singing *One Day When We Were Young*. On the other bed, Tak lies with eyes closed, too deaf to hear her departing footsteps. She'd better be on her way. If he wakes up, he'll demand to go with her.

She flies out the window. The night explodes with light. As she spreads her arms, she notices with amazement her new clothes, resplendent as a rainbow. She flaps her wings and is surprised by the lack of pain. She does it a few more times and still feels no pain. Her arthritis is gone! The stars beckon to her. Father and Mother—they've been patiently waiting.

Chapter 24

Tak cradles his wife on his lap. Dust has gathered overnight on Ming-Jen's urn, at least a dozen specks. He pulls out his handkerchief and rubs circles on the mahogany surface. A *klonk* sounds as he flips over the box to scour the bottom. It's her wedding band inside the urn, the band that binds them forever. He's promised to protect his wife as long as his heart is beating. Last time he checked his pulse, it was.

After blowing at the urn to get rid of the last mote, he gets up from his lazy boy and lovingly places Ming-Jen in her chair. Two cups of tea sit on the table between them, as well as a plate of cookies, same as any other morning in their Spring Meadows suite.

The first time he saw her reduced to the size of a jewelry box, he cried until every drop was drained. Even his bladder dried up so he was cured of incontinence for the day. He would have liked to swallow the whole bottle of Valium, but Cary handed him only two pills and stuffed the rest into her purse.

When death isn't an option, a person has to find a way to exist from one minute to the next, preferably with the least pain possible. After three months of grieving, Tak has found a new philosophy of life and death. The everlasting soul thing hasn't worked for him. The thought of Ming-Jen's spirit floating around the room gives him goose bumps. To him, souls and ghosts are the same species, and they come back only because of unfinished business, such as to revenge a wrong, collect a debt, or fulfill a threat. He doesn't want Ming-Jen to haunt him for the injuries he's done her, especially those she didn't know about while alive.

He'd rather think of Ming-Jen as real, just slightly

transformed. She's shrunk to the size of a Barbie doll, beautiful, ageless, and full of curvatures. Inside the box, this mini-Jen lies curled up, resting, and as safe as can be. Only one harm can befall her. Given her compact size, anyone can stuff her in a bag or under a coat and walk off with her. He has to talk to Cary urgently about this.

"Let me get you some fresh tea," he says. He goes to the kitchenette and turns on the kettle. Three knocks on the door interrupt him. What do they want now? Medicine time is over and it's not lunch yet. Besides, they should know by now he's on a boycott. Since they gave Ming-Jen's place to a new resident, he's refused to eat in the dining room. A bowl of instant noodles with Ming-Jen is better than a three-course meal without her.

He opens the door just enough to peek out with one eye. Seeing it's his neighbor and not an aide, he widens the crack. The woman is neatly dressed in slacks and blouse, a chiffon scarf twirled loosely around her neck. She's one of three able-bodied residents, including himself, who can walk without the support of a cane or walker. She's also quite pretty, her fine features still standing straight in spite of the collapsing ground beneath them. If Tak had met her fifty years ago, he might have flirted with her. She's too old now.

"I was just passing by and thought you may want to go to the sing along," she says.

Tak bows gallantly. "I sing like a frog. You don't want to listen to me."

The woman says something about a prince. Her pert lips appear to be savoring a joke. Is she laughing at him? Uncertain what to do, he turns around to check with Ming-Jen. A halo of light radiates from the polished urn.

"My wife loves to sing," he says. "Can she come too?"

The woman looks bewildered.

"You remember my wife Ming-Jen? She had to go to the hospital for a while, and now she's back."

The woman still looks bewildered. "She's right there," he says, throwing open the door so his neighbor can see the wooden box on the chair.

"I'll see you in the activities room," the woman says, hurrying away.

Tak lines his gym bag with a thick towel and carefully places the wooden box in it. Since Ming-Jen travels everywhere with him in this bag, she should be as comfortable as possible. He doesn't really enjoy watching old women croak and clap their hands like little girls, but he knows Ming-Jen likes that sort of thing. Clutching the precious bag, he shuffles out of the room.

*

I give my three signature taps—one long and two short. This is my morse code to Baba to open up, it's me. I wait, press my ear against the door, and wait some more.

"I heard you went to the sing along," I say the moment Baba appears.

"Who told you?"

"Everyone. Mercy, Jennifer, Heera, Gabriela." I name the social worker, the receptionist, the activities director, the cook.

Baba lowers himself into his lazy boy. I lift my mother from her chair, set her down on the coffee table, and take her seat.

"Why is everyone talking about me?"

"Because they *like* you." Because you're one of two widowers to fifty-eight widows, if truth be told.

"I have something very important to talk to you about," Baba says.

Uh-oh, here it comes.

"You have to move us back to your home."

I take a deep breath. I'll be patient and compassionate toward this old man who recently lost his mate of sixty some years. I won't explode; no, I won't. "Why do you want to do that? You're getting much better care here. Medicines given to you, three good meals a day, a nurse down the hallway. You know I can't give you these services."

"I don't need their *services*. They're all thieves. I can't trust any of them."

"You keep your valuables at my home. You have nothing here that anyone wants to steal."

His eyes point to the urn.

"Nobody is going to steal a box of—" I bite back my tongue. This is my mother we're talking about.

"The wedding ring inside the box is worth a lot," Baba says.

"If you're really worried, I can take her to my home." Actually I'd rather not if I can help it. It will be spooky to have Mami's watchful eyes following me around the house.

"I want her with me!" Baba snaps.

"Fine. Nobody has the chance to steal her anyway. You take her everywhere with you." I think of the evening at the restaurant, where I had to ask the waiter for an extra chair for my mother.

"Give me one good reason I can't move back with you."

"You need a nurse, nursing aide, med tech, cook, and cleaner. I can't do the work of all of them."

"Hire a maid for me then."

"You know how expensive that is? Medicare doesn't cover it, and you don't have long-term care insurance."

"You mean the three of you can't pay for it? What did I raise three children for?"

"We have to think of our retirement too. We don't want to

be a burden to our children like..." The missing YOU streams across the room.

"I'm your father. I demand you move me back!"

"My husband won't allow it!" Regret hits me the moment the words fly out. A modern independent woman should never hide behind her husband. Yet here I am, pushing Steve out to take the blows for me.

"I'm your father. You have to do whatever I say!"

"No, I don't. There's a Chinese saying, when a woman is at home, she obeys her father. When she's married, she obeys her husband." To hell with principles. I'm going to meet my opponent at his level.

Baba is speechless, though not for long. "You lived eighteen years under my roof. I lived only eight years in your home. You owe me ten years."

Aha! I feel elated like a student who's studied for the right exam questions. I was stumped last time Baba wielded this argument. I scoffed and walked away, pretending I had no time for his absurd logic. But the imbalance did bother me. After all, my name is *Yi* for righteousness. I want to do what's just and fair.

One night I sat at my computer and created a two column spreadsheet, one credit and the other debit. The first entries into Baba's credit column (what I owe him) are the obvious big ticket items: room and board, education, and health care. The debit numbers (what Baba owes me) are more recent, so their value is higher due to inflation. To be fair, Baba's credit column should have collected interest during all the years it was outstanding. But what rate should I use? And also what exchange rate, since the first ten years of my expenses were incurred in Hong Kong?

For days I pondered these issues. I finally gave up. There are too many unquantifiable factors. More important than the financial expenses are the emotional credits and debits, the joys and heartaches of each type of caregiving. For example, when a two-year-old throws a tantrum, he's cute. When a ninety-two-year-old does the same, he's *not* cute. So how much should the cuteness factor weigh in the equation? Someday, someone will come up with a Ph.D. dissertation on the subject. Maybe then we'll have an objective method to decide when enough is enough. Meanwhile, a rough estimate will have to do.

"You want to do accounting?" I take up Baba's gauntlet. "Okay, I'll do accounting with you. Your children have been supporting you since you were sixty." (After you got laid off.) "How many years has it been? You're now ninety-two. That makes it thirty-two years."

"What!" Baba slaps the arms of his chair.

"You footed my bills for only eighteen years. I was pretty much on my own in college. Which means you owe me—what's thirty-two minus eighteen? Fourteen years. That makes up for the ten years of living in my home that I owe you. We're even!"

I wait for the next attack. Baba's agitation vanishes, replaced by the cold, purposeful look of a killer on a massacre. His pistol may have run out of ammunition, but there's still the shotgun. His eyes narrow with the meanness of someone about to pull the trigger. "I gave you *life*," he snarls. "How are you going to repay me for that?"

Another easy one! Years ago, my then teenage son taught me the counter strike to this offensive. Although I was the loser in that skirmish, the beauty of my enemy's weapon wasn't lost on me. Good thing I've stored it in my armory for later use.

"I never asked to be born," I say, trying not to look too cute.

Baba slaps the chair some more. "Haiya! You're an ungrateful daughter. How can you say a thing like that?"

"You had children because *you* wanted to. It gave *you* pleasure. You and Mami had fun creating us."

"Haiya, haiya. I don't care what you say. You have to move me back."

"No, I don't."

"Yes, you do."

The decibels escalate with every round. Our conversation has sunk below kindergarten level. Before long we'll be wrestling each other to the ground. One of us has to be the adult.

"Listen to me," I say, placing a hand on Baba's hand to stop it from slapping itself purple. "We want to take care of you, but that doesn't mean you have to live with one of us. That's not what filial piety is about." Mami would be proud of me if she were here. (Maybe she is.) I've downloaded the syllabus of Confucianism 101 and browsed through the books on the reading list.

"Filial piety has to be practiced in context," I explain. "In Confucius' days, China was an agricultural society. People worked the land and never moved away. If you were born in a place, you lived your whole life in that place. Your family kept on growing and growing until it became a village and then a state. That's why historians call ancient China a *family* state. The family was everything to a person. It provided education, employment, protection, insurance—everything a person needed in his lifetime.

"Modern society is very different," I lecture on. "We live in an industrial society—in America we're really post-industrial." Seeing the bewilderment on Baba's face, I decide to keep it simple. "Families are scattered, like ours, because we go where the jobs are. The family has become too small to take care of a person's needs, so other groups have stepped in to fulfill those functions. We have schools for the young and retirement homes for the elderly. I heard even China has nursing homes."

"I don't care! I'm not staying here! I'm your father, you have to obey me!"

I'm delighted for this opportunity. "Confucius says that if a father is wrong, the child should point out his mistake. It's for the father's own good. *Xiao* doesn't mean obeying your father blindly."

"I don't care what Confucius says!"

"It's true. I read it in that book Mami kept at her bedside. As a matter of fact, I brought it with me. You want to read it together?" With both hands I reach into my tote bag for the Chinese bible.

"It's time for dinner. We should go."

"Oh, you go to the dining room now? I brought you beef *chow fun*, but you can have it tomorrow. Let me put it in the fridge."

Baba rocks himself to the edge of the chair.

"You don't have to go yet," I say. "We still have fifteen minutes to read some Confucius."

"I have to go to the bathroom." One, two, three, Baba pushes himself up and makes a "run" for it.

Chapter 25

Tak wakes up with a start. What time is it? He looks out the window and sees a red brow of sun drooping over distant treetops. Oh no, it's getting late. He'd better get going if he's going to catch that plane. As he scoots out of bed, something tugs at his arm. A Band-Aid is stuck to the inside of his elbow with a tube attached to it. How did that get there? He peels off the Band-Aid and yanks the tube. A drop of blood oozes out. He wipes it off with his finger.

He dresses quickly, slips into his shoes, and hurries out of the room. At the doorway he hesitates, not knowing which way to turn. The corridor ends in a wall in one direction and opens into a flood of light in the other. He follows the light, planting one foot in front of the other. The trek seems to go on for miles. He soldiers on, pausing several times to catch his breath. The path finally opens into a bright space where numbers flash from 1 to 2 to 3. His heart elevates. This is a...a...whatchamacallit?

He pushes both buttons, one with a down arrow and the other up. *Ding,* the door opens.

"Sir, where are you going?"

He turns around and sees a giantess looming behind the counter. Her fangs are smeared with blood and she's leaning forward, threatening to smother him with her tremendous bosom.

"Sorry to disturb you," he says with apology. It's best not to offend her. "I'm going to the airport."

The woman steps out from behind the desk, her monstrous body casting a shadow over him. Tak backs away. One swipe from those truncheon arms will finish him. He wants to run, but his legs have frozen into blocks of ice. Her iron claws grip his arm.

She peers at his wrist and says, "Mr. Chan, let me take you back to your bed."

The sight of the bracelet astonishes Tak. How did it get there?

"Sir, please come with me."

Tak wriggles to free his arm. "I have to go to the airport. It's very late. My wife is waiting for me."

"No, it's not late at all. It's actually very early. See that clock?" She points to the huge round face on the wall. "It says 5:20…in the morning. Your wife is probably still in bed."

She starts to drag him back toward where he came from. Tak succumbs—for now. There are other flights to Hong Kong. Cary will find out the schedule.

*

I've been studying Baba's knuckles for an hour (especially the large one that's as smooth and round as a marble), and debating whether to wake him. He should sleep, given the busy night he had busting out of the hospital. At the same time, I have to leave soon for my chamber rehearsal.

"Baba, I've come to see you," I put my hand on his and whisper.

His eyelids flutter open. "Mami, you're here," he says groggily.

I stay still so he can have a better look at me. Caring for the elderly has taught me to ignore whatever the person says during the first waking moments. At that age, sleep and death merge into the same space. Mami often woke up calling me by her dead sister's name. Baba must be just returning from Mami's world. He can use a few more seconds.

After what I judge to be a long enough pause, I say, "Baba, look at me. What's my name?"

"Your name is," he hits his head with his palm like

somebody trying to get ketchup out of a bottle. "Ming-Jen-Chan," he announces.

"Noooo. I'm Cary."

Baba grunts like an irritated walrus. "Stop joking around. We don't have time. There's still a lot of packing to do."

"I'm your daughter *Careeee*," I repeat. "Look around you. What is this place?"

"No ifs, ands, or…" He tries again, "No ands or buts…"

"Don't worry about that, Baba. Do you remember falling, hitting your head, and getting stitches? Here, feel this." I bring his hand to his forehead just above his eyebrow. He runs his fingers over the ugly purple welt.

"Oooh," I cringe. "That must hurt."

"I don't feel anything," he says with a macho shrug.

"You suffered a mild concussion. That's why the doctor wants to keep you here for observation. You're not going anywhere today."

"I can't stay here. We have to go to the airport." He throws off his cover.

I pull it back to cover the diaper peeking out of his gown. "Airport? What are you going to do there?"

"Fly to Hong Kong to meet up with you. What are you doing here?" He looks me up and down as if I were a puzzle to be solved. Then he relaxes, and a bulb lights up in his eyes. "We can take the same flight then. When is Cary coming? She has to drive us to the airport. I hope you have your passport with you."

My skin crawls. This is creepy—my father really believes I'm his wife. This mix-up is much more than his usual wake-up confusion. On the other hand, he hasn't looked as alive since Mami died. His face is flush with excitement, and his up-to-no-good smirk has a hard time keeping away.

"Haiya, have you forgotten where you put your passport?"

Baba scolds.

"It's right here in my purse," I humor him. The doctor has warned me that the anti-seizure medication may cause hallucinations. But if the hallucinations are so pleasant, I wouldn't mind if he had more. His wife is alive and they're going to fly around the world together. I should remember to ask the doctor for a refill.

"Good," Baba says. "I should get dressed now. We better get out of here before the teacher comes back." He grimaces like a schoolboy about to sneak out of class.

I lay my hand on his chest, pushing him back on the bed. "The flight has been postponed till tomorrow. We'll go to the airport tomorrow, okay?"

Baba grabs my hand and pulls me to him. His strength takes me aback. "Now that you're with me, time will pass quickly," he says, puckering his lips.

I leap away as if I've touched a live wire.

"After all these years, you're shy now?" he grins rakishly at me.

"Look at you," I shout, pointing to the black and blue patches on his arm. "The nurses had a hard enough time getting a needle into your vein, and then you had to pull it out. I don't know how many times they had to poke you again."

"All right, all right, you're not in the mood," Baba surrenders. "Let's do something else then. How about visiting Cary?"

"Why do you want to go to Cary's?" An idea buds in my head.

"Have lunch with her."

"Is she a good cook?" I lead him on.

Baba chuckles, "You should know. She learned from you. If you're a good cook, she is too."

What I'm about to do is despicable, but since I can't have this conversation with him in his right mind (which is always as foul as a pig pen), this is my only chance. The sweetest part is he doesn't know he's talking to me about me and thus has no reason to mince words.

"Is Cary a good daughter?" I ask.

He squints at me/Mami as if I were the one out of his mind. "What kind of question is that? Of course, she's a good daughter."

"Do you love her?"

"Why are you asking me so many questions?"

"This is the last one. Just answer me. Do you love her?"

"Of course I love her. Haiiii...Problem is she doesn't love me."

"Why do you say that?" I ask with surprise.

"She doesn't like to spend time with me."

I feel a catch in my throat. Muttering about the darkness in the room, I get up to draw back the curtain. When I return to his side, my voice is steady and my heart sincere.

"I know, Cary is always rushing in and out. But it's not because she doesn't love you. It's because she has her own life to live. Remember how we always taught our children to work hard and do their best? That's what Cary tries to do. You don't want Cary to sit by your side all the time and neglect her work, do you?"

Baba replies with a mischievous grin, "You always say I spoil the children rotten."

"Just the other day, Cary told me what a good father you were," I go on. "Remember those days when Karen and Xiao had gone to college, and I was away taking care of the doctor's brats?" (Oops, shouldn't have used that word since Mami thought they were so precious. Fortunately Baba doesn't notice.) "You always had cookies ready for Cary when she came home from school. You were everything to her—father, mother, brother, sister. She loves you very much. She *told* me so."

Tak cracks a knowing smile. "She looks just like me."

"You two are like twins."

A yawn swallows his face. I glance quickly at my watch, hoping he doesn't see it and interpret it as wanting to get away from him. I can't blame him though, the way I whirl around like a competitor in *Amazing Race*, panting from one stop to another and talking fast and furious as if losing a second could disqualify me for the next episode. Tomorrow there's only one item on my to-do must-do list: You, Baba, I promise.

"You better rest now," I say. "I'll be back tomorrow to spend the whole day with you. And if the doctors think you can go home, we can drop by *Fook Kee* for some salted fish and chicken rice. You like that, don't you?"

He puckers up for a kiss. Stepping beyond his reach, I throw him one.

*

"There you are. You were here and then you disappeared," Tak says. "Where have you been?"

"Everywhere—Beijing, Hong Kong, Paris—"

"Paris! You were in Paris?"

"It was a whirlwind tour, but I saw all the sights you told me about. The Eiffel tower, the palaces and museums, and the Louvre! I was tempted to take one of those paintings home. One thing I don't understand, though, is what's the big deal about Mona Lisa."

"Compared to your beauty, she's far far behind," Tak says, delivering the compliment Ming-Jen is fishing for.

"You know how to talk," she giggles, a hand over her teeth like a well-bred woman.

"Did you go to the underground mall at the Louvre? That was where I saw the fashion shows. They call it *haute couture*," Tak says, showing off his French.

"Oh yes, I went everywhere you've been to, including the night clubs."

Tak looks away. How did she know? He's always told her he was in bed (alone, it goes without saying) every night by nine. After a day of researching the fashion scene and negotiating with customers, he was too exhausted to be out on the town.

"How was Hong Kong? Did you see any of our friends and relatives?" he says to divert the subject.

"I saw everyone we used to know. They all send their regards. Your old friend Mushroom says he's dying to see you again."

Tak feels a tingle at the back of his neck. "How is he? How is...his head?"

"His head is fine and he looks as young as ever."

"Is he still mad at me?"

"Why should he be mad at you?"

"I left him...You know what happened to him?"

"He told me. He said it wasn't your fault. If you didn't run away, the Japanese would have beheaded you too. Two mothers would have been in mourning instead of one."

"Haiii," Tak sighs. "It's better to be dead than to live in shame."

"Believe me, dying is easy. It's living that's the hard part."

"Are you sure Mushroom isn't mad at me?"

"That's what he says."

"You mean Mushroom hasn't been playing tricks on me and ruining my life?"

"You can't blame it on Mushroom. You did it all yourself."

Tak ponders this for a while. "That's not fair. All my life I've been blaming Mushroom for my failures. I never bothered to get back up because I thought he would trip me again. You're telling me now he holds no grudge against me?"

"It was all in your head."

The statement infuriates him. "I want my life back!"

"If you start over again, everything will be different. You wouldn't be moping in your father's store, and I wouldn't meet you there."

"The better for you. You'd marry somebody like your father, a bookworm, a person who loves to study. I *hate* to study. The sight of books gives me a headache."

"You have a point there. I have to admit though, after we got married I found out you have a few good qualities too."

"Me? Good qualities? Like what?"

"You make me believe I'm the most beautiful woman in the world."

Tak gazes at his wife, his heart throbbing irregularly with love. "A movie actress is beautiful because of all the makeup she puts on. *You* are beautiful when you open your eyes in the morning, eyes puffy, hair tousled, and drool caked around the corners of your lips. That's the truth. You can't be *not* beautiful even if you try."

"See what I mean? You just proved what I said." Her eyes flick at him the same way they do every time she wins an argument.

Tak has to think about this for a while. Is she complimenting him, or not? Adoring her is the one "good quality" of his that she mentioned. Doesn't he have other good qualities? He can think of at least one, the most important asset that makes a man a man.

"Can't you think of other ways I make you happy?" Grinning widely, he reaches out.

"Stop, you're messing up my hair." She ducks away. A few strands fly out from her neatly packaged bun, giving her a wild, seductive look. She tucks them in while reproaching him with her eyes. The yellow chrysanthemum on her cheongsam crests like a wave across her chest. Tak's heart aches; this is his wife before she came to the U.S., cut her hair, and started wearing pant suits from K mart.

Ming-Jen slaps his probing hands. "Let me see, how did you make me happy? Well..." She pauses like a politician trying to buy time. "You helped to cultivate my goodness," she finally says.

"Me, cultivate your goodness?! You already have plenty of it. Why would you need my help? I'm the one who's low on goodness. Whatever there is, you squeezed it out of me. That's the truth."

"Your weakness brought out my strength."

Hmm, is that a compliment or not? This discussion is getting too complicated for him.

"Let's go to the airport. The plane must be departing soon," Tak says.

"We don't have to go to the airport. We can fly out from here."

"From here?" Tak looks outside, searching for a plane. Black asphalt stretches below. But it's square like a parking lot and not long like a runway. A lone car drives down the street and stops at the red light. Then all the lights start to dim in unison as if they were connected to the same switch. The traffic light, the red tail lights of the car, the street lamps. Tak rubs his eyes and blinks several times. With every blink, the illumination dies a little more. Before long the asphalt blends into the night and the world turns into a sea of tar.

"Why ...?" Before he finishes the sentence, the glow in the hallway gives a last shudder and expires. In the infinite blackness, Ming-Jen's figure stands out bright and clear, a being from a different time zone. It's daylight where she came from.

"Let's not talk anymore," Ming-Jen says. "It's departure time. Take my hand when you're ready."

"Wait a minute. What about the children? Aren't they coming too?"

"Not now. They'll join us later."

"I can't go without saying goodbye to them. They may think I'm mad at them."

"All right. You can stop by their homes on your way out."

"Do you have their addresses? I want to visit each one of them—Karen, Xiao, and Cary."

"We've been to their homes so many times. We'll find them even with our eyes closed."

"Don't I need to pack my toothbrush and things?"

"You won't need them. We've got everything we need at our new home."

"But I have to get dressed. I can't go out in this." He pinches close the backside of his gown.

"Why are you dilly-dallying? Are you afraid?"

"Of course not. I'm not afraid of anything, not even dying."

He's miffed that she should imply he's a coward. Then again it's hard to stay mad at his wife for long. He gazes longingly at her radiant face. Her skin is fair and unblemished, a splendid contrast to the black shiny braid flung over her shoulder. This is the Ming-Jen he'd laid eyes on the first time. Love pours into his heart, filling his chest into a helium balloon. He takes her hand and together they float above the bed. Oof, he hits a snag. A little string jerks him back.

"Let go of your attachments," Ming-Jen says. "Don't be afraid."

"I *told* you I'm not afraid."

Yet he can't help closing his eyes when Ming-Jen yanks him through the window. He braces himself for the shattering of glass. A drop in temperature tells him he's outside. He touches the crown of his head to see if anything is broken. His scalp is smooth, even the stitches are gone.

A flash reveals a field below. Three children are running around, chasing each other, their childish laughter as sweet as wind chimes. He looks closer and recognizes them, each a virtue, *Ren, Yi,* and *Xiao.* He loves them all the same.

Standing close by is a man, watching the children with a pleasure that only a father can have. His thick jet-black hair is slicked back, his full-moon eyes brim with love, his lips wear a playful smile, and his muscular shoulders roll as he walks toward the children. What a handsome dude, Tak thinks.

No, he won't change anything. Not a single thing.

Chapter 26

Voices wake me. I lie still, listening carefully: one male, the other female, and some weird animal sounds, like a pig snorting and a goose honking. The noise comes through the wall from Baba's old study now converted into Steve's entertainment center. I look to my right. Steve faces me, his cheeks and jowls sagging to one side on the pillow. I want to nudge him and say, "You forgot to turn off the TV *again*." But my heart softens at seeing him in his most vulnerable state. My old man is getting forgetful, and I better be extra nice to him. In the not too distant future we'll both be deaf and arthritic. We'll be shuffling around the house, yelling at each other and pining for our children to visit. The picture brings a crooked smile to my lips.

I get out of bed and stumble toward the door, my limbs heavy with sleep. So this is how people fall in the middle of the night. Light flickers from the room next door. Just as I suspected, Steve has done it again. This is becoming a new habit of his, dozing off during the late-night news and staggering to bed without turning off the TV. I pick up the remote and point it at the box, a finger poised to press the off button. The clock on the DVD player reads 2:46 am.

My drowsy eyes pop open. Two people are wrestling on the screen, a man and a woman. And they're buck naked! I quickly turn it off. This is no late-night news. This is Baba's Playboy channel! Was Steve watching it, or can it be…?

I picture Baba clad in a trench coat, collar turned up, slipping out the back door of the hospital and hopping into a taxi. He has my house keys too. Wide awake now, I hurry down to the basement. It's dark there, but Baba could have gone to bed in my former bedroom and present guest room. I turn on the light. The bed is empty.

I move on to my study. Laozi raises his head slowly and blinks at the light. His eyes are milky with cataracts. I'm sure he can't see me since he's always bumping into furniture and walls. Poor Laozi has gone blind and deaf. A gang of robbers can strip the house bare and he won't notice. I crouch down to pet the loose skin, which has grown looser because there's nothing but bones under it. "Everything's all right, sweetie. You go back to sleep."

I try to heed my own advice, but as I lie in bed, my mind can't stop spinning around the unsolved mystery. I'm tempted to wake Steve up and ask if he was watching Playboy. Not that I mind. I'm not a prude or a hypocrite who condones my father's vice but not when it's practiced by my husband. I just want to know. That's not unreasonable, is it?

The phone rings. My heart jumps into my throat. A call at this hour is like a death knell.

*

Across the country, another clock flashes: 11:46 pm. George glances anxiously at the time. He's been lying in bed for more than an hour, trying not to disturb his sleeping wife while he tosses and turns inside his prickly conscience. Baba is in the hospital. If anything happens to him before they reconcile, George fears he'll never sleep a wink in his life again. The last time they talked on the phone was three months ago, when the conversation ended with Baba spitting insults and him slamming down the phone. Since then he's instructed his secretary to say he's at a meeting whenever Baba calls. On his home phone, caller ID screens the unwanted calls.

He must see Baba soon. After the board meeting next week, he can fly out to the East Coast for a long weekend, which may well turn into a very very long weekend if they have a row. Without Mami's civilizing influence, Baba is a cave man. His father knows where to club him too. Calling him a good for nothing son, un-*Xiao*, and disobedient, is brutal enough. Yet nothing can be more savage than branding him a "coward." It's an affront to his manhood to say he can't perform his filial duties because he's afraid of his wife.

Of course, he's afraid of his wife. Any man who claims he's above such fear is either a liar or one who has a mistress waiting in the wings. As he's neither, he has to watch his step. His wife almost left him once over his parents. He can't let it happen again.

If only they hadn't called her the Red Guard—Mami behind her back and Baba to her face. For their information, his Red Guard wife is actually a devout practitioner of filial piety. She sends her parents in China enough spare change to pay their rent and a full-time maid, plus calling them every other day and visiting twice a year. No cultural revolution can take the *Xiao* out of a Chinese.

Karen once emailed him an article about a study comparing eastern and western cultures. When a westerner talks about himself, one part of his brain lights up. When he talks about his mother, another part turns on. For a Chinese, the same spot lights up whether he's talking about himself or his mother. *Thanks a lot, Karen, for telling me I can't escape from my parents short of a brain transplant.*

A chill sweeps over his chest. He gropes for the blanket. Where is it? He tries to open his eyes but can't; his eyelids are glued together like sealed envelopes. Suddenly something wooly and warm unfurls, up past his thighs and continues over his chest and shoulders. A presence hovers over him, breathing warm air on his brows. "Don't move him," Baba whispers. "Let him sleep with us tonight." George had loved dozing off in his parents' bed, where a little boy could enjoy undivided parental love, free from annoying sisters.

Once again nestled between his parents, George falls asleep with a child's abandon.

*

Karen steps on the gas to climb the steep hill. Her station wagon chugs on, as tired and ready to retire as the driver. It's been a long day stretching into the night. Aside from the usual hallway fights and classroom disruptions, she's also had to deal with unruly parents. The PTA meeting to discuss budget cuts turned into a witch hunt. As the highest school administrator present, she became the scapegoat for everything wrong, from the dropout rate to the unemployment rate and crime rate. Smeared and battered, she'd escaped into her office to regroup before heading home. The unfinished needlepoint tucked in her bottom drawer is her savior on days like today, so she took it out and stitched another flower. It was past eleven when she left the office.

For all the years she's driven in San Francisco, its roller coaster roads still give her the jitters. She's now close to the top, at the blind spot where all she can see is the brown hood of her wagon and the night sky. Her stomach lurches as if she's about to plummet down a cliff. Fortunately the suspense doesn't last long. The asphalt reappears and levels into a four-way stop intersection.

Another roller coaster ramp looms ahead. She floors the pedal to whip the mule on. She's been meaning to replace the car before it reached two hundred thousand miles, but work always gets in the way. She's been meaning to do a number of personal things, such as calling Cary to see how Baba is. His fall doesn't sound too serious, though one never knows with an old-old person. She'd closed her door at lunch and browsed the Internet for information on concussion. Confusion, memory loss, and dizziness are some of the symptoms. But Baba suffers all of the above on any given day. How can the doctor tell if his dementia is from the usual wear and tear or the trauma of the fall? Doing too little is harmful, but so is overly aggressive treatment. It's too late to discuss with Cary now. Tomorrow, she'll call on her way to work.

At the stop sign, she darts her eyes around and sees a car approaching. I got here first, she thinks, and drives on. A light beams at her. She glances over and sees it's very bright very fast very oh-my-God! She closes her eyes, her mind screaming: I have the right of way!

Her body jolts forward. She opens her eyes and sees the reflection of a fiery streak zooming past her tail. It just missed her!

The clock flashes 11:46 pm. She looks down at herself, checking off each part with disbelief—her lungs are pumping, her heart beats, oh yes, like a maniac, hands intact, head in place. She looks further down and sees her feet resting on the floor. Wait, she doesn't remember ramming down the pedal. Even if she had, the old wagon couldn't have bucked as fast as it did. The scientist in her says there's got to be a logical explanation. Perhaps her reflex is faster than she thought, the old buggy more powerful…

From out of nowhere, her lips pop the word Baba. Now, why did she think of him?

Chapter 27

Ming-Jen and Tak get their wish at last. After years of haranguing and cajoling, they've finally convinced their children California is the best place for them. Most of the clan lives here, and the weather is mild and sunny year round. Although real estate prices are on the high side, they don't need much land. Their children have bought them a little plot on the southern outskirts of San Francisco, just beyond the reach of the nippy Bay fog. The ground here is always warm.

They've gotten an extra bonus too—a free plane ride. Like other passengers, they went through X-ray at security. Unlike other passengers, they didn't need tickets. They sat side by side in the overhead bin in the plane. It was a smooth ride that went by like a blip in the chart of infinity. They were taken straight to George's home in Palo Alto; rightly so, as he was the eldest son.

And now, they're all gathered at George's church. Everyone who owes his life to the two of them is there, plus the in-laws and a number of friends (not their own but their children's). Had their peers been alive, every pew would have been filled, instead of just half. Two larger than life photos of them loom from floor to ceiling on the wall screen. This is a picture taken in Cary's living room on their sixtieth wedding anniversary. The grand family reunion they wanted at the time hadn't materialized as their other children and grandchildren couldn't coordinate their schedules. They'd been grumpy all day until the photo session. For a few seconds they set aside their gripes and smiled to leave a good impression for posterity. Their foresight is paying off now.

Ming-Jen and Tak wait patiently for the minister to finish

his prayer. They're not Christian and don't believe in heaven and hell. For them, the ideal resting place is where their children and grandchildren are. To gather with them all in one place is heaven enough for them.

Finally the moment they've been waiting for arrives. Karen ascends the altar to deliver the eulogy. Ming-Jen and Tak smile on her as she addresses the congregation. Ming-Jen is delighted to see how well put together her daughter is: an elegant black dress wraps around her slender figure, which she inherited from her mother, and around her neck gleams a string of pearls, also inherited from her mother.

Karen begins, "When my students complain to me about their parents, I always tell them that parents are the most important people in a person's life. No matter what kind of scrapes they get into, their parents will always be there for them. Believe me," she commands her listeners, "Your parents watch over you more than you realize."

Tak grins at the private joke. Only he and Karen know what she's referring to.

"I tell my students: yes, I know, parents can be a nuisance. My children will attest to that." She winks at the three young people in the second row. "However, if you give them a chance, you'll discover that parents are the most reliable people in the world. They'll always do their best for you. And I talk from personal experience, as both a mother and a daughter."

Ming-Jen nods with approval. Having previewed Karen's speech, she doesn't expect any bombshells. Don't get her wrong, she didn't censor anything—George took care of that. After the siblings nominated Karen for delivering the eulogy, George laid down the ground rules. A eulogy is by definition a tribute to the dead, he said, and therefore should contain only praises. While the living are never perfect, the dead have no faults. Mami was the most loving mother in the world, and Baba was the most loving father in the world, and that was that. All other information, such as Mami's impossibly high standards for her eldest child (supposed to have trickle-down effects on younger siblings) and Baba's struggle with depression, met the fate of George's delete button. Only cute anecdotes with heartwarming endings survived his editing.

After reading her script faithfully, Karen looks out at the assembly. Years of practice have trained her headmistress eyes to speak to each individual as if he or she were the only person in the room. "I also tell my students that the key to a good relationship with their parents is compassion. *Ren*, Chinese for compassion, is a major Confucian virtue. It also happens to be my name."

"This isn't in your draft!" Ming-Jen says with shock and dismay. Oh no, what's up Karen's sleeve? Her firstborn, who has a sharp tongue that can cut a person to shreds, has never had a kind word for Confucius. She also hates her name.

"Compassion is putting yourself in another person's shoes and understanding where he comes from," Karen continues. "Compassion is allowing others to be human, something we often don't realize with parents. Although they want you to think they're gods, they're *not*. They're only humans who have lived through a history you often don't know and don't understand. If you're willing to accept that, you will judge them kindly.

"Shortly before my mother passed away, I went to Virginia to celebrate her ninetieth birthday. We had a wonderful time together. Whatever fights we had in the past, and we had our share, became insignificant in the big picture of our love. The day she passed away, I talked to her on the phone and told her I..." Her shoulders heave. "I love her..." Her voice cracks.

Ming-Jen whispers in Cary's ear, "Go help your sister." Cary sidles out of her pew. Karen calms down and signals to her sister to return to her seat.

"Baba and Mami," Karen resumes, her take-charge self

again. "Thanks for giving me a better life than you had yourself. May you rest in peace. I love you."

Whew, Ming-Jen huffs. It wasn't so bad after all.

The next officiant is George. Balancing a gigantic basket of flowers with both hands, he approaches the altar solemnly and sets the bouquet in front of his parents. He's designed his own ritual and hasn't said much about it except that he won't be speaking. Ming-Jen and Tak are relieved their son isn't going to make a blubbering fool of himself.

George steps back, rotates toward his mother's image, and bows from the waist. Straightening up, he gazes into his mother's eyes.

"My beloved son, I've given you the hardest virtue," Ming-Jen says. "Karen only needs to be compassionate, Cary to do what's right and just, but you have to do them all. *Xiao* requires you to repay your parents and also to love them even when they're cranky and demanding and too demented to know it. You've accomplished both with excellence."

George takes a second bow, this time for Baba.

"Hey, George, I heard you're going to Las Vegas for a conference next week. Remember the time you took me to Las Vegas, just the two of us? I had a grand time at the casinos, and well, you know what I liked best, the club where the dancing girls sat on my lap. I hope you have a good time. I'll be floating around like a lazy cloud, drifting wherever the wind blows."

George takes a third bow for both parents and walks down the altar, passing Cary on her way up. Ming-Jen is happy to see her sloppy daughter dressed in a navy blue pant suit. The outfit begs for a brooch, such as the diamond-studded leaf Ming-Jen bequeathed her, but that would be asking too much of Cary. Ming-Jen's pulse quickens as Cary reaches the piano. She always gets nervous at her daughter's recitals. Once, Cary got stuck in the middle of a piece, and the teacher had to go up and prompt her. Watching her little girl fumble, Ming-Jen died a thousand deaths. She prays Cary won't have a memory slip on this of all occasions.

Tak starts humming. He can imagine his fingers flying over the keyboard, although he's never taken a lesson in his life. He may not have accomplished much in ninety-two years, but when his children achieve something, he feels he's done it too.

*

Standing next to the grand piano, I'm tempted to wave to the familiar faces. *Oh my, you've grown up so much... Haven't seen you in a long time, you look great... Let's get together after the funeral...* Instead, I hear my voice say, "I'm going to play the first two movements of the *Italian Concerto*, by Johann Sebastian Bach."

I stare at the piano keys. What am I supposed to do with these black and white things? The bustle of the day has kept me from going through my pre-performance preparation, which is a three-step process of torment, death, then resurrection. Without it, I'm at a loss. Where on earth is middle C?

My left arm lifts, my fingers spread out and land on the cool surface. The opening chord vibrates up the ceiling, and the pall of mourning crashes down. The F major chord announces the party has begun, followed by another emphatic line in C proclaiming, it's true, the party really has begun. The Italian Concerto is a joyous piece, which is why I chose it to celebrate my parents' lives. It's also polyphonic, which means, if you close your eyes, you won't believe it's just my two hands pounding away. You'd think a musician is plucking on his violin strings, another blowing into his trumpet, and another tweeting on his flute. Only Bach could write a piece for the piano (actually, its predecessor, the harpsichord) and make it sound like an orchestra playing. Which is the second reason I chose this piece. The celebration of my parents' life deserves no less than an orchestra.

I marvel at my fingers running, flipping, and vaulting like little gymnasts. This is every performer's dream, to be able to let his muscles take over while he sits back and watch the show. Except that there's something strange about my hands. They don't seem to belong to me. Where have I seen these hands before?

The first movement ends back in F major. I hold down the chord, which sounds as contented as a fat man declaring he's eaten and drunk his full. Electricity buzzes in my fingertips and sweeps through the spacious church.

The second movement, marked *Andante*, is a prayer. I imagine Bach peeping at God through half-closed eyes when he was writing this part.

I start with my eyes open. By the fourth bar, they're closed. The line unravels slowly as if someone up there is cranking a giant spool, winching the soul out of my body and hoisting it higher and higher. Listening to it is a transcendental experience. Performing it, however, is a treacherous affair. If the player isn't careful, the line can snap, the soul crash to earth, and everyone will wake up with a jolt. For this reason, I force my eyes to flicker at every jump of more than an octave, and there are many.

My pinkie lands securely on the low G. I stare at my hand with astonishment. I recognize it now—it belongs to Baba—the clay brown skin and the wide blunt nails that seem manicured by a hatchet. That first knuckle, spherical as a marble, can only be his. I've spent many hospital hours studying it.

Oops, the hands have climbed too high. Hiding any trace of panic on my blissful face, I noodle a few improvisations and then circle back to the beginning of the phrase. My eyes are open now, and I stay alert until a sigh in D minor releases me. The music has safely deposited my parents in heaven. I get up to return to my seat, glad of my decision to skip the third movement. Bringing them back for a romp in *Presto* would be cruelty beyond reason.

A hairy hand wraps around mine and squeezes. I look up

at Steve with an apologetic smile. Although he doesn't know it, I've wrongly accused him of watching late night porn. The call from the hospital absolved him instantly. Baba died around a quarter to three, the same time my TV came on, and the same time George felt somebody pull the cover over him, and Karen escaped a car crash. Baba had come to say goodbye. The three of us have no doubt in our minds, but we've agreed to keep the encounters to ourselves.

The minister begins to read a passage from the Bible. I sit motionless while excitement crackles inside me, and it isn't just from the leftover adrenaline. Somewhere in the middle of the heavenly second movement, my account with Baba suddenly squared. Finally the debit and credit columns match. The entry on the left reads, "Life," for the life Baba gave me. My repayment to him, registered on the right, is "An extension of life." Although the hands that played the *Italian Concerto* are attached to my wrists, which are attached to my arm and so on, they're unmistakably Baba's. As long as I can play the piano, so can he.

The words "resurrection of the dead" catches my ears. I want to raise my hand and interrupt the minister. *Excuse me, sir. The dead are still alive.*

*

I survey my parents' new home while Steve drives. The place looks tidy and well managed. A few grassy knolls undulate here and there, probably manmade to add relief to the landscape. Otherwise there's nothing but row after row of tombstones.

"So many dead people here," Mami remarks in my ear.

I shrug. "Try coming out at midnight. You may make some friends."

Baba groans, "Please leave me alone in my hole."

"You did well," Steve says, waking me from my daydreaming. "It's the best I've heard you play that piece."

Coming from the person who's listened to me play the Bach a million and one times including this last, the compliment is more momentous than if it had come from a New York Times critic.

"Yeah, Mom, it was beautiful," Fred agrees in the back.

"I wanted to jump up and yell bravo! But I guess you're not supposed to do that at a funeral," Maggie says.

"Thanks, everyone," I say, turning around to my children. They're both dressed in black, looking unusually grownup. Between them sit their grandparents. Their urns don't spook me anymore. I've come to view their ashes as clippings on the floor after a haircut, keepsakes for the living to hang on to. The rest of my parents have been transformed into heat and light, wind and rain, carbon and oxygen. Their particles are everywhere, which may be why I think of them every time I vacuum my house.

I've been waiting for a good time to discuss with my children the subject of elder care, modern parlance for filial piety. What can be better than when the audience is held captive in a car?

"Remember, a while back, you said you would take me into your home when your dad and I grow old? Is that a standing invitation?"

"Sure," Fred says without hesitation. "It will be a long time before you guys get to that point. But yeah, whenever you're ready."

"Filial piety is the number one virtue," Maggie says with a thumbs-up. "If filial piety is not pursued from beginning to end, disasters are sure to follow."

"Hey, where did you get that from?" I say.

"You don't think I listen to Popo? She said it at least a dozen times on every visit."

"I'll never be like your Popo," I say defensively. "Your dad and I plan to stay independent as long as we can. We'll live our own lives and let you live yours. When the time comes though, when we're too weak to take care of each other, we won't hesitate to lean on you. We won't be as demanding as our parents, but we're not like those Americans who refuse help from their children no matter what."

"Speak for yourself," Steve says. "I'm one of those Americans."

"Fine. I'll go live with the kids, you live in a nursing home."

"I won't care when I'm duh…" His jaws hang slack.

I punch him in the arm. "Seriously," I say, returning to the children, "We don't have to live in your home, but we should be within a twenty-mile radius of one of you. Otherwise you can't get to us regularly. Wherever we are, in a nursing home or our own place, we'll need an *advocate*." I let it sink in, the new term I recently picked up in an elder care article. "Don't worry, when I get to that stage, I don't intend to hang on long. I'll make it very clear in writing when to pull the plug. You go by that and not by what I say when I'm confused and scared. I don't want any of you to be burdened with that kind of decision. Anyway," I cut myself short, afraid to frighten my children. "I just want to give you the experience of taking care of me."

"Do I have to change your diapers?" Maggie says.

"You may have to. I'm sorry." I reach over to pat the soft, baubled hand, which I hope will change lots of baby diapers one day.

Maggie scrunches her nose.

"Think of it as an experience," I say. "You'll get to see the process of aging in all its glory. Remember how you like to flip to the end of a mystery novel?"

"I still do," Maggie says.

"Once you know the ending, you become more aware of the clues planted along the way, right? It's the same with life. When you can see the end, you can better interpret the present."

"Mom, there's something I've been wanting to tell you," Fred interjects. "You've been so busy with the funeral and stuff, I thought I'd wait till tonight."

Uh-oh, this doesn't bode well, I think. The last time he dithered about telling me something was when he wrecked my car.

"But since we have some time now, I might as well…" Fred drags out the suspense.

A worm is taking big bites of my stomach. I want to shriek: get it over with!

"Annette and I are getting married," Fred says.

I hear what I hear but my brain can't absorb it.

"We haven't picked the date yet, but we figured sooner is better than later since… you know…"

"Wait a minute," I say, remembering a past conversation. "You once said you have no reason to get married unless you plan to start a family. Do you mean…?"

Fred's answer is as loud as a trumpet. My son blushes, my wonderful, gorgeous son who's going to make me a grandmother! The car breaks into whoops of congratulations and I have to remind Steve to steer clear of the tombstones.

"She just got through her first trimester," Fred says. "The wedding should be soon, before she gets too big. It will be informal, just the family and a few close friends."

Steve and I echo approval. How can we, an eloped couple, criticize other people's wedding formats? To appease our parents we later staged a fake wedding officiated by Steve's ex-roommate. No, the ceremony doesn't matter. It's what happens after the ninth month that will change our lives. Only the other day, Steve griped that he wasn't a grandpa yet at sixty-six. I wanted to say, "What about me, I'm almost sixty and not a grandma yet." But since he complained first, I had to say, "Be patient, it will happen."

I roll down the window and take in a lungful of Mami, then Baba. Lately the law of conservation of energy has hailed back from high school physics to haunt me. I'd liked the subject as much as a dental drill in my tooth, and am thus quite amazed at myself for looking it up on the Internet. A number of sites appeared. One was full of mathematical formulas, which I immediately clicked out of, but several others were catered to science retards like me.

The law states that energy can't be created or destroyed. Like the swing of a pendulum, the back and forth motion goes on forever unless somebody sticks in his hand to stop it. Energy doesn't die; matter doesn't disappear. They can be transformed, yet the sum of all within a system is constant.

Our motorcade arrives at Plot N, Section 100-500. I watch the people emerging from their vehicles: my brother and sister and their spouses and children. Everyone is outfitted in parent-approved best, beautiful and throbbing with energy. Karen locates the freshly dug grave and directs us to form a circle around it. Joining hands, we sing *One Day When We Were Young* while Fred and Maggie lower the urns into the grave.

I look around at my family and my heart overflows. I never dreamed I would say this: Thank you, Confucius, for bugging me to practice filial piety. When a circle is complete, nothing is ever lost. We're all here, the living, the dead, and those to come.

Conk-la-reeeeeee, a call draws our heads upwards. A red-winged black bird perches on a nearby tree. As though aware of being the center of attention, he puffs out his chest for an encore: *Conk-la-reeeeeee.*

"Baba," I whisper. For some totally insane reason, the bird reminds me of my father. Perhaps it's the black coat and red patch. When dressing for an occasion, Baba liked to accent his finery with a red handkerchief folded just so in his breast pocket. That must be it. There can be no other reason.

"That bird looks like Gunggung," Maggie says, craning her neck for a closer look.

How I want to hug my daughter. When she makes an outrageous statement, nobody balks because we all know Maggie is offbeat, and we love her for that. If I were to say the same, people would think my brain has gone mush with grief.

"Why do you say that?" her Aunt Karen quizzes.

"It's the way he holds his tail up, looking all excited like Gunggung when he was about to do something wicked."

A faint *Seeeee-yeeeee* calls from a distance. Gunggung jerks his head in that direction. He opens his wings, waves his brilliant handkerchiefs at us, and is gone before any mouths can close.

"That's Mami calling," George says.

We all laugh. It's a joke. Of course, it's just a joke.

Homa & Sekey Books Titles on China

MASTERPIECES OF THE ORAL AND INTANGIBLE HERITAGE OF HUMANITY SERIES
(A Set of 15 Titles, Paperback, Color Illustrated, Art/History)
Shaolin Kungfu by Lv Hongjun. Order No. 1089, ISBN: 9781931907866, 104p, $24.95
Taijiquan by Yan Shuangjun. Order No. 1090, ISBN: 9781931907873, 213p, $34.95
Chinese New Year Painting by Wang Shucun; Wang Haixia. Order No. 1091, ISBN: 9781931907880, 149p, $29.95

FORTHCOMING:
Anshun Local Drama in China
Dehua Porcelain in China
Huzhou Writing Brush in China
Mount Tai Steles in China
Bamboo and Silk Music in Southern China
Bronze Drums in China
Folk Legends of Gengcun in China
Quanzhou String Puppetry in China
Cantonese Opera in China
The Glove Puppet Show in China
Sichuan Opera in China
Violet Sand Crafts in China

Jack Ma: Founder and CEO of the Alibaba Group by Chen Wei. Order No. 1105, ISBN: 9781931907200, Hardcover, 208p, $27.95, Business/Biography

The Historical Architectural Map of Beijing (Color Illustrated) by Li Luke, et. al. Order No. 1098, ISBN: 9781931907316, Paperback, 804p, $99.95, Travel/Culture/History

The China Well-being (Minsheng) Development Report 2012 by Renwu Tang, et. al. Order No. 1097, ISBN: 9781931907941, Hardcover, 393p, $149.95, Social Studies/History

Decoding Critical Genes of Enterprises: The Bionic Laws for Organizational Longevity by Bin Yan. Order No. 1094, ISBN: 9781931907910, Paperback, 219p, $49.95, Business/Management

Salt in Ancient China by Song Jupu and Jing Hong. Order No. 1093, ISBN: 9781931907903, Paperback, 163p, $39.95, Culture/History

The Illustrated Book of Chinese Tea by Wang Jianrong and Guo Danying. Order No. 1093, ISBN: 9781931907897, Paperback, 202p, $29.95, Culture/History

Reading the Times: Poems of Yan Zhi. Order No. 1087, ISBN: 9781931907842, Hardcover, 132p, $19.95, Poetry

Chinese Civil Procedure and the Conflict of Laws by Chen Weizuo. Order No. 1086, ISBN: 9781931907835, Hardcover, 178p, $79.95, Law

Understanding China's Criminal Procedure by Yi Yanyou. Order No. 1085, ISBN: 9781931907828, Hardcover, 330p, $99.95, Law

Disappearing Shanghai: Photographs and Poems of an Intimate Way of Life. Photographs by Howard W. French, Poems by Qiu Xiaolong. Order No. 1084, ISBN: 9781931907811, Hardcover, 126p, $29.95, Art/History

Beauty of Stone Windows: A Cultural Interpretation of Stone Windows of Sanmen by Editoral Board. Order No. 1082, ISBN: 9781931907798, Paperback, 160p, $69.95, Art/Culture/History

A Concise Illustrated History of Chinese Printing by Luo Shubao. Order No. 1071, ISBN: 9781931907675 , Paperback, 151p, $39.95, History

The Three Character Classic: A Bilingual Reader of China's ABCs (2nd Edition) by Dr. Phebe Xu Gray. Order No. 1081,

ISBN: 9781931907781, Paperback, xx, 191p, $24.95, Language/Culture

Managing China's Modernization: Perspectives on Diplomacy, Politics, Education and Ethnicity by Dr. Edwin Pak-wah Leung. Order No. 1078, ISBN: 9781931907743, Hardcover, xvi, 338p, $59.95, History/Politics

China's Terracotta Army and the First Emperor's Mausoleum by Yuan Zhongyi. Order No. 1072, ISBN: 9781931907682, Paperback, 152p, Color illustrations throughout, $29.95, Culture/History/Art

Folk Culture in China's Zhejiang Province: The Flowing Mother River by Tong Shaosu, trans. by Yu Jianqing and Shen Mingxia. Order No. 1066, ISBN: 9781931907620, Paperback, 216p, Color illustrations throughout, $29.95, Culture/History

EDUCATION IN CHINA SERIES (Hardcover)
Educational System in China by Ming Yang. Order No. 1060, ISBN: 9781931907569, 410p
Educational Policies and Legislation in China by Xiaozhou Xu et al. Order No. 1061, ISBN: 9781931907576, 275p
Basic Education in China by Libing Wang. Order No. 1062, ISBN: 9781931907583, 147p
Higher Education in China by Jianmin Gu et al. Order No. 1063, ISBN: 9781931907590, 227p
Technical and Vocational Education in China by Xueping Wu et al. Order No. 1064, ISBN: 9781931907606, 283p

Seven Kinds of Mushrooms: A Novel of the Cultural Revolution by Zhang Wei, trans. by Terence Russell. Order No. 1059, ISBN: 9781931907552, Paperback, 214p, $16.95, Fiction

Two Lifetimes: A Novel by Joanne Guo. Order No. 1058, ISBN: 9781931907545, Paperback, 242p, $16.95, Fiction

The Art of Mogao Grottoes in Dunhuang: A Journey into China's Buddhist Shrine by Fan Jinshi & Zhao Shengliang. Order No. 1057, ISBN: 9781931907538, Paperback, 172p, Color illustrations throughout, $29.95, Art, Buddhism

Everything I Understand About America I Learned in Chinese Proverbs by Wendy Liu. Order No. 1056, ISBN: 9781931907521, Paperback, 173p, $16.95, Social Studies

September's Fable: A Novel by Zhang Wei, trans. by Terrence Russell & Shawn X. Ye. Order No. 1050, ISBN: 9781931907460, Paperback, 495p, $29.95, Fiction

The Bitter Sea: "Morphing" and Other Stories by David Ke, PhD. Order No. 1048, ISBN: 9781931907446, Paperback, 226p, $16.95, Fiction/Asian Studies

www.homabooks.com

Ordering Information: Within U.S.: $5.00 for the first item, $1.50 for each additional item. **Outside U.S.:** $25.00 for the first item, $12.50 for each additional item. All major credit cards accepted. You may also send a check or money order in U.S. fund (payable to Homa & Sekey Books) to: Orders Department, Homa & Sekey Books, P. O. Box 103, Dumont, NJ 07628 U.S.A. Tel: 800-870-HOMA, 201-261-8810; Fax: 201-261-8890; Email: info@homabooks.com.